SHOOTOUT OF THE
MOUNTAIN MAN

SHOOTOUT OF THE MOUNTAIN MAN

William W. Johnstone
with J. A. Johnstone

PINNACLE BOOKS
Kensington Publishing Corp.
www.kensingtonbooks.com

PINNACLE BOOKS are published by

Kensington Publishing Corp.
119 West 40th Street
New York, NY 10018

PUBLISHER'S NOTE
Following the death of William W. Johnstone, the Johnstone family is working with a carefully selected writer to organize and complete Mr. Johnstone's outlines and many unfinished manuscripts to create additional novels in all of his series like The Last Gunfighter, Mountain Man, and Eagles, among others. This novel was inspired by Mr. Johnstone's superb storytelling.

All Kensington titles, imprints, and distributed lines are available at special quantity discounts for bulk purchases for sales promotions, premiums, fund-raising, educational, or institutional use. Special book excerpts or customized printings can also be created to fit specific needs. For details, write or phone the office of the Kensington special sales manager: Kensington Publishing Corp., 119 West 40th Street, New York, NY 10018, attn: Special Sales Department; phone 1-800-221-2647.

ISBN-13: 978-0-7860-1920-5
ISBN-10: 0-7860-1920-4

First printing: December 2010

10 9 8 7 6 5 4 3 2 1

Printed in the United States of America

Chapter One

Smoke Jensen was in Longmont's saloon playing cards with a few of his friends. Louis Longmont wasn't playing, but he was nearby, leaning up against the wall, adding his own comments to the conversation that flowed around the card table.

Smoke was only partially participating in the conversation, and was only partially participating in the card game, as was demonstrated when he failed to respond to the dealer's request.

"Smoke?" Garrett said. Garrett, a stagecoach driver, was one of the other players.

"What?"

"How many cards?"

"I pass."

"What do you mean you pass? You've already matched the bet."

"Oh, uh, I'll play these."

"Smoke what's got into you?" Louis asked. "You seem to be somewhere else."

"I fold," Smoke said.

Laying his cards facedown on the table, Smoke

got up. Not until he stood could anyone get a good enough look at him to be able to gauge the whole of the man. Six feet two inches tall, he had broad shoulders and upper arms so large that even the shirt he wore couldn't hide the bulge of his biceps. His hair, the color of wheat, was kept trimmed, and he was clean shaven. His hips were narrow, though accented by the gun belt and holster from which protruded a Colt .44, its wooden handle smooth and unmarked.

Smoke walked to the bar, moving to the opposite end from a young man who had come in a few minutes earlier. Smoke had noticed him the moment the young man came in. He was wearing his pistol low on his right side, with the handle kicked out. He was sweating profusely, though it wasn't that hot. He had ordered one beer as soon as he came in, but hadn't taken more than one sip the whole time he was there.

Smoke had seen men like this before, young gunsels who thought the fastest way to fame was to be known as the man who had killed Smoke Jensen. He knew that as soon as the young man got up his nerve, he would make his move. It was that, the upcoming confrontation with this man, that had taken Smoke's mind away from the conversation and the game.

Louis came over to the bar.

"Are you all right, Smoke? You're acting rather peculiar."

"Better not stand too close to me, Louis," Smoke said under his breath.

"What?"

Smoke nodded toward the young man at the opposite end of the bar. The young man was leaning over the bar, staring into his beer with his hands on either side of the glass.

Louis looked toward the man, then saw what Smoke had seen. It appeared that the nervous young man was trying to gather his nerve.

"Draw me a beer, will you?" Smoke asked.

Louis nodded, walked over to draw a mug of beer, then set it before Smoke. Without glancing again at the young man at the far end of the bar, Louis stepped away from Smoke, giving him all the room he might need.

Smoke did not overtly stare at the young gunman, but even though it appeared that he was uninterested in his surroundings, he was maintaining a close watch. Because of that, he was ready when the young man finally made his move.

"Draw, Jensen!" the young man shouted, turning away from the bar as he made a grab for his pistol.

"I already have," Smoke replied calmly.

The young man had his pistol only half withdrawn when he realized that he was staring down the barrel of a gun, the pistol already in Smoke's hand.

"What the—how did you do that?" the young man asked, taking his hand off his pistol, then raising both of his hands. "Don't shoot, don't shoot!" he begged.

By now, all conversation throughout the saloon had stilled, the card game had stopped, and everyone was paying attention to the drama that was playing out before them.

"Pull your gun out, very slowly, using only your thumb and forefinger," Smoke ordered.

"What are you goin' to do, mister?" the young man asked. "Are you goin' to kill me?"

"Why not? You were going to kill me, weren't you?"

"Yeah, I reckon I was," the young man answered.

"Drop your pistol in there," Smoke said, pointing to a nearby spittoon.

"In the spittoon? No, I won't do that," the young man replied.

"Oh, I think you will," Smoke said. He thumbed back the hammer, and the deadly double click of the sear engaging the cylinder sounded exceptionally loud in the now-quiet saloon.

"All right, all right," the young man said. Stepping over to the spittoon, he made a face, then dropped the pistol into it. It caused the brown liquid to splash out onto the floor.

Smoke holstered his pistol.

"Louis," he called.

"Yes, Smoke."

"Give the young man a new beer. On me."

"Ma—make it whiskey," the young man said.

Louis poured a shot and gave it to the would-be gunman. With a shaking hand, he lifted the glass to his lips, then tossed it down.

"What's your name?" Smoke asked.

"The name's Clark," the young man answered. "Emmett Clark."

"Why did you want to kill me, Emmett Clark?"

"It's a matter of honor," Clark answered.

"Honor? You think it is honorable to kill someone?"

"If you call them out and do it face-to-face,"

Clark said. "And if you're payin' someone back for somethin' they done to you."

"Boy, I've never done anything to you," Smoke said. "I've never even heard of you."

"Not to me, you ain't. But you done it to my kin. You kilt my pa. I was only fourteen when you kilt him, but I taught myself how to shoot so's I could get things all square."

"What was your pa's name?"

"Clark, same as mine. Rob Clark. He was a banker in Etna, and you shot and kilt him when you was holdin' up the bank. You do remember that, don't you?"

"Yes, I remember that bank robbery. But I didn't have anything to do with it, or with shooting your father."

"Don't tell me that, mister. You was found guilty of killin' him. You was found guilty and sentenced to hang. I wanted to watch you hang, but my ma wouldn't have nothin' to do with that. She went back to live with my grandparents in Kansas City, and I didn't have no choice but to go back with her. It was a long time afore I found out that you didn't actually hang. You escaped."

"Yes. I escaped, and I proved my innocence," Smoke said.[1]

"Ha! Proved your innocence? You expect me to believe that?"

"You should believe it, son, because it's true," Sheriff Carson interjected. Stepping into the saloon a moment earlier, Monte Carson had stood just inside the door as a silent witness to the

---

[1]*Betrayal of the Mountain Man*

interplay between Smoke and Clark. "I got the wire that said Smoke had been completely cleared. He was set up by the folks who actually did rob the bank and kill your pa. I've still got the wire down in my office if you need to be convinced."

"I'm sorry about your father, boy," Smoke said. "But as the sheriff said, I didn't have a thing to do with it. It was someone else who killed him."

Clark was quiet for a long moment. "Where are they?" he asked. "The ones that killed my pa, I mean. Where are they now?"

"They're dead," Smoke said.

"How do you know they are dead?"

"Because I killed them."

"Damn," Clark said. He pinched the bridge of his nose for a moment. Then he grabbed a towel from one of the bar hooks, got down on his knees, and fished out his pistol. Everyone watched him warily as he began drying it and his hands off. Then, grasping his revolver by the barrel, he held it out toward Sheriff Carson.

"I reckon you'll be wantin' to put me in jail now," he said.

Carson looked beyond the boy toward Smoke. Almost imperceptibly, Smoke shook his head.

"Why would I be wanting to put you in jail?" Carson asked.

"I don't know. Attempted murder, I guess."

"From what I can put together, there wasn't that much attempting to it, was there?" Sheriff Carson asked. "I'll bet you didn't even get your pistol out of the holster."

Inexplicably, Clark laughed, then shook his head. "No, sir, Sheriff, I reckon you've got me there," he said. "Mr. Jensen sort of put a stop to it before it ever got started."

"What do you think, Smoke? Should I put him in jail?" Carson asked.

"Clark, you said you were a man of honor," Smoke said to the young man. "Is that true?"

Clark nodded pointedly. "I ain't got no family now. My ma died last year. Never had no brothers. I ain't got hardly no money either. I reckon the only thing I got that is worth anything is my honor, so, yes, sir, I would say I am a man of honor."

"Then I'm going to hold you to that honor, Clark," Smoke said. "I'm going to let you ride on out of here, trusting that you aren't going to be lying in wait somewhere, aiming to shoot me."

"You got my word on that, Mr. Jensen. I'm satisfied that you didn't have anything to do with killing my pa. Makes sense to me anyway, now that I think about it. If you were guilty, there'd be paper out on you, and, though I've looked, I haven't seen any."

"Let him go, Sheriff," Smoke said.

"Go on, boy," Sheriff Carson said. "But I'd appreciate it if you would leave town."

"Yes, sir," Clark said. "I really have no reason for staying now anyway." He made a motion toward returning his pistol to his holster, then looked at the sheriff as if asking for permission.

Sheriff Carson nodded that it would be all right.

"Clark, have you ever used that gun?" Smoke asked.

"Just to shoot at varmints and such," Clark replied. "I've never used it against a man."

"Do you plan to?"

"For the last few years, all I've thought about was finding you and killing you. And I didn't even figure that would be wrong, seeing as how you had been sentenced to hang but escaped. I don't have any plans to use it against a man, but I figure I could if it ever come to that."

"Are you good with it?"

"Yes, sir," Clark answered. "I'm damn good with it."

"There will always be someone better," Smoke said. "Remember that."

Clark nodded. "Yes, sir, well, I reckon you just proved that to me, didn't you?"

Smoke and the others in the saloon watched as the young man walked out through the batwing doors. A moment later, they heard the sound of hoofbeats as he rode away. Louis Longmont was standing at the window watching, and he called back to the sheriff.

"He's gone," Louis said.

Not until then was the saloon reanimated as everyone began to talk at once.

"I must say, Smoke, you seemed awfully easy on him," Sheriff Carson said.

"I reckon I was," Smoke said. "But then I look at him, and I see myself when I was on the blood trail after the ones who killed folks that were close to me."

"You comin' back to the game, Smoke?" Doc Colton called from the poker table.

Smoke shook his head. "No, I expect I'd better get on back out to the ranch. I have been in town long enough."

"What he's saying is that he doesn't want Miss

Sally to come into town, grab him by the ear, and lead him home," David Tobin said, and the others laughed.

"Yeah, well, if you ever had your ear grabbed by Sally, you would understand why," Smoke said with a good-natured smile, and again the others laughed.

Smoke went outside to the hitching rail, untied his horse, then swung into the saddle. He looked in the direction young Clark had taken and saw him, now a long way out of town, growing smaller as the distance between them opened.

His horse, Seven, whickered as Smoke approached him. Smoke squeezed his ear.

"You about ready to go back home, are you, boy?" Smoke said as he untied the reins from the hitching rail. Seven dipped his head a couple of times, and Smoke laughed.

"I should have never built that new stall for you. You like it too much. You're going to get so lazy you'll never want to leave it."

Smoke swung into the saddle, then started out of town, the hollow clump of Seven's hooves echoing back from the buildings that fronted the street. It was five miles to Sugarloaf, and because Seven was showing an anxiousness to run, Smoke decided to give him his head.

Chapter Two

As Smoke Jensen was leaving Big Rock, back at his ranch, Sugarloaf, his wife, Sally, was sitting on a flat rock, high on an escarpment that guarded the north end of the ranch, protecting it from the icy blasts of winter. Sally had discovered this point of vigil, which she called Eagle Watch, shortly after she and Smoke were married and moved here into the "High Country" to start their lives together.

Reached by a circuitous and often hidden trail, Eagle Watch was covered with a mixture of pine and deciduous trees that offered green all year, while also providing a painter's palette of color in the spring when the crab apple and plum trees bloomed, and again in the fall when the aspen and maple leaves changed. In addition, the meadow itself was blanketed with wildflowers of every hue and description.

Sally had come up here in her first week at the ranch to write a letter to her father back in Vermont, to try and give him an idea of what she felt about her new home.

Smoke and I make our debut here in this wonderful place where the snowy mountains will look down upon us in the hottest summer day as well as in the winter's cold, here where in the not too distant past the wild beasts and wilder Indians held undisturbed possession—where now surges the advancing wave of enterprise and civilization, and where soon, we proudly hope, will be erected a great and powerful state, another empire in the sisterhood of empires.

It was very much like Sally to express her thoughts in such a poetic fashion. She was a young woman of education and passion, sensitive to the rugged beauty of the home she shared with her husband, and filled with unbridled enthusiasm for their future. The letter had been written some years earlier, and since that time, Colorado had become a state. But though dated, the letter still remained appropriate to the way Sally felt about this place.

From here, Sally could see the house Smoke had built for them, a large two-story edifice, white, with a porch that ran all the way across the front. It had turrets at each of the front corners, the windows of which now shined gold in the reflected sunlight. Also in the compound were several other structures, including the bunkhouse, cook's shack, barn, granary, and other outbuildings. She could also see many of the thousands of acres that made up Sugarloaf Ranch.

Abandoning her contemplation of the ranch, she turned her attention to the road that ran from Sugarloaf into Big Rock. There, she saw a plume of dust, then, just ahead of the plume, a

galloping Appaloosa. She smiled at the sight—
Smoke was coming home at a gallop.

Mounting her own horse, Sally started back
down the trail toward the ranch compound.
Though the trail down was too steep to allow a
gallop, her horse was sure-footed and nimble
enough to traverse the distance rather quickly,
thus allowing her to reach the house before
Smoke. Dismounting, she climbed up onto the
wide porch so she could watch his arrival.

The road, which on the state and county maps
was called Jensen Pike, ran parallel with a long
fence, before it turned in through a gate that had
the name of the ranch fashioned from wrought-
iron letters in the arch above. But, as Sally knew
he would, Smoke did not come through the
gate. Instead, he left the road, then urging Seven
into a mighty jump, sailed over the fence almost
as if on wings. After successfully negotiating the
fence, he galloped into the compound before
pulling the horse to a stop and leaping down
from the saddle.

"Seven, you are the greatest horse in the world!"
Smoke shouted, patting the hard-breathing
animal on its forehead.

Sally laughed. "You said that to the other three
horses you named Seven, and the two you named
Drifter."

"They were the greatest horses in the world
too," Smoke said.

"Don't be silly. There can only be one greatest,"
Sally reminded him.

Smoke held up his finger and waved it back
and forth. "No, that's the schoolteacher in you
talking," he said. "If you love horses, you know

there can be as many greatest horses as you want."

Again, Sally laughed. "All right," she said. "I guess I can't argue with you on that. How was your trip to town? Did anything interesting happen?"

"Not really."

Sally arched her eyebrows. "Not really? That means something actually."

"Tell me, woman, when I think something, do words just appear on my forehead for you to read my thoughts?" Smoke teased.

"Yes," Sally said. "Now tell me what happened."

Smoke told Sally of his confrontation with Emmet Clark, finishing with the fact that he let him ride away.

"Oh, Smoke, do you think that was smart?" Sally asked.

"I don't know if it was smart," Smoke said. "You are the smart one of the family. But I think it was right. I believe him when he said that he is a man of honor. And I respect honor."

"That's because you are a man of honor," Sally said. "Take care of Seven and wash up. I'll have dinner ready soon."

Esmeralda County, Nevada

A brilliant streak of lightning lit up the night sky and in its flash, Bobby Lee Cabot could see the four men who were with him, their ponchos pulled about them, scrunched down in their saddles. It was raining hard, and Bobby Lee readjusted his own poncho as he waited with the others alongside a railroad water tank. Under the frequent flashes of lightning, the steel tracks of the Nevada Central Railroad glistened in the rain.

"What if the train don't come?" Conklin asked.

"The train comes ever' night," Dodd answered. "What makes you think it won't come tonight?" Frank Dodd was the leader of the group. Dodd was just under six feet tall with broad shoulders and powerful arms. In his middle forties, he had spent more than half his life in prison. In a prison fight, another inmate had cut off half of his left eyelid, as well as a piece of his upper lip, leaving him permanently scarred. That same encounter had left the man who scarred him permanently dead.

"What if this here train don't have no money on it?" Conklin asked.

"What if I just put my boot up your ass for askin' so damn many dumb questions?" Dodd replied irritably.

"I'm just askin' is all."

"Well, don't ask."

The five men were waiting alongside the track halfway between Lone City and Cloverdale, Nevada. They were here, in the middle of the night in the middle of a rainstorm, because it was their plan to rob the train when it stopped for water. Actually, it was only the plan of the other four. Unbeknownst to the others, Bobby Lee was a railroad detective with the Western Capital Security Agency. He had worked his way into the gang in order to find a way to bring them to justice.

Shortly before departing on this train robbery expedition, Bobby Lee sent a letter to Herman Wallace, the sheriff of Esmeralda County, notifying him of the gang's intentions. In the letter, he asked Sheriff Wallace to be riding in the express car with enough deputies to end the train robbing spree of Frank Dodd, Walter Conklin, Wayland Morris, and Jules Stillwater.

That would go well for Bobby Lee, who had spent six months tracking them, then getting himself into position to stop the bandits. He was sure that the railroad company would give him a bonus for his part, but it wasn't the bonus that motivated him. It was the satisfaction of taking out a gang of robbers who had been a thorn in the side of the railroad for the better part of two years.

The rain stopped and some of the clouds rolled away, revealing a full moon which illuminated the area almost as bright as day.

"This ain't good," Conklin said. "Moon bright like it is, they're goin' to be able to identify us."

"You think they ain't goin' to know who we are?" Dodd asked.

They heard the train whistle in the distance.

"All right boys, get ready. It'll be here soon," Dodd said.

They waited a moment longer until they could hear the puffing of the steam engine as the train worked its way up the long grade, approaching the water tank. Now the great headlamp was in view, but as the moon was bright, the lamp was projecting no visible beam of light. When the train rounded a curve, it exposed its entire length so the men could see all five cars behind it, every window of each passenger car showing light. As the train grew closer to the water tower, it began braking.

"Wait until it comes to a complete stop," Dodd ordered.

With a squeal of brakes, the train stopped. Then the relief valve began opening and closing, each cycle emitting a loud puffing sound. The fireman left the engine, then climbed up onto the tender and reached up for the water spout.

"All right, they ain't payin' no attention to us now," Dodd said. "Let's ease on down there."

As the others approached the train, Bobby Lee dropped back behind to be in position. Any moment now, the car doors would open and Sheriff Wallace and his deputies would be waiting. They would confront the robbers and if Dodd tried to make a run for it, Bobby Lee would be in position to stop him.

"Conklin, you and Wayland get up into the engine cab. Make sure that engineer don't suddenly decide to take off," Dodd ordered.

"He ain't goin' to go nowhere with the fireman up on the tender like that," Conklin said.

"Just do what I told you to do," Dodd said. "Stillwater, you and Cabot come with me."

The two men rode down to the engine cab, then with guns drawn, yelled up at the fireman.

"You! Put your hands up!" Conklin called out.

"Where'd you come from?" the fireman shouted, his words audible over the rhythmic rush of the steam relief valve.

"It don't make no never-mind where we come from."

"What's goin' on here?" the engineer called down from the cab. He stuck his head out through the window, but when he saw to two armed riders, he jerked back inside.

"Huh-uh, Mr. Engineer," Conklin called up to him. "If you don't want the fireman kilt, you better stick your head and arms back out the window and keep 'em there where we can see you."

The engineer complied.

While that was going on, Dodd and Stillwater approached the express car. With Bobby Lee remaining slightly behind the other two, Dodd banged on the door with the butt of his pistol.

"You boys in there got two choices!" he shouted. "You can either open the door and not get hurt, or keep the door closed and more'n likely get kilt when I blow up the car with dynamite!"

"Oh, they are going to open the door all right," Bobby Lee said aloud, though saying the words too quietly to be heard. He chuckled at the thought of Dodd being surprised when the sheriff and his deputy made their sudden, and unexpected, appearance.

But it wasn't Dodd who was surprised. It was Bobby Lee. When the door to the express car opened, there was nobody there but one frightened express agent. Where was Sheriff Wallace?

It took very little persuasion for the express agent to pass down two large cloth bags. Dodd opened them and looked down inside, then let out a shout of joy.

"Yahoo! Boys, these is all twenty-dollar bills! There's gotta be a couple thousand dollars or more! Come on! Let's get out of here!"

Conklin and Wayland came back from the engine, and the robbers made ready to ride away. Before they left, though, Dodd turned back toward the train and shot the express agent, who grabbed his chest, then fell to the ground from the car.

"Why did you do that?" Bobby Lee yelled in shock and anger. "You didn't have any call to shoot him."

"He seen our faces," Dodd replied. "Come on, let's go!"

Bobby Lee started to ride away with the other four, but he stopped, then turned and rode back to the train. Dismounting, he hurried over to the still form of the express man. He put his hand on the express man's neck to feel for a pulse, but there was none. The man was dead.

Damnit! He thought. This didn't have to happen. Where was the sheriff? Where were his deputies?.

By now, some of the passengers had stepped down from the train, and three of the men, holding pistols in their hands, approached Bobby Lee.

"Mister, shooting him was dumb enough," one of the armed passengers said. "But coming back here to gloat over what you done is 'bout the dumbest thing I've ever seen."

Bobby Lee stood up. "Is the sheriff on board this train?" he asked.

"Don't need no sheriff. I reckon we can handle you till we get you to town," the passenger said.

"No, you don't understand. My name is Bobby Lee Cabot, I'm with the Western Capital Security Agency. I told Sheriff Wallace about this robbery. This was supposed to be a set up to capture the robbers."

"Well, if you and the sheriff are such good friends, then I reckon you two can get it all worked out when we get to town. Get his gun, Joe."

The passenger named Joe pulled Bobby Lee's pistol from his holster. Bobby Lee offered no resistance. There was no sense in it. The man holding the gun on him was right. It would be all worked out once he and Sheriff Wallace got together.

"What are we going to do with him?" one of the men asked.

"I say we hang him," another suggested.

"Look here!" Bobby Lee said, suddenly frightened over the possibility that he might be lynched right here, before he could clear himself. "I told you, I wasn't with them!"

"Mister, do you take us for fools? We saw you with them."

"Yes, I was with them, but I was setting a trap for them. I thought the sheriff would be on this train and he could arrest them."

"A likely story."

"I say let's hang him."

"No," another passenger said. By now, several other passengers had come down from the train. The passenger who called out was a tall, silver-haired, dignified-looking man. "I saw it too, and this man isn't the one who did the shooting."

"What difference does it make who did the shooting? He was with them, that's all that matters as far as I'm concerned."

"If you men hang him, you are going to have to shoot me as well. And you'll be doing it in front of every other passenger on this train. Do you want a double murder on your hands?"

"What? No, what are you talking about? Hanging this fella wouldn't be murder. It would be justice."

The silver-haired man shook his head. "No, it wouldn't be justice, it would be lynching. The only way I'm going to let you do that is if you shoot me first. And I think that even you would admit that shooting me would be murder."

"Maybe the old geezer is right," one of the original three men said. "I ain't no murderer."

"Me neither," the second of the three said.

The spokesman of the group acquiesced. "All right," he said. "All right. Let's get some rope and tie the son of a bitch up. We'll turn him over to the sheriff as soon as we get to Cloverdale."

"Thanks, mister," Bobby Lee said to the man who had stopped the lynching.

"Don't thank me, mister," the man replied. "I hope you do hang. The only thing is, I want to see you legally hanged—I don't want to see these good men get into trouble because of you."

Bobby Lee offered no resistance when the armed train passengers bound and gagged him like a trussed-up calf, then threw him bodily and painfully onto the floor of the express car. More gently, they lifted the messenger into the car with him. Then one of the armed passengers climbed into the car to keep an eye on their prisoner.

With two short blasts on the engine's whistle, followed by a series of jolts and jerks, the train got under way again.

"Mister, you picked the wrong train to rob," his guard said, his glaring eyes gleaming in the glow of the car lamp. "Yes, sir, there was some of us on board who won't put up with nothin' like that."

Bobby Lee wanted to explain to him about his

plan to set up a trap for Frank Dodd, to prove to him that he was indeed an employee of the Western Capital Security Agency, but the gag prevented him from talking. There was nothing he could do now but lean back against the side of the car and make himself as comfortable as possible for the remainder of the ride.

Bobby Lee Cabot was twenty-four years old. He was a slender man, with more strength than his appearance suggested. His hair was sun bleached, and his eyes were a cross between gunmetal gray and sky blue. Women found him rather appealing, and men weren't intimidated by him. That sort of low-key combination worked well for him in his profession as a private detective, because it enabled him to blend easily with his surroundings.

The first part of it had worked well. He had been accepted into Frank Dodd's gang. Perhaps it had worked too well, because he had not only convinced Dodd and his men that he was one of them, but now the train passengers were equally as convinced.

It was late at night, and there would be another two hours before they reached Cloverdale. As a result, Bobby Lee's guard fell asleep. Bobby Lee worked himself out of the ropes, and removed the gag. Then, quietly and carefully, he took the gun from the sleeping guard's hand. Having freed himself, he returned to his position against the side of the car.

It was just after dawn as the train began braking for its approach into Cloverdale. The guard, awakened by the change of sound and motion, stretched and yawned, then suddenly realized where he was and what he was supposed to be doing.

"What the hell?" he shouted in alarm when he saw that Bobby Lee was sitting against the side of the car, holding the pistol. The would-be guard threw his arms up. "No, mister, don't shoot! I've got a wife and kids! Don't shoot!"

"Relax," Bobby Lee said. "I'm not going to shoot you. I told you, I'm not one of outlaws. I want to see the sheriff. I plan to get this all straightened out." He handed the pistol back to the guard. "I believe this belongs to you."

Cloverdale was awakening on the new day when the train arrived. The stagecoach was waiting for any passengers who might need a connection to the nearby towns that weren't served by the railroad. Freight wagons were already beginning their morning runs, stores were opening, and citizens were moving about. Word that the train had been robbed was quickly spread through the town so that soon, a rather substantial crowd had gathered around the depot to watch, sadly, as the messenger's body was taken down.

"Who done it?" someone asked.

"Frank Dodd, who else?"

When Bobby Lee was taken from the train, tied and watched over by at least two armed men, a gasp of surprise passed through the crowd.

"Ain't that Bobby Lee Cabot?"

"What's he doin' all tied up like that?"

"Someone said he was ridin' with Dodd."

"You don't say."

"I don't believe it."

"What do you mean you don't believe it? They caught him red-handed is what they done."

Sheriff Wallace arrived then, pushing his way importantly through the crowd. "Open up here, let me through, make way," he called repeatedly. Anyone looking down from an elevated position would have seen the crowd parting, then closing in behind him as he made his way to the platform alongside the express car where the two armed passengers were holding Bobby Lee prisoner.

"Here he is, Sheriff," one of the two armed passengers said. "We caught this fella red-handed, right after the train was robbed and the messenger was kilt."

"I want to thank you men for bringing him in," Sheriff Wallace said. "This will save me the trouble, and the county the expense of having to go after him."

Sheriff Wallace was a very big man, six feet six inches tall. He had a round, bald head that sat on his shoulders with very little visible neck. His ears were so small that they seemed mismatched for his head. He wasn't just tall, he was big, weighing right at three hundred pounds.

"What do you mean, save you the trouble of going after me? What's this about, Sheriff?" Bobby Lee asked, surprised by the sheriff's reaction.

"This is about bringin' you to trial, findin' you guilty, and hangin' you," Sheriff Wallace said. "That's what it's about."

"Sheriff, uh, maybe I ought to tell you something," the man who had been watching over Bobby Lee said.

"What?"

The passenger cleared his throat and looked at the others. "Well, sir, I fell asleep while we was comin' in this mornin', and when I come to, this here fella was free, and holdin' my gun."

"You should have been more careful," Wallace said.

"Yes, sir, but my point is, he could have got away, only he didn't. He give my gun back to me. It sort of makes you think, don't it?"

"Think about what?" Sheriff Wallace said.

"Well, it makes you think about whether or not he's guilty. I mean, if he was guilty, wouldn't he have maybe kilt me, then got away?"

"Maybe," the sheriff agreed. "Or maybe he just figured it would make him look innocent."

The expression on the passenger's face changed, from one of concern to one of anger over being used.

"Yeah," he said, glaring at Bobby Lee. "Yeah, I wouldn't be surprised if that wasn't it."

"Come along, Cabot," Wallace said. "I've got a jail cell waitin' for you."

Bobby Lee was about to say something else, but he held his tongue when he decided that perhaps the sheriff was merely trying to protect his undercover status. He remained quiet until the sheriff took him down to his office.

"I have to confess that you had me worried there for a moment," Bobby Lee said. "But I understand now what you are doing."

"Do you?"

"Yes. You are protecting my identity. You are going to wait until they leave town before you let me out."

"What do you mean I'm protecting your identity? You are Bobby Lee Cabot, and soon as we start the trial, the whole world is going to know who you are. And what makes you think I'm going to let you out?"

Again, Bobby Lee was surprised, and this time he was also worried. There was no one present but the two of them, so the sheriff had no reason to talk like this. "I expect you to let me out because of the arrangement we had."

"What arrangement? What are you talking about?" Sheriff Wallace asked.

"Sheriff Wallace, you are beginning to make me uncomfortable. You know damn well what arrangement we had. We not only talked about it in some detail, I also sent you a letter, telling you about the robbery. I asked you to be in the car with deputies. If you had done what I asked, we could have stopped this," Bobby Lee explained. "That messenger would still be alive, and you would have Frank Dodd and his entire gang in jail."

"We never had any such conversation, and I did not receive a letter from you."

"Of course you received it. You have to have received it. I sent it to you in plenty of time."

"I don't know what kind of trick you are trying to pull, Cabot, but you aren't going to get away with it," Sheriff Wallace said.

Chapter Three

In the parlor of the house Smoke had built for his wife at Sugarloaf, on the wall opposite the windows, there was a picture that Smoke particularly liked. Sally found it rather jarring, but tolerated it because of her love of Smoke. The picture, cut from a calendar, was a full-color Currier and Ives print of two night trains, racing out of Washington, D.C., sparks flying from the stacks and with every window in every car shining brightly. It was a dramatic, if unrealistic, representation. Just below the calendar was the stove, cool now as there was no need for it, but with the faint aroma of smoke from last year's use still clinging to the black iron. Next to the stove was a large mahogany, coiled spring-driven, disc-operated music box. It was playing now, and the music it produced was full throated and vibrant, resonating throughout the room.

Sally was doing some crochet, while Smoke was looking at a new stack of stereopticon photographs. At the moment, he was looking at a picture of London's Big Ben. They were equally involved in their pursuits when Pearlie knocked on the front door.

"Come in, Pearlie," Sally called.

Removing his hat, the young foreman came into the room.

"Something I can do for you, Pearlie?" Smoke asked, looking up from the stereoscope he was holding in his hands.

"Yes, sir, I reckon there is, if you are of a mind to allow it, that is."

Smoke put the instrument down. "Allow it? What is it I am to allow?"

"Me and Cal have been thinkin'," Pearlie started.

Smoke chuckled. "Now that is something I would like to have seen. Imagine, you and Cal both thinking at the same time."

"Smoke, don't tease so," Sally scolded.

Smoke laughed. "All right, I'm sorry. But it did seem like a funny thought to me."

Pearlie chuckled as well. "Yes, sir, well I admit that thinkin' ain't somethin' me an' Cal do all that well. But thinkin' is what we was doin' all right, and what we'd like to do is ride off to Denver and see if me an' him couldn't ride in that there rodeo they are a' holdin'. We could win us some money."

"Are you saying I don't pay you two enough?"

"No, no!" Pearlie said quickly. "We don't mean nothin' like that. It's just that, well, sir, me an' Cal is both pretty good riders an' we would just love to prove it, is all."

"Smoke, stop teasing them so. You knew they were planning this. I told you all about it."

"I know," Smoke said. "I was just having a little

fun is all. I'm sorry, Pearlie, of course you and Cal can go. When are you leaving?"

"The rodeo is a couple of weeks from now. We figure on leavin' about Monday of the week of the rodeo. That is, iffen you don't mind."

"What do you think, Sally?"

"I have no problem with them going," Sally said. "But his grammar?" She screwed up her face. "It is positively atrocious."

"Now who is teasing him?" Smoke asked.

"I'm not teasing, I am teaching."

"You plan on being a teacher forever, do you?" Smoke asked. "You gave up that job a long time ago."

"Teaching isn't a job," Sally replied. "It is a never-ending commitment. Yes, I will continue to teach for as long as I live."

Getting up from the table where he had been looking at the three-dimensional pictures, Smoke walked over to Sally, then leaned down to kiss her on the forehead.

"And I will continue to learn as long as you are willing to teach," he said.

"Me too," Pearlie added.

Sally laughed. "Pearlie, you are—a challenge," she said.

Three days after Bobby Lee was brought into Cloverdale under guard, his trial got under way when Judge Briggs came through town as part of his circuit. Briggs arrived in a carriage that was driven by a black man who was also his bodyguard. His Honor, Judge Jeremiah J. Briggs, was a tall, thin—some might even describe him as cadaverous—man. He had a sallow complexion, sunken cheeks, deep-set eyes that were so brown that there was little delineation between iris and pupil, dark, bushy eyebrows, and dark hair. He wore a black suit with a burgundy vest and matching cravat. Because there were only two lawyers in town, Briggs appointed one as the prosecutor and the other as defense counsel. Arriving at ten in the morning, Judge Briggs gave the lawyers, both for the prosecution and the defense, until two o'clock that afternoon to prepare their case.

"I expect to have this case tried and adjudicated before supper," he said. "Do you think we can do that?"

Ray Roswell, who had been appointed as the prosecutor, nodded confidently. "Your Honor, I have an entire trainload of passengers who were witnesses to the murder. I expect this to be a quick and easy trial."

"Mr. Reid, will you have time to prepare you case by two o'clock?" Judge Briggs asked the defense counsel.

"Easily, Your Honor," Reid said. "There is little to prepare for. Unfortunately for me, it seems to be an open-and-shut case against my client."

"Very well, court will convene at two o'clock sharp," Judge Briggs said.

Reid went directly from the meeting in the judge's hotel room to the jail, where he asked to speak with the prisoner.

"He's back there," Deputy Harley Beard said.

Bobby Lee was lying on the bunk with his hands laced behind his head when the door from the sheriff's office opened and a fat man with a florid face and thin, blond hair stepped into the back. He was sweating profusely, and he held a sweat-soaked handkerchief in his hand.

"Bobby Lee Campbell?" he asked.

"Cabot."

"I beg your pardon?"

"Bobby Lee Cabot," Bobby Lee said. "That's my name."

The fat man pulled a piece of paper from his pocket and looked at it, his lips moving as he read the print.

"Yes, Cabot," he said. "That's you?"

"It is."

"My name is Jack Reid. I've been appointed as your defense attorney."

Bobby Lee extended his hand, but saw that Jack Reid made no effort to reciprocate, so he pulled his hand back.

"Why am I being appointed an attorney?" Bobby Lee asked. "I can afford my own attorney."

Reid wiped sweat from his face before he answered. "There are only two counselors in Cloverdale," he replied. "The judge has appointed Mr. Roswell as prosecutor, so that leaves me for you."

Bobby Lee nodded. "I guess that answers my question, doesn't it?"

"I'm here to help prepare for your defense. We go to trial at two o'clock this afternoon."

Bobby Lee looked up at the clock that hung from the wall at the end of the small corridor that separated the two jail cells from the back wall of the sheriff's office. It read twelve-fifteen.

"That's only an hour and forty-five minutes," he said. "That doesn't leave us much time, does it?"

"It's time enough for the defense I have planned," Reid said.

"What defense is that?"

"I have looked at the case of the prosecution, Mr. Cabot. And my advice to you is to plead guilty, and throw yourself upon the mercy of the court."

"What?" Bobby Lee replied sharply. "I'll do no such thing! I was not a participant in the robbery, I was trying to stop it."

"Mr. Cabot, the entire train saw you riding with Dodd and the others," Reid said.

"Yes, of course I was riding with them. It was all part of the plan. I was to ride with them and gather information as to when and where their next robbery would take place."

"But the entire train saw you with them," Reid said again, as if he had not understood a word Bobby Lee said. "It will be their word against yours."

Bobby Lee shook his head. "I don't deny I was riding with Dodd. The passengers did see that, but what the passengers could not see was my intent. Why was I riding with Dodd?"

"Is that really the case you want to make?" Reid asked.

"Of course it is the case I want to make. It is the truth, so I can do little else."

"All right, I'll do what I can, but don't expect much," Reid said without enthusiasm. He turned to leave. "I'll see you in court at two o'clock."

"Wait, that's it? You are leaving now? That's all the preparation you are going to do?"

"What else is there to prepare?" Reid said. "You tell me that you were with Dodd because, somehow, you had planned to trap him and the others. Right?"

"Yes," Bobby Lee replied.

"Then I am prepared."

Bobby Lee watched his lawyer waddle through the door and close it behind him. Now, for the first time since being put in jail, he began to think that he was not going to be able to get out of this.

At two o'clock that afternoon, Deputy Beard led a handcuffed Bobby Lee into the courtroom, which was actually the ballroom of the Depot Hotel.

"Sit over there behind that table," Beard said, pointing to a table at which sat the still-sweating Jack Reid.

"Good luck, Bobby Lee," someone called, and looking toward the crowded gallery, he saw Doc Baker, the man who had called out to him, Nate Nabors, and Minnie Smith. Nabors owned the Gold Strike Saloon and Minnie worked for him.

Minnie smiled bravely at him, and Bobby Lee smiled back.

Those three seemed to represent the only friendly faces in the entire crowd. In the face of nearly every other person present, he saw anger and hatred of the man they had already convicted in their own minds. Just across from Bobby Lee sat Ray Roswell, the prosecutor. He was tall, dignified-looking, with piercing blue eyes and silver hair and a neatly trimmed silver beard. He was wearing a suit that fit his slender body well. Bobby Lee groaned inwardly. If the jury was going to make its decision on the appearance of the respective lawyers, he had already lost.

When he looked toward the jury box, Bobby Lee saw not one friendly face. He only recognized one juror, and it was a man he had beaten in a game of poker a few weeks earlier. The man had lost a considerable amount of money, and had accused everyone else at the table, including Bobby Lee, of cheating.

Sheriff Wallace came in through another door, stood just inside the door, and called out in a loud voice.

"Hear ye, hear ye, hear ye! This here trial is about to commence, the Honorable Jeremiah J. Briggs, presiding. Everybody stand respectful."

The Honorable Jeremiah J. Briggs came out of a back room. After taking his seat at the bench, he put on his glasses, fitting the earpieces very carefully over each ear, one at a time, then cleared his throat.

"You may be seated," he said.

There was a rustle of clothing and the scrape of chairs as the gallery, large enough to overflow the courtroom, responded.

Judge Briggs picked up a piece of paper and looked at it for a moment before speaking.

"There comes now before this court defendant Bobby Lee Cabot, charged with murder, pursuant to the shooting death of August Fletcher on the night of August twenty-first in the current year. Is the defendant represented by counsel?"

"Yes, Your Honor, I am counsel for the defense," Reid answered.

"Is the state represented by counsel?"

"Yes, Your Honor," Roswell answered.

"Very well, we may proceed. Would the bailiff please bring the accused before the bench?"

Sheriff Wallace, who was acting as bailiff for this trial, walked over to the table where Bobby Lee sat next to Jack Reid.

"Get up, Cabot," he growled. "Present yourself before the judge."

Bobby Lee was still handcuffed, and had shackles on his ankles. He shuffled up to stand in front of the judge. Reid went with him.

"Bobby Lee Cabot, you stand accused of the crime of murder, specifically the murder of August Fletcher, Mr. Fletcher being at the time of his demise a messenger for the Nevada Central Railway Company. How do you plead?"

"Not guilty, Your Honor," Bobby Lee said, speaking the words loudly and distinctly so that everyone in the courtroom could hear him.

"Prosecutor, make your case," Judge Briggs said. Folding his arms across his chest, he leaned back in the chair and watched as Roswell rose from his seat, then approached the jury.

"Gentlemen of the jury," he began. "You have been assembled here today to adjudicate the case of murder. It is a difficult duty, but a duty of great honor, for in it lies the entire underpinnings of our republic. You are exercising the rights and privileges secured for us by thousands of brave young men who died upon fields of battle, men who gave their last full measure of devotion so that, for as long as our republic shall endure, men like you can perform the noble duty of providing a fair trial for those such as the accused."

Ray Roswell was smooth in appearance and language, and it was immediately apparent that he had won the respect of the jury. He gave an impassioned opening argument to the jury, calling upon sympathy for the slain messenger, evoking the image of a loving husband and father of three, taken from his family by the brutal act of murder.

"Defense may claim that his was not the finger that pulled the trigger, but by law, that does not matter," Roswell pointed out. "He was in the act of committing a felony and, during the commission of that felony, an innocent man was killed. That makes everyone concerned equally guilty. I am confident, in fact I fully expect, that at the conclusion of this trial, you will exercise the most solemn duty of your purview, and that is to find guilty, and recommend the penalty of death by hanging for the defendant Bobby Lee Cabot."

"No!" a woman's voice called out from the gallery, and though Bobby Lee recognized the voice as that of Minnie Smith, the judge did not know who had called out.

"I will have no more verbal responses from this gallery," the judge said sternly. He looked toward the defense table. "Counselor, present your defense," he said.

Reid put his sweat-dampened handkerchief on the table, then walked over to the jury. By contrast to Roswell's smooth and dignified appearance, Reid's suit hung in such a misshapen fashion that he looked for all the world like a stuffed sausage. His voice was thin, and difficult to hear.

"That Mr. Cabot was there, we cannot deny. It

was a full moon that night, and though it had rained earlier, the clouds moved away, which meant that my client was seen by nearly everyone on the train, bending down over the body of poor Mr. Fletcher. In fact, three passengers from the train disarmed Mr. Cabot and brought him here to jail. But"—Reid held up his finger as if making a salient point—"Bobby Lee Cabot is not the man who did the actual shooting. And I ask you to bear that in mind."

As Roswell had just pointed out to the jury that it didn't matter whether Bobby Lee had been the shooter or not, everyone in the court looked at each other and shook their heads in total contempt for Reid's efforts.

"You are fired," Bobby Lee said when Reid sat back down.

"You can't fire me. I'm the only other lawyer in town."

"I'll defend myself."

"You know what they say. The man who defends himself has a fool for a lawyer."

"I couldn't have a worse fool for a lawyer if I chose the town drunk," Bobby Lee said. "Your Honor, I am firing my counselor," he called out.

"Your Honor, I object," Reid said.

"You object to what, Counselor?"

"I object to this man firing me."

"Objection overruled. He has every right to fire you, and every right to defend himself."

"Thank you, Your Honor," Bobby Lee said.

"Don't thank me, young man," Judge Briggs said. "I fear you have chosen an impossible task for yourself. You may present your case."

Bobby Lee held out his hands. "Could I have these handcuffs removed?"

"Remove the handcuffs, but keep the shackles on his ankles," the judge said.

The sheriff walked over to the defendant's table and removed the handcuffs. Bobby Lee stood, and rubbed his wrists for a few seconds before he began to speak.

"Your Honor, I was not a member of Frank Dodd's gang," Bobby Lee said. "I am an employee of the Western Capital Security Agency, and I had infiltrated his gang not for any personal gain, but for the sole purpose of setting a trap for him. That's why I sent a letter to Sheriff Wallace, explaining what I was doing, providing him with information as to the date and time of the holdup—Wednesday, July twentieth, at ten-thirty, and the place, which was the watering tower ten miles south of Lone City. In that same letter, I asked him to be in the car with his deputies in order to facilitate the arrest of Dodd and his confederates."

"Objection, Your Honor," Roswell called. "The letter is not in evidence."

"Can you produce the letter, Mr. Cabot?" Judge Briggs asked.

"No, sir. I sent the letter to Sheriff Wallace, so I don't have it. But I can prove that I sent it."

"How can you prove it?"

"I would like to call as my first witness Minnie Smith. I told her about the letter."

"Objection, Your Honor," Roswell called. "That would be hearsay."

"Sustained. You cannot call Miss Smith."

"Then I would like to call Dr. Baker to the stand."

"Did Dr. Baker actually see you mail the letter?" Judge Briggs asked.

"No, sir, he didn't see me mail the letter, but I told him that I was going to mail the letter. And I told him before I sent it."

"Objection," Roswell called.

"Sustained."

"May I call Nate Nabors?" Bobby Lee asked, his voice almost pleading.

"Are you calling Mr. Nabors as a character or a material witness?" Judge Briggs asked.

"I'm not sure I understand the difference."

"A character witness will testify as to your character," Judge Briggs explained. "He will tell what a fine upstanding citizen you are, when you are not murdering Western Capital Security Agency messengers."

The gallery laughed, and Bobby Lee fumed, knowing that the joke and the laughter were at his expense.

"A material witness's testimony will provide testimony that provides direct evidence pertaining to the case."

"In that case, Your Honor, Mr. Nabors is a material witness."

"You may call him."

"Nate?" Bobby Lee called.

"Your Honor, may I inquire if the defendant is going to ask the witness about the supposed letter?"

"Are you going to ask about the letter?" Judge Briggs asked.

"Your Honor, I told Mr. Nabors about the letter."

"Did you show him the letter? Did he see you mail it?"

"No, Your Honor."

"Your Honor, I object to this witness."

"Objection sustained. You may not call the witness, Mr. Cabot."

"Your Honor," Bobby Lee said in obvious frustration. "If you won't let me call any witnesses, then I don't know how I'm going to prove that I sent that letter."

"If the only witnesses you have are people that you told about the letter, then their testimony would be considered hearsay and is not admissible," the judge said. "Have you anything else to offer in your defense?"

"Wait a minute," Bobby Lee said. "What about Fred Welch?"

"Who is Fred Welch?"

"I am Fred Welch, Your Honor," a man said. He was sitting in the gallery.

"Mr. Cabot, what is Mr. Welch's relationship to this case?"

"He is the postman, Your Honor. He delivered the letter."

"Is that right, Mr. Welch?" the judge asked. "Did you deliver the letter in question?"

"I don't know," Welch replied.

"You don't know?"

"Your Honor, I deliver hundreds of pieces of mail every day," Welch said. "And I deliver a lot of mail to the sheriff. I don't ever notice who the mail is from, only where it is going. It could be that I delivered the letter that Mr. Cabot is talking about, but if I did, I don't remember it."

"Your Honor, if this witness cannot support the defendant's claim as to the delivery of the

letter, then I see no merit to his being called,"
Roswell said.

"I agree, Mr. Roswell," Judge Briggs said. "Defense move to call Fred Welch as a witness is denied."

"Your Honor, you have not let me call any witnesses at all," Bobby Lee said.

"That's because you have not presented a witness who is material to the case," Judge Briggs said. "Now, I will ask you again. Have you anything further to present in your defense?"

Bobby Lee shook his head. "Only that I didn't do it. I mean, yes, sir, I was there, but like I say, I was there trying to catch the Frank Dodd gang. And if Sheriff Wallace had done what I asked him to do in the letter, if he had been there like he was supposed to, then more than likely Mr. Fletcher would still be alive, and Dodd and the others with him would be in jail."

"Objection, Your Honor," Roswell said. "As the letter is not in evidence, it cannot again be mentioned, either in presentation or summary."

"Sustained. Do you understand what that means, Mr. Cabot?" Briggs asked.

"I'm not sure that I do understand, Judge."

"It means that this letter, whether real or supposed, is of no use to you in your defense. You may not mention it again. Do you understand it now?"

"Yes, sir. Uh, yes, Your Honor."

"Do you have anything else to present in your defense?"

"No, Your Honor."

"Very well. Mr. Roswell, make your case," the judge said.

"Your Honor, prosecution calls Sheriff Herman Wallace to the stand," Roswell said.

"Sheriff Wallace, take the stand, please," Judge Briggs said.

Wallace stood, hiked up his trousers, then walked to the front of the courtroom. After he was sworn in, he took the stand, which was a chair next to the table Judge Briggs was using as his bench. Wallace was so big that once he sat down, none of the chair could be seen. As a result, it almost looked as if he were just squatting in the front of the room, and for some reason, despite the severity of the moment, Bobby Lee found the picture funny. He laughed out loud.

"Do you find these proceedings funny, Mr. Cabot?" Judge Briggs asked sharply.

"No, Your Honor," Bobby Lee replied.

"Then please display the proper decorum in my courtroom."

"Yes, Your Honor."

"Counselor, you may continue with your direct," Judge Briggs said.

"Thank you, Your Honor," Roswell said. He then turned his attention to his witness.

"Sheriff Wallace, defense claims that the two of you were working together. He further claims that he provided you with all the information as to time and place regarding the robbery, and that you were to secrete yourself in the express car for the purpose of arresting Dodd when the robbery was attempted. Are any of those claims true?"

"No, they are not," Wallace replied forcefully.

"Let's dismiss this subject of a letter once and

for all. Did you receive a letter from the defendant, outlining all or any of these proposals?"

"I did not."

"Would you have acted if you had received such a letter?"

"Absolutely," Wallace said. "For the opportunity to take out the Dodd gang, I would have done anything necessary. But I never received such a letter."

"Do you know Minnie Smith, the person that Cabot attempted to call on his behalf?"

"I know who she is, yes."

"Assuming the judge had allowed her to testify, would her testimony have been credible?"

"I doubt it," Wallace replied.

"Why not?"

"Miss Smith is—uh—I don't like to say it in mixed company."

"Come, now, Sheriff. We are all adults and we bear a serious responsibility with this trial. So I ask you again. Why do you feel that Miss Smith's testimony would not be credible?"

"She is a—soiled dove."

"I beg your pardon?"

"She is a whore," Wallace said.

Roswell nodded, then looked toward the young woman who was sitting in the front row. "Is her profession the only reason you would find her testimony untrustworthy?"

"No, sir. Like all whores, I suppose, she has her favorite. And for reasons unbeknownst to me, Bobby Lee Cabot seems to be that one, though what she sees in him, I'll never know."

The gallery laughed.

"I object!" Bobby Lee shouted.

"What is your objection, Mr. Cabot?" Judge Briggs asked.

"I object to them calling Miss Smith a whore."

Again the gallery laughed, and Judge Briggs made use of his gavel. When the laughter stopped, he looked over at Bobby Lee. "I am going to accept your objection, Mr. Cabot, but not for the reason you stated. It had already been ruled that Miss Smith cannot testify. Therefore any reference to her in any way will not be allowed." Briggs turned toward the jury. "Please disregard everything you have heard about Miss Smith's reliability as a witness, as she will not be a witness." He then addressed Roswell. "And Counselor, if you introduce her again during the course of these proceedings, I will hold you in contempt. Do you understand me, sir?"

"I do, Your Honor."

"You may continue with your direct."

"Thank you, Sheriff. No further questions." Roswell turned toward Bobby Lee. "Your witness," he said.

Bobby Lee made no reply.

"Mr. Cabot, do you wish to cross-examine this witness?" the judge asked.

"I beg your pardon, Your Honor?"

Judge Briggs sighed, then stroked his chin. "Do you wish to ask this witness any questions?"

"Yes, Your Honor."

"Then now is the time to do so," Briggs said.

Bobby Lee walked over to stand near the sheriff. "Sheriff, when those people from the train brought me in to you as their prisoner, did one of the men who had been guarding me tell you that during the night he had fallen asleep, and that I had loosened my bonds and took possession of his pistol?"

"Yes."

"And did that same man tell you that when he awoke the next morning, I returned the pistol?"

"Yes."

"Do you not think that if I were truly guilty, I would have escaped during the night?"

"The train was running," Sheriff Wallace said.

"Has no one ever jumped from a running train before?"

"I suppose they have."

"Don't you think that the reason I did not try to escape was because I knew I was innocent, and I believed you would back me up?"

"No. I think you just wanted to try and fool the guard into believing you were innocent."

"What would be the advantage of that? He had no authority to clear my name. Only you have that authority."

"I don't know what you mean?"

"Yes, you do, Sheriff. You knew what we had planned. Don't you think I had every reason to believe that you would let me go?"

"I don't know. Maybe you were crazy."

There was more laughter from the gallery, and again, the judge gaveled them quiet.

"Sheriff, did I not tell you when we returned to the jail that I was surprised that you weren't in the express car? Did my letter not ask you to do that?"

"Look here, I never got this letter you are talking about," Wallace said, pointing at Bobby Lee.

"Objection, Your Honor, this supposed letter has already been dealt with," Roswell shouted.

"Your Honor, you said the others couldn't testify because I had only told them about the letter," Bobby Lee said quickly. "The sheriff is the person I sent the letter to. If I did send it, and he denies it, then he is lying under oath, and isn't that called perjury?"

Briggs thought for a moment, then he nodded. "It is indeed called perjury, Mr. Cabot. Prosecution's objection is overruled. You may continue."

"Thank you, Your Honor. Sheriff Wallace, knowing that you are under oath, I ask you again. Did you receive the letter I sent?"

"No."

"Without regard to the letter, in conversation did I or did I not tell you that I had joined Dodd's gang for the purposes of setting a trap for him, and that I wanted you and your deputies to be in the express car?"

"I don't recall any such conversation."

"You are denying that we spoke about this, and you are denying that you received a letter from me."

"Objection, Your Honor, questions have been asked and answered."

"Sustained. Counselor, I believe you have taken this line of questioning about as far as you can take it," Judge Briggs said. "Do you have any questions of a different line?"

Dejectedly, Bobby Lee shook his head. "No, sir, Your Honor."

"Redirect, Mr. Prosecutor?"

"No, Your Honor."

"Do you have any further witnesses, Mr. Roswell?" Judge Briggs asked.

"I have no further witnesses, Your Honor, but

I do have a letter from the WCSA that I would like to read into the court records as evidence," Ray Roswell said.

"And the WCSA is?"

"The Western Capital Security Agency, Your Honor. It is the private detective group for which Bobby Lee Cabot claims he was working undercover."

"You may read the letter," Judge Briggs said.

Roswell cleared his throat, then began to read aloud.

"The Western Capital Security Agency has no record of recommending that Mr. Cabot associate himself with the outlaw Frank Dodd. On the contrary, we would strongly oppose such an idea. If Mr. Cabot was functioning as a part of the Dodd gang, it was for reasons of his own, and not for any type of investigative operation."

There was a collective gasp from the gallery.

"Hell, that proves it right there!" someone shouted. "No need to go on any further with this trial! Hang the son of a bitch!"

"Quiet! Quiet in the court!" Judge Briggs said, making aggressive use of his gavel.

"Your Honor, that doesn't prove anything!" Bobby Lee shouted. "I didn't tell the agency that I was doing this."

"Are you putting that in the form of an objection, Mr. Cabot?" Judge Briggs asked.

"An objection, yeah. Uh, I mean, yes, sir, Your Honor."

"Objection overruled." Judge Briggs looked at Roswell. "You may continue, Counselor."

"Yes, Your Honor. I would like to point out to the jury that because of Cabot's connection with the Western Capital Security Agency, he would know all the schedules, and he would know which trains would be carrying large amounts of money. This would make him a valuable asset to someone like Frank Dodd. And with that, prosecution rests."

"Thank you. Summation, Mr. Cabot?"

"I beg your pardon?"

"This is where you make your final appeal to the jury."

Bobby Lee didn't even stand. Instead, he looked directly at the jury. "I can't prove that I'm innocent, because neither Miss Smith nor Doc Baker nor Nate Nabors could stand up here and tell you what I told them about the letter, and Sheriff Wallace, who was the only witness I spoke to, lied. Also, I know that the letter from the WCSA makes it look bad for me, but everything I said is true. I worked my way into the Dodd gang so I could set it up for the sheriff to capture them in the act. Only, the sheriff wasn't there, so nothing went the way it was supposed to. So here I am, on trial for my life, and there doesn't seem to be anything I can do about it except tell you that I'm not guilty."

"Mr. Roswell, your summation?"

Taking his cue from Bobby Lee, Roswell didn't stand either.

"Gentlemen of the jury, I believe my case has been made," he said. "All you have to do is consider the facts in evidence. I am confident you will come up with the verdict of guilty of murder in the first degree."

After the judge charged the jury, the twelve men retired to one of the other rooms of the hotel to consider. It took but ten minutes for them to return a verdict of guilty.

"Will the defendant stand before the bench, please? Mr. Reid, approach with him."

"He fired me, Your Honor," Reid replied.

"Nevertheless, you are the court-appointed attorney of record. I don't want any technicalities coming up after the fact. Please approach with him."

"Yes, Your Honor."

"Bobby Lee Cabot, you have been found guilty as charged. It is therefore the order of this court that a gallows be built sufficient to provide the mechanism needed to extinguish your life by hanging, said event to take place on the thirty-first of this month. May God have mercy on your soul. Sheriff, remove the prisoner."

"No!" a woman shouted out loud.

"Bailiff, remove that woman from my court," Judge Briggs ordered.

As the sheriff put the cuffs back on Bobby Lee, he saw one of the sheriff's deputies escort a weeping Minnie Smith from the hotel ballroom cum courtroom.

"I'll come see you, Bobby Lee. I promise, I'll come see you!" Minnie shouted.

"Bake him a cake, Minnie! Bake him a cake and put a file in it!" someone called, and to the raucous laughter of all in the court, Bobby Lee was removed and taken back to the jail.

Chapter Four

Smoke stood looking at the baby in the cradle. He reached down and pulled away the cover so he could see the baby's feet. Then he reached down to play with the baby's toes. The baby smiled up at him. He heard a soft laugh behind him.

"Why do you love to play with his feet so?"

"I don't know. I guess because his toes are so tiny."

"Of course he has tiny toes. He is just a baby."

"Isn't he a handsome little thing, though?" Smoke asked.

"Ha! I've never heard of anyone being so vain," the baby's mother said.

"What do you mean vain?"

"He looks exactly like you. For you to say he is handsome is the same thing as your saying you are handsome."

"Well?" Smoke teased. "Didn't you tell Preacher you thought that I was a handsome man?"

"You are hopeless," she said, laughing at him as she picked up a pillow and hit him.

Smoke took the pillow away and grabbed her, then pulled her into his arms and kissed her.

"Uhmm, careful," she said. "You know what happened the last time we started this, don't you?"

"What?"

She nodded toward the baby in the crib.

"That happened," she said.

"So, would it be so bad for little Art to have a brother?"

"Ha! Are you that sure it would be another boy?"

"I was right the first time, wasn't I? I think we should just see if I'm right this time." Swooping her up, he carried Nicole to bed.

Nicole? But how can this be?

With a start, Smoke set up in bed. His breathing was labored, and he felt a heavy pain in his heart. Looking over at the woman who was sleeping beside him, he saw, not Nicole, but Sally.

His wife, Nicole, was long dead now, brutally murdered by three men: Potter, Richards, and Stratton. The same three men had also killed their baby, Art. Even now, the very mention of their names brought Smoke's blood to a boil.

Smoke had tracked them down to the town of Bury, Idaho. As events developed, the name of the town was prophetic, because the three men wound up being buried there.

The dream of Nicole had been unbidden, and unexpected. But now as he sat up in the dark of the bedroom he shared with Sally, he wanted to remember. He wanted to take some comfort from the fact that justice had been done. He'd burned down the entire town, then dealt with the killers of his wife and son.

* * *

. . . *Richards, Potter, and Stratton stood at one end of the block. A tall, bloody figure stood at the other. All their guns were in leather.*

"You son of a bitch!" Stratton screamed, his voice as high-pitched as a woman. "You ruined it all." He clawed at his .44.

Smoke drew and fired before Stratton's pistol could clear leather. Potter grabbed for his pistol. Smoke shot him dead, then holstered his gun, waiting.

Richards had not moved. He stood with a faint smile on his lips, staring at Smoke.

"You ready to die?" Smoke asked the man.

"As ready as I'll ever be, I suppose," Richards replied. There was no fear in his voice. His hand appeared steady. "Been a long run, hasn't it, Jensen?"

"It's just about over."

"What happens to all our holdings?"

"I don't care what happens to the mines. The miners can have them. I'm giving all your stock to decent, honest punchers and homesteaders."

A puzzled look spread over Richards's face. "I don't understand. You did . . . all this"—he waved his hand—"for nothing?"

"I did it for my wife and my baby son."

"But it won't bring them back!"

"I know."

"I wish I had never heard the name Jensen."

"You'll never hear it again after this day, Richards."

"One way to find out," Richards said with a smile. He drew his Colt and fired. He was snake-quick, but he hurried his shot, the lead digging up dirt at Smoke's feet.

Smoke shot him in the right shoulder, spinning the man around. Richards grabbed for his left-hand gun and Smoke fired again, the slug striking the man in the left side of his chest. He struggled to bring up his Colt.

He managed to cock it before Smoke's third shot struck him in the belly. Richards sat down hard in the bloody, dusty street.

He opened his mouth to speak. He tasted blood on his tongue. The light began to fade around him. "You'll . . . meet . . ."

Smoke never found out who he was supposed to meet. Richards toppled over on his side and died.[2]

Slowly, the memories drifted away. Why had he dreamed of Nicole? There had been many years that had passed since she and Arthur were killed, and yet, in his dream, Nicole was so real that he half expected her to be lying next to him when he awoke.

But it wasn't Nicole, it was Sally, and looking over at her now, he knew that she did not have to feel threatened by the dream, just as he knew that his love for Nicole did not end with her dying. Getting out of bed carefully so as not to awaken Sally, Smoke padded barefoot across the bedroom floor, where he stood at the window looking out at his ranch, Sugarloaf.

The ranch was not only big. It was also one of the most profitable cattle operations in the entire state of Colorado. From this window, he could see the barn and corral, the bunkhouse, the cookhouse, and the rolling pasture beyond, all painted in silver and black under the full moon that floated high in the night sky above. Kirby Jensen had come a long way from the wild Missouri boy who grew up in the mountains under

---

[2]*Return of the Mountain Man*

the tutelage of one of the most storied mountain men in history, a man who was known far and wide as Preacher.

After avenging Nicole's murder, Smoke met a schoolteacher named Sally Reynolds. And though he had thought no woman could ever replace Nicole, Sally had done just that. She had not eliminated Nicole, for the memory of Smoke's first wife would forever be kept green. But Sally had certainly established her own claim to his heart.

"Smoke?"

He had not wanted to awaken her, but he realized now that she had probably been awake from the moment he got out of bed. In the quiet, dark room, Sally's voice was soft, resonant, and comforting. "Smoke, are you all right?"

Smoke looked back toward the bed. Sally had raised herself up on her elbows to look over at him. The white silk of her nightgown shimmering in the moonlight. Why did he dream of Nicole? Was his dream of his first wife a betrayal of this one?

No, surely not, just as his concern about the dream was not a betrayal of Nicole.

"I'm fine," he said. "I'm sorry if I woke you."

"What are you doing up?"

"I don't know, I just woke up."

"Did you have a dream?"

"Yes."

"A nightmare?"

"A nightmare?" Smoke thought of the dream, and of the warmth and love he had felt for Nicole and the baby in that dream. "No," he said. "No, it wasn't a nightmare."

"Would you like me to get up as well? I could make us some coffee," Sally said.

Smoke walked back over to the bed and sat down on her side. He reached for Sally and pulled her to him, then kissed her deeply.

"Uhmm," she said. "Whatever your dream was about, I like it."

"About the coffee?" Smoke said.

"Yes?"

"I don't think we are going to need it." Crossing around to the other side of the bed Smoke climbed into bed beside her, then pulled her to him. Outside their window, the limb of an aspen tree was moved by a gentle breeze, the leaves catching the moonlight, to send a sliver of silver through the night.

The aroma of freshly made bear claws drifted out of the kitchen and into the yard, all the way over to the bunkhouse. Pearlie noticed it first and he began sniffing the air.

"What are you doing?" Cal asked.

Without answering, Pearlie pulled on his boots, then started for the door. Before he reached the door, Cal got a whiff as well and, even though he only had on one boot, he ran after Pearlie, hopping and skipping across the yard with one boot on his left foot and the other in his hand.

"No, you don't!" he called out after Pearlie. "You ain't goin' to get ahead of me!"

The two young men burst into the kitchen just as Sally was taking the pastries from the oven.

"My, oh, my, do them smell good!" Pearlie said.

"It's do 'those' smell good," Cal corrected.

Sally smiled. "Very good, Cal. I'm impressed."

"Seems to me like somebody that can't speak English good probably ought not to get any bear claws," Cal said, putting on his other boot.

"Oh, I'm afraid that would leave you out as well," Sally said.

"Why?"

"It's can't speak English well," Smoke put in, coming into the kitchen then.

"Oh, well, I was just teasin'," Cal said. "Sure I want Pearlie to have some."

"That's very generous of you, sharing my bear claws like that," Smoke teased.

"Your bear claws? That's funny, I thought I was the one that made them," Sally said.

"Well, you didn't make 'em all for yourself, did you, Miss Sally?" Cal asked.

Sally put the pan on the table. "No, I didn't make them all for myself. You can have one as soon as they are cool enough for you to—oh, never mind," she added with a little laugh when she saw Cal and Pearlie each grab one, then toss it from hand to hand until they could raise it to their mouth.

"Must be a special occasion for you to make bear claws this morning," Smoke said. "Anything I might know about?"

Sally smiled. "Maybe," she said.

Smoke knew she was referring to their intimacy during the night, and he smiled back, then reached for a bear claw. "Always glad I could please," he said.

"What? Why, you!" Sally sputtered.

"What are you all talking about?" Cal asked.

"Cal, are you going to put that boot on, or just

stand here in my kitchen with it dangling from your hand?" Sally asked.

"Oh. I'm going to put it on," he said. And with the bear claw hanging from his mouth, he sat on the floor and pulled the other boot on.

"What are you two boys going to do today?" Smoke asked.

"Ride fence up in the north quarter," Pearlie answered.

"You'll be out all day. Better have the cook put you up a lunch."

"Yes, sir, I thought we would."

"And maybe?" Cal asked, mumbling the word around the pastry.

"You can each take a couple more with you," Sally said.

"Thank you!"

The two young cowboys grabbed the bear claw–shaped doughnuts, then hurried out of the kitchen to begin their daily chores.

"I wish someone would invent a machine to let you look inside a person," Smoke said as Pearlie and Cal hurried across the yard to the barn. "I swear, the only innards either of them have is stomach."

Sally laughed. "You aren't far behind," she said.

"It's your fault," Smoke said as he reached for a second. "You are just too good a cook."

"Smoke, may I ask you a question?"

"Sure."

"What was your dream last night?"

Smoke hesitated for a moment. "I dreamed about Nicole," he said.

"I hope it was a pleasant dream."

Smoke walked over to Sally, put his arms

around her, and pulled her to him. He brushed her hair away from her forehead and kissed her there.

"It was," he said. "But you have no reason to be jealous."

"I'm not in the least jealous," she said, turning her head up so his kiss came to her lips.

Chapter Five

Back in the jail cell in Cloverdale, Nevada, Bobby Lee Cabot was lying on his bunk, his hands laced behind his head as he stared up at the ceiling. Outside the jail, he could hear the sawing and hammering on the gallows that was being constructed for his hanging.

"Are you scared, Bobby Lee?"

The question came from the prisoner who was in the cell next to his. Andy Emerson was a small man, around five feet five inches tall, with a sweeping mustache that seemed oversized for his short stature. He was also a cowboy who drank too much. He was never a mean drunk, though he did, in his own words, sometimes develop "a mountain lion's attitude in a pussycat's body." He often manifested this mannerism when confronting Sheriff Wallace or one of his deputies, and as a result, Wallace had a personal grudge against him. Andy spent a lot of time in jail for public drunkenness when others, who were often drunker, were given a pass.

"I guess I'm a little frightened," Bobby Lee confessed.

"A little frightened? If I was about to be hanged, I'd be so scared I couldn't even talk," Andy said. "You're about the bravest person I ever met."

"I'm not that brave, Andy, believe me," Bobby Lee said. "What's the sheriff got you in for now?"

"I was at the Gold Strike last night," Andy said. "I had a few drinks, sure, but I wasn't drunk, you can ask anybody there. But the next thing you know, Wallace was in there accusin' me of getting drunk and causing a disturbance." Andy paused for a moment. "The thing is, well, he just kept pushin' until I got mad and I shoved him. Then I really was causin' a disturbance. But only 'cause he sort of drove me to it."

"Andy, we've talked about this before," Bobby Lee said. "You really do have to cut back on your drinking. You've gotten yourself on the sheriff's bad side and he's just going to keep riding you till you really do get in trouble."

"I know, I know," Andy said. "You've always been straight with me. I ought to pay attention to you."

At that moment, they heard the sound of the door that led from the front half of the building back to the jail cells being opened. Deputy Harley Beard came into the back and opened the door to Andy's cell. "You can go now," he said. "But next time we catch you drunk in town, you'll wind up in here again."

"Yeah," Andy said, reaching back onto the bunk for his hat. He put it on, then looked over at Bobby Lee.

"Bobby Lee, when it happens—uh, I mean,

when they hang you—I ain't goin' to be there watchin'. I hope you understand. I've always figured you for a friend, and I don't think I want to watch a friend get his neck stretched. That don't mean I'm not goin' to be thinkin' about you. It's just that I don't want to be here when it's happenin'.'"

"I understand," Bobby Lee replied.

"Bye, Bobby Lee."

"You goin' to hang around jabberin' with him, or are you goin' to get out of here?" Deputy Beard asked. "'Cause if you're just goin' to hang around, I can put you back in jail and you two folks can just visit all you want."

"I'm goin'," Andy said.

Beard waited until Andy left before he turned to Bobby Lee's cell.

"Cabot, you got a visitor," Deputy Beard said.

"Who is it?"

"Who is it? It's the whore. Who else would waste their time comin' to see you?"

"Good, please send her in."

Beard disappeared into the front of the building, but Bobby Lee could still hear him talking.

"Better let me search you, to make sure you ain't takin' him no weapons." There was a decided leering tone in the sound of his voice.

"Watch your hands." There was irritation in the woman's voice.

"Ha! Like you haven't had hands there before," Beard said. "All right, you can go in."

Standing at the front of his cell, Bobby Lee watched as Minnie Smith came into the back. Minnie was a pretty girl, and would have been prettier, Bobby Lee believed, if she would just let nature take its course. But, defying nature, she had dyed her hair, which was naturally auburn, a henna-tinted red. Her eyes were shaded, her cheeks were rouged, and her lips were painted.

The dye and makeup was because of Minnie's occupation, which technically was saloon hostess, though other sobriquets were used, such as hurdy-gurdy girl, parlor girl, and soiled dove. In truth, she was a prostitute, but Bobby Lee saw more than that in her. Minnie had been present all during his trial, and had cried bitter tears when Bobby Lee was sentenced.

"Oh, Bobby Lee," she said. "I can't stand it. I know you sent that letter to Sheriff Wallace, you told me about it. But I can't get anyone to believe me. I'm so sorry."

"Don't worry about it," Bobby Lee said.

"How can I not worry about it?" She pointed toward the front of the building. "Do you know they are building a gallows right now in front of this very building?"

"Yes, I've heard them at work. Minnie, I need you to do something for me."

"What? What do you want?" Minnie asked. "I'll do anything you ask."

"I want you to send a telegram for me."

"A telegram? To the governor?" She shook her head. "It won't do any good, Bobby Lee. I've already sent a telegram to the governor."

"No, not to the governor," Bobby Lee said. "I want you to send this to a friend of mine. If there is anybody in the world who can do anything for me, it will be him."

"All right, give me the name of the person, tell me what you want to say and where you want it to go," Minnie said. "I'll send it."

After Minnie received her instructions and left, Bobby Lee lay back down on his bunk again to resume staring at the ceiling above. Outside, he could hear the sounds of the men as they continued to work on the gallows.

"All right, boys, lift up the cross tree," one of the carpenters shouted. "There you go. Hold it in position while I get it nailed down."

The carpenter's vocal instructions were followed by the banging of the hammer.

Realistically, Bobby Lee knew the chances were only about one in one hundred that the telegram would reach its destination. According to the sentence of the judge, he was to hang on the thirty-first. That was only one week away.

Bobby Lee was sure that Minnie would send the telegram—he had that much faith in her—but he really had no sense of confidence that the telegram would actually get through. He had asked her to send it to Buck West, rather than Smoke Jensen, believing that by so doing it would get Smoke's attention more quickly. Now he wondered if perhaps he had been too smart by half. What if the telegram didn't reach Smoke? For that matter, what if the telegram did reach Smoke, but because it was addressed to Buck West, he chose to do nothing about it?

One thousand miles east from the Cloverdale Jail, in the town of Big Rock, Colorado, a rather sizable crowd was watching a spirited horseshoe pitch. A tossed horseshoe hit the peg, made a loud clang, spun around the peg, then settled down.

"Ringer!" Jason Whitman shouted. "Looks like Smoke beat you, Floyd."

"Damn," Floyd said. "Smoke, is there anything you can't do? 'Cause if there is, I sure want to give you a go on it."

"Sally says I can't knit worth a damn," Smoke said.

"Is that a fact? Well, I'll tell you what," Floyd said. "I believe I'll just take up knittin' so's I can find somethin' I can beat you at."

The others laughed at the barber's lament. Floyd Carr had been the champion horseshoe thrower for Big Rock for three years running. He had about convinced himself that he was the best in the entire state of Colorado, and didn't believe it when he was told by those who had seen Smoke throw horseshoes for fun out at his ranch that Smoke was better.

Reluctantly, Smoke had taken up Floyd's challenge, and had just beaten him in three straight games.

Accepting the accolades of those gathered for the match, Smoke begged out of a celebratory drink at the Longmont Saloon by explaining that he had to get back to the ranch.

"You mean you'd rather go back home than have a few drinks with your friends?" Whitman asked.

"Whitman, that's about the dumbest question I've ever heard," Sheriff Carson said.

"What's so dumb about it?" Whitman asked.

"What friends at Longmont's are you talking about?"

"Well, Louis will be there. Floyd will. You'll be there too, I reckon. And I'll be there."

"Uh-huh," Carson said.

"So?"

"Think about it, Jason," Carson said. "We'll be at Longmont's. Sally is at Sugarloaf."

"Oh," Whitman said. "Oh, yeah, I see what you mean."

The others laughed, then shouted their good-byes to Smoke when he swung into the saddle for the ride home.

As Smoke rode by the Western Union office, the telegrapher stepped into the front door and called out to him.

"Smoke, I've got a telegram here that's addressed to Sugarloaf Ranch. It came late yesterday afternoon, and I was goin' to get a boy to bring it out to your place today, but seeing as you are here, maybe you'll take it."

"Thanks, I'll take it."

"Yes, sir," the telegrapher said. "The only thing is, it's addressed to a fella by the name of Buck West, and I don't believe I've ever heard of him. Do you know such a person?"

The name Buck West got Smoke's attention. For a while, Smoke had been on the dodge, and he'd used the name Buck West. There weren't too many people around who knew about that part of his life. And certainly anyone who knew to send a telegram to Sugarloaf Ranch would know that he wasn't using that name anymore. It made him very curious.

Smoke gave the telegrapher a quarter, then

stuck the telegram in his pocket. He planned to wait until he got back to the ranch before he read it, but curiosity got the best of him so, about a mile out of town, he reached into his pocket and pulled out the telegram.

BOBBY LEE CABOT TO BE HANGED AUGUST 31 IN CLOVERDALE NEVADA STOP COME QUICK TO GOLD STRIKE SALOON MINNIE SMITH

Bobby Lee Cabot had been Nicole's half brother. He'd been younger than Nicole, she had partially raised him, and for a while Bobby Lee had even lived with Nicole and Smoke. Bobby Lee had practically worshiped the ground Smoke walked on, and Smoke remembered him fondly. He had no idea who Minnie Smith was, but if she had sent him a message addressed to Buck West, then he knew that it was authentic. She could only have been given that information by Bobby Lee.

Smoke rode about another half mile toward home while he contemplated the message. He was glad that Bobby Lee had thought to contact him, because he was absolutely not going to let him be hanged—of that he was sure. What he was not sure about was what he was going to do to stop it.

Then, with a smile, Smoke came up with an idea. But in order to make the idea work, he was going to have to ride back in town to visit the printing shop. Turning back toward town, Smoke slapped his legs against the side of his horse, causing the animal to break into a ground-eating lope. He reined up in front of the sheriff's office, then stepped inside.

"Smoke," Carson called to him. "Come back to lord it over Floyd a bit, did you?"

"No," Smoke said. "I need a favor from you, Monte."

"Ask, you've got it."

Smoke explained his idea.

"I don't know, Smoke," Carson said. "What you are asking for doesn't make a lot of sense to me."

"Will you do it?"

"Yes, of course I will," Carson said. "Just because it doesn't make sense to me doesn't mean it isn't a bad idea. You're one of the smartest men I know, so I figure you've probably got it worked out in a way I haven't considered yet."

"Thanks," Smoke said.

Sheriff Carson wrote out a note, then handed to Smoke. "Show this to Curly," he said. "And if he still has questions, tell him to come see me."

Curly Latham listened to Smoke's request.

"Let me get this straight," the printer said. "You want me to print just one?"

"One is all I need," Smoke replied.

"I've never heard of such a thing," Curly said.

"Will you do it? Or do I have to go find another printer somewhere?"

"Look here, Smoke, you know how this works. It will cost you as much to have me print just one as it would to have me print one hundred. You know I'm going to do it for you if that is what you really want. I just hate taking advantage of you like this."

"I know," Smoke said. "But one is all I need. In fact, I very specifically do not want more than one printed. This isn't something I want anyone else to see, and I can control it much better this way."

"What about the sheriff? What does Monte think about it?"

"I stopped by to see Sheriff Carson before I came here. Here is a note from him," Smoke said.

Curly, please do as Smoke says. Just print one.
Sheriff Carson

Curly Latham shook his head in confusion. "All right, Smoke, if this is what you and the sheriff both want, I'll do it. But I sure as hell don't know what good just one of these things will do for you."

"Thanks, Curly. Oh, and would you put in an envelope and have it waiting for me at the sheriff's office? I have to get back out to the ranch, but I'll be taking the late train out tonight and I want to take this with me."

"It'll be there waitin' for you," Curly promised.

Sugarloaf Ranch, adequately timbered and well watered, with ample grass, was the culmination of all Smoke's dreams and aspirations. But he had not always been the "gentleman rancher." There was a time when he had ridden what many might call "the outlaw trail." And while he operated with equal alacrity between law and lawlessness, he had never crossed the line between right and wrong. Of course, there were some things that he considered right that might be questioned by others, such as hunting down and killing the men who had killed his father, then going on the vengeance trail yet again to kill those who had murdered Nicole and his young son, Arthur.

Most of the people who knew Smoke now thought they knew everything there was to know about him. But there were very few of his current acquaintances who knew there had been a wife before Sally. Smoke loved Sally, there was no denying that, but had Nicole not been murdered, he would have never even met Sally. Most of the time the shadows of his past remained just that, shadows. It served no purpose to bring those memories to the surface, but this telegram had done that.

It was funny. He had just had a dream about Nicole, which was unusual in more ways than one. It was unusual because, though she still occupied a part of his heart, he had managed, quite successfully until the dream, to put her out of his mind. And it was unusual because, in a way, his dream of Nicole seemed to presage this telegram from her brother.

Was it just a coincidence? Or had the dream been a warning of what was to come? He knew that the Indians put great store in the power of dreams, and, for that matter, so did Preacher. He had always respected Preacher, and if Preacher felt that way about dreams, then he figured there might be something to it—but until this incident, he had never encountered the power of the "dream spirit."

When Smoke arrived at his ranch, he saw Pearlie sitting at an outside table just under a spreading oak tree. There was a saddle on the table in front of his foreman, and Pearlie was doing some repair work. A peal of laughter rang out from over by the little cluster of houses, where the families of some of his Mexican workers lived, and Smoke smiled when he saw Cal chasing after the laughing children as he swung a lariat over his head. In many ways, Cal was still a kid himself.

Both Pearlie and Cal waved at him, and he returned their wave, then went into the big house.

"Hello, darling," Sally said, greeting him with a big smile. "How did you do at horseshoes?"

"I won."

"I never had any doubt. By the way, I'm making a chicken pot pie for supper tonight. We'll call it a celebration of your winning at horseshoes. I hope you are hungry."

"How soon can you have it ready?" Smoke asked.

Sally laughed. "My goodness, I guess you really are hungry."

"No it's not that," Smoke said. "I have to catch a train tonight."

Sally's expression changed from one of a smile to one of curious concern. "Is something wrong?"

Smoke showed Sally the telegram. She read it, then looked up at him with a quizzical expression on her face. "You are going to Nevada?"

"Yes."

"That's a long way to go, isn't it?"

"Darlin', if they were about to hang Bobby Lee in China, I would go see what I could do to help."

"That brings up the next question. Who is Bobby Lee Cabot?"

"He is Nicole's brother," Smoke said.

Sally nodded. No further explanation was needed.

"I'll hurry supper, then I'll pack your things," she said.

Although Pearlie and Cal frequently ate with the other cowboys, they were more like family than hired hands, so just as frequently they ate with Smoke and Sally. They especially did so on nights like tonight when Sally had gone out of her way to fix something special.

It was Pearlie who noticed it first— Smoke's saddlebags, neatly packed, as well as his rifle and canteen, over by the wall.

"Are we going somewhere?" Pearlie asked, nodding toward the gear.

"We aren't," Smoke replied. "I am."

"Wait a minute," Cal said. "That ain't right, Smoke. We always go as a team."

"That isn't right," Sally suggested.

"See, even Sally agrees."

"I was correcting your grammar."

"Oh."

"Cal, this is something personal," Smoke said. "Very personal. It concerns something that happened before you, before Pearlie, even before Sally."

"Well, yeah, but I mean—"

"You heard him Cal," Pearlie said, interrupting

the younger cowboy. "Some things are, like Smoke said, personal."

Looking around, Cal saw the expressions on the other faces, and those expressions told him he was in the wrong.

"Oh, uh, yeah, I see what you mean," Cal said. "I'm sorry, Smoke. You go on by yourself if you want to. You won't hear nothin' else from me."

Sally drew a breath to correct his grammar yet again, but she left the words unspoken. She was not a schoolteacher anymore, and she had about decided that Cal was a lost cause anyway. Besides, he was obviously feeling rejected right now, so there was no need to add to his discomfort by more grammatical corrections.

Smoke smiled at Cal. "I'm glad I have your permission."

"My permission? No, I didn't mean it like that. I mean, of course you can go anywhere you want. You don't never need my permission a'tall."

"Oh. Well, I'm glad to hear that."

Smoke laughed, as did the others, at Cal's reaction. Smoke reached out and ran his hand through Cal's hair.

"I was teasing you, Cal," he said. "Look, ordinarily I would want Sally, Pearlie, and you with me. But trust me, this isn't a normal thing. Besides, you and Pearlie have that rodeo to go to, remember?"

"Oh, yeah, I nearly forgot that."

"How can you nearly forget that?" Pearlie challenged. "We just been practicin' for it for near a month now."

"Well, I didn't really nearly forget it, I just nearly

forgot it is all," Cal said, as if his explanation made any sense at all.

"Smoke has a train to catch tonight," Sally said. "What do you say that any more conversation we have, we have while we are eating?"

Chapter Six

Sally, Pearlie, and Cal rode with Smoke into town. There, they stopped by the sheriff's office to pick up the document Smoke had printed, then went on to the railroad station so they could see Smoke off on the train.

"If you would, Charley, book me only on trains that have an attached stock car. I plan to take my horse with me."

"All right," the stationmaster replied. He worked on the tickets for a few moments, then handed a packet of them to Smoke.

"You'll leave here at eleven tonight," Charley explained. "You will arrive in Colorado Springs at one in the morning, where you will change trains, then depart Colorado Springs at two a.m., arrive in Cheyenne, Wyoming, at eleven tomorrow morning. Because you will need a stock car, you won't be able to depart Cheyenne until three o'clock tomorrow afternoon. Then comes the long ride, from Cheyenne to Battle Mountain, Nevada. You will reach Battle Mountain at eight a.m. the next day. I'm afraid you are going to have to spend the entire day in Battle Mountain, because you won't leave until ten that evening. You'll reach Cloverdale at eight o'clock on the following morning. It will be an all-night trip, but your passage should be quite comfortable, as the train is equipped with Pullman cars."

"It's good to see that you have it all worked out for me," Smoke said.

"Oh, and Smoke, I don't know how dependable the shipping people are at all these stations, so if I were you, I would keep an eye on your horse at each place."

"Thanks, Charley, I intend to," Smoke replied.

Tickets in hand, Smoke sat inside the depot with Sally and his two friends as they waited for the midnight special. It was called that, even though most of the time it was scheduled to arrive at about eleven.

"What kind of a fella is this Bobby Lee?" Cal asked.

"I'm not sure," Smoke said. "He was not much more than a kid the last time I saw him, but he was as fine a kid as I've ever known. I've only heard from him once or twice since Nicole died. I think he rode shotgun on a stage for a while, and was a deputy somewhere up in Wyoming. I don't know how he got to this place in Nevada, and I have no idea why they are about to hang him."

"Do you think he is innocent?" Cal asked.

"I don't know. But I don't care whether he is innocent or not."

"You mean, even if he was guilty, you would go try to rescue him?" Cal asked.

"I'm not going to *try* to do anything," Smoke said. "I am going to do it."

"Cal, quit asking such dumb questions," Pearlie said. "You mind how when I was in jail that Smoke come to rescue me?"[3]

"Yeah, but you hadn't been convicted yet," Cal replied.

"Do you think that would have mattered?"

"No," Cal said. "I don't reckon it would have mattered. Smoke would have rescued you, just like he's going to try to rescue this fella Cabot."

"I told you, there is no try about it," Smoke said. "I'm going to do it." He reached out to put his hand on Sally's hand and looked deep into her eyes.

As Smoke gazed deeply at her, Sally could almost look back in time to see the Smoke she had not known, the Smoke that had come before.

"I know that you will," Sally said.

They heard the whistle of the far off train.

"Sounds like the train is comin'," Cal said, stating the obvious.

Smoke had checked his rifle through with his saddle, but he kept his saddlebags with him, and he reached down to scoop them up.

"What do you say we go out onto the platform and watch that big beast roll in?" he suggested.

"All right," Sally answered.

Smoke draped the saddlebags over his right shoulder, then put his left arm around Sally's waist and pulled her closer. She leaned into him.

"You've got nothing to be jealous about, Sally," Smoke said quietly.

"Oh, darling, I know that. I'm not in the least

---

[3]*Savagery of the Mountain Man*

jealous," Sally said. "I think the fact that you can still have such a feeling for Nicole even though she has been dead these many years is one of the reasons I love you so. It's comforting in a way. It reassures me that if anything happened to me, you would still love me."

"Forever," Smoke said, squeezing her more tightly.

By the time they stepped out onto the platform, the train was already approaching the station with its big headlamp sending out a long beam of light ahead, catching hundreds of fluttering night insects in its glow. The exhaust valve was venting off the used steam so that huge puffy clouds of white swirled about the engine, reflecting in the platform lamplights so that they appeared to glow. The loud puffs echoed back from the sheer, red wall of Big Rock Cliff, just on the other side of the tracks. It was this cliff from which the town had taken its name. The bell clanged incessantly as the engine, a two-four-two, rolled up alongside them. The engine was so heavy that Smoke could feel the vibration in his stomach, and he saw small, burning embers dripping through the grates of the firebox and laying down a long, glowing trail to smolder between the tracks. The engineer was leaning on the sill of the cab window, eyes forward, with his hand on the brake valve.

Smoke heard the hiss of air as the brake cylinders were closed, followed by the squeal of iron on iron as the braking pads gradually clamped down on the wheels, bringing the train to a stop. For a moment, the train sat there, and all who were near the engine could hear the bubbling, gurgling sound of the boiling water, as well as the loud whoosh of excess steam pressure being bled off by the rhythmic opening and closing of the relief valve.

The conductor, impressive looking in his blue uniform and with the shining railroad badge on his cap, stepped down from the first car. He was carrying a small step-assist with him, and he put that in front of the boarding step that hung down from the car. Then, turning toward the car, he waited as three people got off. Because of the size of the town, Smoke knew almost everyone who lived here, and he recognized Mr. and Mrs. Dumey as they stepped down from the train. They weren't ranchers, but owned a small farm just outside of town. They also had a daughter in Colorado Springs, and Smoke was reasonably sure they were just now returning from a visit there.

Dumey verified that fact when, a second later, he saw Smoke standing there.

"Smoke, what do think?" Dumey called out to him. "We have a new granddaughter!"

Smoke smiled back. "Good news, Dumey. I hope she gets her looks from Carol and your daughter, and not from you," he teased.

Dumey laughed. "I think you are right there. I would not want her looking like this ugly face."

"Oh, Chris, what are you talking about? I think you are a very handsome man," Carol replied.

"Ah, you see, Smoke. I still have her fooled," Chris called back, eliciting more good-natured laughter.

Smoke recognized the drummer too. It was Phil Roach, and he sold ladies' notions.

"Hello, Phil, I hope you are having a successful outing," Smoke said.

"I'm doing well, thank you, Smoke," Phil replied.

Those were the only three people to get down from the train, and Smoke was the only one waiting to get on.

"You're it, Mr. Jensen," the conductor said. "Time to get on board."

"Thanks, Sam," Smoke replied. He looked over at Pearlie and Cal. "I expect you two boys to do me proud at the rodeo," he said.

"We will," Cal promised.

"Smoke . . ." Sally began, but she didn't finish her sentence.

"You were going to tell me to be careful, weren't you?" Smoke asked.

"No," Sally replied. "I wasn't going to—"

"Sally?" Smoke challenged.

"All right, yes, I suppose I was," Sally said. "But this will be the first time in a long time that you have gone anywhere without any of us. And you know yourself that there has been more than one incident where having us along was a good thing."

"I'll admit that, yes," Smoke said.

"We won't be with you this time."

"So?"

Sally laughed. "You are going to make me say it, aren't you?"

"Why not? You are dying to," Smoke said.

"All right. Be careful."

With another laugh, Smoke kissed her good-bye. Then he waved at Pearlie and Cal before stepping up into the car.

The car was dimly lit by six wall-mounted lanterns, three on either side, in the front, middle, and back of the car. Smoke found a seat midway through the car on the depot side, and sitting down, he raised the window and looked out at Sally, Pearlie, and Cal. They were still there, and would remain there, Smoke knew, not only until the train left the station, but until it was well out of sight.

It was odd, he thought, how a person's life took such turns and twists. As he sat there, looking out at the woman who was now so much a part of his life—a part of him, really—he could well believe that she was the only one ever for him. And yet, if Nicole had not been killed, he would have never even met Sally, and he knew, with no diminishment of his feelings for Sally, that he would have been just as happy and satisfied.

The engineer blew the whistle two times, then with a rattle of couplings, a squeak of bearings, and a few jerks to take up the slack, the train started forward. Within less than a minute, the train had reached its normal running speed of twenty-five miles per hour.

This train was not equipped with sleeping berths, so Smoke made himself as comfortable as he could under the circumstances. He pulled his hat down over his eyes, folded his arms across his chest, and quickly fell asleep.

He was going to be on a train for a long time.

When the town of Desolation, Nevada, was laid out, it was with the absolute assurance and confidence that the Nevada Central Railroad would come through. Instead, the railroad passed ten miles to the west. As a result, the town that had started with such high hopes was now withering on the vine.

There were some attempts to revive the town— talk, for example, of running a spur track from the main line to Desolation, much as had been done at Austin, which was ten miles south. A few stores hung on, depending upon area ranchers and miners to provide them with a customer base. But the most successful business establishment in Desolation was the New Promise Saloon.

Desolation had no city marshal. The nearest law was the Lander County sheriff, who was located in Austin, and he provided no deputies for the dying town. This complete lack of law meant that Desolation was a town where even those who had wanted posters being circulated on them could come without fear of being arrested. The citizens of Desolation had mixed feelings about this. Some welcomed the business of the outlaws since most of the outlaws not only had money, but had nowhere else to spend it except with the merchants of Desolation. In addition, others pointed out that, in a perverse way, the outlaw element was itself a form of protection, for none of the outlaws wanted to create a disturbance in the only place where they could feel welcome.

At the moment, Frank Dodd was sitting at a table in the back of the New Promise Saloon, eating pickled pig's feet and drinking beer.

"Dodd," Jules Stillwater said. "I got them two boys for you to meet."

Dodd gnawed at one of the pig's feet, pulling back the tough skin to get to a little piece of meat.

"What two boys?" he asked. He spit a piece of gristle onto the floor.

"Phillips and Garrison, the two I told you about. You said you wanted to get a couple more men to make up for losin' Cabot."

Dodd finished off the pig's foot, then set the white bone down with a little pile of white bones.

"All right bring 'em in."

Stillwater went back out front, then returned a moment later with two men. They were both of average size, and both were badly in need of a shave and in even worse need of a bath. One of them had a gun stuck down in his waistband; the other was wearing a well-worn holster.

"Either one of you ever used one of those before?" Dodd asked, pointing to the guns the men wore.

"Yeah, sure, lots of times," one of them replied. "Me 'n Garrison's done some robbin'."

"Where?" Dodd asked.

"Here and there."

"You ever held up a train?" Dodd asked.

Phillips, who was the one doing all the talking, shook his head no. "Don't reckon I have," he said.

"You think you've got the nerve to do it?"

"I reckon I do."

"What about you?" Dodd asked Garrison.

"Whatever Phillips says is fine by me," Garrison replied.

"Yeah, well, if you ride with me, it ain't what Phillips says, it's what I say. You'll be followin' my orders. You got that?"

Garrison nodded. "Yeah," he said. "I got that."

"Good."

"Why did you ask about robbin' a train?" Phillips asked. "Is that what we're goin' to do?"

"It may be," Dodd said.

"When?"

"When I tell you," Dodd replied.

Chapter Seven

It was the middle of the night when Smoke changed trains in Colorado Springs. The train had an extended stop in Denver, but it was still the dark of the morning and Smoke dozed in his seat, barely aware of the stop. It was nearly noon by the time he reached Cheyenne, and after making certain that his horse was off-loaded and put in the stable to be ready for the next leg, Smoke checked his saddlebags with the station-master, then found a saloon where he could kill a few hours.

"Do you serve meals here?" he asked.

"Ham, fried potatoes, and biscuits," the man behind the bar replied. He was wearing a white shirt with sleeve garters, and a string tie. "Not sure what kind of pie we have today. I think it's apple."

"Sounds good enough, I'll take it," Smoke said. He pointed to an empty table. "I'll be over there."

"All right," the bartender replied with a nod.

Smoke glanced toward two young men who

were standing at the far end of the bar. This wasn't the first time he noticed them. He had seen them when he first stepped into the saloon. And though he had never seen these two particular men before, he had seen men like them in saloons and bars from Montana to New Mexico and from Kansas to California.

They wore their guns low, and they had a way of slouching, as if showing their disdain for the rest of the world. They were men who earned a living with their guns, either directly, by robbery, or indirectly, by hiring their guns out.

It was the latter that concerned Smoke—not that someone might have hired them to come after him—as far as he knew, right now, he had no particular enemies after him. Also, he was not a wanted man, and had not been wanted for many years.

But if these men were hired guns, what stronger recommendation could they have than that they were the ones who had shot and killed Smoke Jensen? It was the same thing he had initially thought about young Emmett Clark, though ultimately, Clark had been on a mission of honor.

There was nothing honorable about these two.

One of them noticed that he was looking at them.

"Hey, old man," he said. "What are you looking at?"

"Barney, leave my customers be," the bartender said.

"You stay out of this, Troy. You just stand back there and polish glasses like a good little bartender," the one called Barney replied.

The other young man with Barney laughed at the comment.

"What do you think, Clay?" Barney asked his friend. "Should I leave the customer be?"

"Depends on the customer," Clay replied. "Hey, customer, are we bothering you?"

"Not too much," Smoke replied.

"There you go, barkeep, did you hear that?" Barney called. "He said his ownself that we ain't botherin' him all that much."

"How come it is that we ain't botherin' you all that much?" Clay asked.

"I guess it's because I've been around braying jackasses like you two all my life," Smoke said easily. "I've just learned to turn them off."

The others in the saloon, who had suspended their own conversations and activities to monitor the developing drama, laughed loudly at Smoke's rejoinder.

The two young punks were angered by the remark, and both of them stepped away from the bar, then stood facing him, their legs slightly spread, their arms hanging loose with their right hands curled and hovering just over the butts of their pistols.

"Mister, do you know who you are talking to?"

"From what I gather, your name is Barney and his name is Clay. Am I right?"

"Yeah. I'm Barney Hobbs, this here is Clay Vetters. I reckon you've heard of us?"

"Can't say as I have," Smoke replied.

"That don't matter none. I reckon that after we kill you, just about ever' one will know who we are. That's right, ain't it? Killin' you is goin' to make us famous, don't you think?"

"Who is this fella?" one of the customers asked, saying the words much louder than he intended.

Smoke still said nothing.

"Of course, seein' as you'll be dead, it won't make no difference what you actual think, will it?"

Again, Smoke remained quiet.

"You don't talk a lot, do you?" Barney asked.

"Well, if I don't talk much, it seems to balance out, because you two can't seem to shut up," Smoke said.

There was more laughter, though by now, the laughter was somewhat strained as everyone in the saloon realized that the Rubicon had been crossed and there was no going back. This was going to end in bloodshed.

"Before we start this little dance, I need to know that we are killin' the right man. You are Smoke Jensen, aren't you?"

"If I told you I wasn't, would it make any difference?"

"Nah. You've done shot your mouth off too much. I reckon we're goin' to kill you, no matter who you are."

"I am Smoke Jensen."

Now there was a collective gasp from all who were in the saloon.

"I know'd that was him soon as he come in here," a quiet voice said from somewhere else in the saloon.

"This here is goin' to be interestin' to watch," yet another voice said.

"I'm glad you come clean with that—Mister—Jensen," Barney said, setting the word "Mister" apart from the rest of the sentence. "Now we will have witnesses who can back up our claim as to who you are."

Smoke shook his head. "The witnesses aren't going to do you any good," he said.

"What do you mean they ain't goin' to do us any good? Why, word will spread all over 'bout you bein' kilt and 'bout who the ones was that kilt you," Clay said.

"It's not going to do you any good because you'll be dead," Smoke said to Clay. Then he looked directly at Barney. "Both of you will be dead."

Smoke's comment was followed by a beat of silence.

"If you boys are going to make your play, do it now and be damned," Smoke said. "I've got my lunch comin', and I don't figure on lettin' it get cold."

Smoke's voice was calm, cold as ice. His face was an indecipherable, blank mask. Only his steel-gray eyes showed any animation, and one could almost imagine that they were windows, opening on to hell.

"Maybe you ain't noticed Mr. High-an'-Mighty Smoke Jensen, but there's two of us," Barney said. "I wouldn't be pushin' it if I was you. That is, unlessen you're all that anxious to die."

"I don't have all day, gentlemen," Smoke said. "Are you going to draw? Or do you plan on trying to talk me to death?"

Smoke fixed the two young men with a cold death stare, and he could see they were beginning to have second thoughts. Perhaps they had made a mistake, perhaps the fact that there were two of them did not necessarily mean they could take him. They began to back away from their truculence. Beads of perspiration broke out on their foreheads, and Clay's lower lip began to quiver.

"Barney, what are we doing?" he asked quietly.

Barney forced a grin.

"We do what we said we was goin' to do," Barney said.

"What?" Clay replied, fright obvious in his voice.

"We've been spoofin' you, Mr. Jensen. But to show you there's no hard feelin's, we'd like to pay for your lunch," Barney said. "Barkeep, bring us the bill."

Sensing that the tension had been eased, the others in the saloon relaxed, breathed more easily, and renewed their conversations. A young woman came from the kitchen carrying a tray laden with the meal Smoke had ordered.

Smoke touched the brim of his hat and nodded at the two men. "I'm much obliged," he said.

Barney and Clay returned to their private conversation at the far end of the bar, while Smoke ate his lunch.

After he finished his meal, he looked around the room and seeing a player leaving one of the card games, went over and inquired politely if he could join.

"It would be an honor to have you join us, Mr. Jensen," one of the players said, and the others agreed.

He was well into the game, betting cautiously not wanting to lose, but not that concerned about winning. What was more important to him was just that he be able to entertain himself for a couple of hours, and he was doing that, all the while keeping an eye on the clock so as not to miss the train. The other players were cordial, and as no one was winning or losing very much, it was a very pleasant way of passing time.

With a final glance at the clock, Smoke noticed that it was within twenty minutes of the arrival time of the next westbound train.

"Gentlemen," he said, folding his cards and pulling in his personal bank, "I thank you for inviting me in to your game. It has made my wait for the train much more pleasant."

"Mr. Jensen, you were indeed a welcome visitor," one of the other players said.

Smoke put the money back in his pocket and started toward the door.

"Smoke, look out!" one of the card players shouted.

Almost concurrent with the player's shout was the crash of gunfire. Only the fact that Smoke had reacted to the warning saved his life, for the bullet whizzed by his ear so closely that he could feel the wind of its passing.

Smoke drew and whirled around in one motion. As he did so, he saw Barney and Clay standing in the middle of the floor. Barney had just fired at him, as evidenced by the smoke that was curling up from the barrel of his pistol. Clay was raising his pistol to fire.

Smoke fired twice, the shots coming so close on top of each other that to most of the witnesses, it sounded as if there was only one shot. And yet, two men went down. It had all happened too quickly for any of the others in the saloon to try and get out of the line of fire. Most were still moving, though by now it was all over.

Barney was killed instantly, but Clay was still alive. He sat up and tried to reach for the pistol that was lying on the floor just in front of him. Smoke was to him in a few quick steps and, using the toe of his boot, he kicked the pistol across the floor, out of reach of the wounded man.

"I'm dying," the wounded man said.

"Yes, you are," Smoke said. "Why did you shoot at me? Why couldn't the two of you just leave it alone?"

"Because you are Smoke Jensen," Clay answered.

"What have I ever done to you?"

"Barney said that iffen we was to kill you, we'd make a lot of money," Clay said. "I shouldn't a' listened to him. The sumbitch got me kilt is what he done."

Clay coughed once, and blood spilled from his mouth. Then his eyes rolled back in his head and he fell over.

"Damn, Mr. Jensen, do you get this all the time?" one of the cardplayers asked.

"Too many times," Smoke replied. He put his gun away just as the city marshal came in.

The marshal saw the two bodies on the floor, and the others standing around looking down at them. The marshal had his gun drawn as well, but seeing nobody with a drawn weapon, he put his pistol back in his holster.

"Someone want to tell me what happened here?" he asked.

Everybody started talking at once, and the marshal, in exasperation, held up his hand.

"Hold it, hold it!" he called. "I need just one person to tell me what happened."

Most of the people looked directly at Smoke.

"I have a feeling you're involved in this," the marshal said.

"If the fact that I killed them means I'm involved, then yes, I'm involved," Smoke said.

"Why did you kill them?"

"He didn't have no choice, Marshal," someone said, and everyone else in the saloon agreed with him.

The marshal shook his head and again, held up his hands for quiet. "What's your name?"

"Jensen. Kirby Jensen, though most people call me Smoke."

A big smile spread across the marshal's face. "Smoke Jensen?" He stuck out his hand. "Damn if I wouldn't like to shake your hand. That is, if you don't mind. Though, I reckon just about every one you meet wants to shake your hand."

"It's not the people who want to shake my hand that I have a problem with," Smoke said. He glanced back toward the two bodies that were lying on the floor. "It's the people who want to kill me that give me trouble."

"Yeah," the marshal said, nodding and looking as well at the bodies. "I see what you mean. Are you going to be here long, Mr. Jensen?"

"You running me out of town, Marshal?" Smoke asked, though the tone of his voice softened the words so that it was not a challenge.

"What? No, no," the marshal replied. "You're free to stay here as long as you want. I was just wonderin' if there were likely to be any more incidents like this. I mean, fellas tryin' to make a name for themselves."

"I'm not staying, Marshal. I'll be leaving on the

next train. That is, unless you need me to stay for an inquest."

"Won't be necessary, Mr. Jensen," the marshal said. "Unless someone in here has a different story from the one I've been hearing."

There were several then who spoke up, but all were in agreement with the initial report that Smoke Jensen had acted in self-defense. There was not one word in opposition.

"I'd say that you are free to go," the marshal said.

Chapter Eight

Believing that Smoke Jensen was the man who killed his father, Emmet Clark had dedicated himself to finding and killing Smoke. When he learned that Smoke was not guilty of the act, and that the men who actually were responsible for the murder of his father had already been taken care of by the very man he had been hunting, he felt unfulfilled. He had dedicated a significant part of his life to one objective, only to discover that it was the wrong objective. The result of having spent so much of his life pursuing a false goal left Emmett Clark with a huge sense of emptiness. So, what would he do now? He had skills with a gun—incredible skills, but what was he to do with them?

In the weeks following his confrontation with Smoke, Clark began a western drift with no specific sense of purpose or destination. One day, quite by accident, he happened upon a stagecoach robbery in progress. The driver, two women, a child, and an old man were standing on the road beside the coach with their hands in the air. A highwayman, wearing a hood over his face, was holding a gun.

Without a second thought, Clark pulled his pistol and, urging his horse into a gallop, started toward the scene. The robber, hearing the sound of the approaching horse, turned toward Clark, and seeing that Clark was bearing down upon him, fired. Clark heard the bullet whiz by him and he returned fire. One shot was all it took. The would-be robber dropped his pistol, clasped his hands across his chest, then fell.

"Is anyone hurt?" Clark shouted, leaping down from his horse as he arrived.

"Just him," the driver said. In a gesture of derision, he spit a stream of tobacco on the robber's prostrate form.

Clark squatted by the man he had shot, then reached down to pull off the mask. The robber's eyes were open, but unseeing. Clark had never killed anyone before, and he didn't know how he would feel about it. He was surprised by the fact that he felt nothing at all. It was simply something that had needed to be done and he had done it.

"Damn, boy, you know who that is?" the driver asked. Then, answering his own question, he continued. "His name is Bates. Corey Bates. I seen a poster on him in the stage office back in Concordia. Looks to me like you just earned yourself five hunnert dollars."

"Five hundred dollars?"

"Yes, sir, five hunnert dollars. That's the bounty on him." The driver chuckled. "That's near 'bout a year's pay for me, and you made that much in just a few seconds."

"I never thought about him havin' a bounty," Clark said.

"Then if you wasn't after the bounty, what was you doin'? I mean, you come in here with your gun blazin'. Not that I'm complainin' or nothin'," the driver said. "I figure you come along just in the nick of time."

"I don't know," Clark said. "I just happened to be riding through when I saw him holding up the stage, so I did what I thought was right."

"Well, sir, doin' what you thought was right just earned you five hunnert dollars. If you'll give me a hand, we'll throw his carcass up on top of the stage and you can turn him in to the sheriff when we get to Bonanza City. He can put through the reward for you."

"Thanks."

"I don't know, the way you come ridin' in here like you done, I guess I just figured you was one of them men who hunted down outlaws for the reward that's been put on 'em."

"I never considered anything like that," Clark said. "How does one become such a person?"

"Son, you just do it," he said. "Course, some folks that does things like this ain't much better than the men they are chasin', so if you get into that trade, you need to be careful lest you don't become an outlaw yourself."

It took two days for the sheriff of Bonanza City, Idaho, to authorize the payment of the reward money to Clark. He thanked the sheriff profusely, then, sticking the money and a handful of wanted posters down into his saddlebags, rode out of town, still heading west, but no longer in a purposeless drift. He was now riding in pursuit of his new profession, and although he did not think of it in that term, he was now a bounty hunter.

It was sometime later when Clark rode into the town of Eberhardt, Nevada, hot, thirsty, and with a mouth full of dust. Tying up in front of the Red Dog Saloon, he patted himself off as best he could, then went inside. There were at least a dozen customers, all engaged in what seemed to Clark to be simultaneous conversations.

"Beer," he ordered, slapping a dime onto the counter. The bartender delivered the mug and started to slide a nickel back in change, but Clark waved it away. "No," he said. "This one is for thirst. I'll need another one to enjoy."

Clark downed the first beer, then picked up the second and turned his back to the bar to look out over the saloon in a casual study of the men just to see if any of them fit the descriptions of any of the posters he had out in his saddlebags. It was then that he began to catch bits and pieces of the conversation.

"Mr. Fiddler said he got near six hundred dollars."

"And he's sure it was Dewey Gibson?"

"Yeah, he's sure. You might remember that Gibson used to ride for one of the ranchers here about. Mr. Fiddler recognized him right away."

Clark had never seen Dewey Gibson, but it was a name he recognized, for his name and a likeness was on one of the reward posters he was carrying.

Clark called out to the bartender.

"What robbery are they talking about?"

"Dewey Gibson robbed Fiddler's Mercantile this morning," the bartender said.

"He always was a no-account," someone said.

"Well, he ain't a no-account no more," one of the others said. "They's a three-hundred-dollar reward out for him now."

"This morning, you say?"

"About two hours ago."

"Interesting," Clark said. He finished his beer, wiped his mouth with the back of his hand, then walked down the street to Fiddler's Mercantile. After talking with Fiddler for a few minutes, Clark went out in pursuit. Unlike the first outlaw, who he'd happened across by accident, Clark was purposely after Dewey Gibson.

He hadn't tracked Gibson too far before he noticed that Gibson's horse had broken stride badly. It was easy enough to read the sign. Gibson had been so anxious to put distance between himself and the town where he'd stolen the money that he'd ridden his horse into the ground. The four-hour lead he had on Clark was meaningless. Clark would catch up with him before nightfall.

Clark found Gibson's horse by early afternoon. Ironically, with rest, the horse had recovered, but Gibson had been so desperate that he'd abandoned it and was now proceeding on foot. Clark took a drink of water, poured some into his hat for both horses, then began walking, following Gibson's footprints across the hot, desert sand.

The sign was as easy to read as if it had been printed in a newspaper. Shortly after abandoning his horse, Gibson had been so frightened that he'd started running. He'd managed to run for about half a mile; then he'd walked for another couple of miles. Then the desert had begun to extract its toll from him. Gibson had started throwing things away, his spurs, his shirt, and finally an empty canteen. Clark left the shirt and spurs, but he picked up the canteen, thinking that if he found water he would refill it, giving him an extra canteen. In this heat, an extra canteen could be a lifesaver.

Soon, it became obvious that Gibson was having a hard time staying on his feet. It was clear from the sign that Gibson would fall, crawl for a few feet, then get up and lunge ahead for a few feet farther before falling again.

Then Clark saw him, a solitary figure staggering across the desert.

"Gibson!" Clark called.

Startled at hearing his name called, Gibson started to run.

Clark had been leading both horses, his and Gibson's, and because the animals were now fairly well rested, he swung into the saddle, then started after Gibson, catching up with him within less than a minute.

"Gibson, come on," he said. "You're going to die in the desert unless you come back. Come on. I've got an extra canteen. I'll give you a drink of water."

"Why don't I just take your canteen and horses?" Gibson said, his voice surprisingly strong. He pulled his gun, pointed it at Clark, and pulled the trigger.

"Gibson, no!" Clark shouted, but even as he called out, he heard the bullet buzz by his head.

Clark had no choice but to draw his own pistol and shoot.

Gibson went down with a bullet hole in his forehead.

"Damn, why did you do that?" Clark asked in a puzzled voice. "You probably wouldn't have gotten much over a year for what you did."

With a sigh of frustration, Clark picked Gibson up, then laid him, belly-down, over his horse. Then, giving both animals another drink, he turned and started back.

The little town of Eberhardt, Nevada, lay just ahead of Emmett Clark, baking like a lizard under the sun. A heat-induced dust devil rose in front of him, then skittered across the road, causing sand to blow into his face and sting his cheeks. He was riding one horse and leading another, and he turned to check on Dewey Gibson, who was belly-down on the horse behind him.

He allowed himself to drink the final few swallows of one of the canteens, and even though the water was warm, it eased the thirst. Besides, he knew that now he was but a few minutes from a cool beer.

Dewey Gibson was only the second prisoner Clark had brought in since embarking upon his new career as a bounty hunter. He had killed the stagecoach robber, Corey Bates, during the actual stage holdup. It had not been his intention to kill Gibson, but Gibson had given him no choice. Gibson had fired first, and Clark had been forced to return fire to defend himself.

Clark hooked his canteen back onto the saddle

pommel, then looked around at the little town he was entering. Nearly all the buildings were built from wide, unpainted, and weathered rip-sawed boards. Having collected the day's heat, the town was now giving it back in shimmering waves that were so thick they distorted the view.

There was no railroad coming into Eberhardt, but there was a stagecoach station with a schedule board announcing the arrival and departure of four stagecoaches per week. He had known many towns like this: isolated, inbred, and stagnant.

Clark rode down the street taking inventory of the town's commerce: a livery, a hardware store, a blacksmith shop, and a general store. The proprietor of the general store, wearing a white apron, was out front, sweeping the porch, the stiff straw broom making loud scratching noises. The scratching stopped as the grocer paused in his sweeping long enough to look at Clark, and to pay particular attention to the body Clark had draped over the horse behind him.

Clark located the hotel, a restaurant, and of more particular interest to him, the saloon. By now, others had come out to watch him, drawn by their morbid interest in the body on the horse behind him. At the far end of the single street, Clark saw the jail and marshal's office.

Riding up to the hitching rail in front of the jail, Clark dismounted, and patted his shirt and pants a few times. The action sent up puffs of white dust, which hovered around him like a cloud. He cut a quick glance up and down the street, aware now that he was the center of intense interest. A few buildings away he saw a door being closed, while across the street, a window shade was drawn. A sign creaked in the wind, and flies buzzed loudly around the piles of horse manure that lay in the street.

Clark didn't have to open the door of the jail; it was opened for him. Someone wearing a badge—whether the marshal or one of his deputies Clark didn't know—stepped out onto the porch. The lawman was overweight and his shirt pulled at the buttons, gapping open in the middle. He stuck his hand inside his shirt and began to scratch.

"Find him dead on the trail, did you?"

"No," Clark replied. "I killed him."

The lawman got a surprised expression on his face and his eyes grew wide.

"Look here! Are you telling me you killed him, and you are bringing him into town to brag about it?"

"I didn't come to brag, I come to collect my reward," Clark said.

"What reward?"

Clark pulled a dodger from his pocket and showed it to the lawman.

WANTED

BY THE STATE OF NEVADA

Dewey Gibson

Reward: $300.00

"This is Gibson," Clark said.

"Yeah? You don't mind if I take a look, do you?" the deputy asked.

"Do you know Gibson?"

"Yeah, I know him. We've had him in jail here two or three times." The deputy stepped down from the porch and walked back to take a look at the body that was draped across the horse. He nodded. "That's him, all right. What did you kill him for? I know he held up Mr. Fiddler's store here, but as far as I know, Gibson never kilt nobody."

"He was trying to kill me," Clark said.

"Why did you bring him here? Gibson is from here. He's likely to have a few friends around that won't take too kindly to him bein' kilt and all."

"I was here earlier, I heard that he had held up the store, so I went after him. Being as this is where he did his latest crime, I figured I would come here to claim my reward."

"I ain't got no three hundred dollars to give you," the lawman said. "I ain't even got three dollars."

"That's all right," Clark said. "All I need from you is a receipt saying I brought him in. I can turn it in to the state and get the reward."

"I can give that to you. But, uh—"

"Uh, what?"

"What am I supposed to do with the body?"

"Do you have an undertaker in town?"

"Yes."

"I'd say get in touch with the undertaker and let him take care of it."

"Yeah, I guess you're right," the deputy said.

"But before you do that, make out that receipt."

"The receipt. Oh, yeah," the deputy said. "All right, come on in." He looked back toward the body. "I reckon ole Dewey will be all right there—it ain't like he's goin' to be goin' anywhere."

"You might want to get the undertaker fairly soon, though," Clark said. "He's been in the sun for a couple of days now and he's getting a mite ripe."

"Yeah, I'll do that, soon as I make out the receipt for you," the deputy said.

Once inside the marshal's office, Clark stepped over to a wall that was festooned with reward flyers. Seeing a poster with Corey Bates's name and description, he tore it down. "You don't need to keep a poster up for this man anymore."

"Why not?"

"He's dead."

"Did you kill him?"

"Yes."

"I suppose you'll be puttin' in for the reward?"

"I already collected the reward."

"Five hundred dollars," the deputy said. "That was a pretty good payday. But if you really wanted some money, you should go after Frank Dodd."

"Frank Dodd?"

"This man right here," the deputy said, pointing to a reward poster. "Reward on him is five thousand dollars."

Clark whistled. "Five thousand? That's a lot of money. The state has put that much money up?"

The deputy shook his head. "It ain't the state that put up the money," he said. "The money was put up by the Western Capital Security Agency."

"Hmm. I reckon I'll take a look into that."

The deputy chuckled. "Yes, you and about a hundred other folks who are tryin' to catch him." He handed the receipt to Clark. "I tell you what.

If you don't want to wait for your money, you can take this to the bank tomorrow and they'll give you ninety percent face value on it."

"Thanks."

"Where you goin' to be later this afternoon?" the deputy asked. "Just in case the marshal wants to talk to you."

"I'll be down at the Red Dog Saloon, having a beer," Clark replied. "Maybe having a lot of beers."

Leaving the marshal's office, Clark walked down to the saloon. Several ollas spaced around the inside of the saloon allowed water to evaporate, doing a reasonably effective job of cooling so that, compared to the sun-baked street outside, it was quite comfortable.

"You was here a few days ago, wasn't you?" the bartender asked.

"Yes."

"What brung you back?"

"You serve good beer here," Clark said.

The bartender laughed. "We serve good beer," he said. "Did you hear that, gents? This fella came back to the Red Dog 'cause we serve good beer."

"That ain't why he come back," one of the customers said.

"It ain't?" The bartender put a beer in front of Clark and picked up the nickel. "Then why did he come back?"

"He come for the reward. Ain't that right, mister?" His questioner moved up alongside him. "You the one I seen ridin' in a while ago leadin' another horse, ain't you?"

Clark prepared himself for a confrontation. "That was me."

"I couldn't see all that well from here, but

looked to me like the fella you had draped across that horse was Dewey Gibson."

"That's who it was."

"Uh-huh, like I said, you come back for the reward."

"And the beer," Clark said, smiling and lifting the mug of beer in an attempt to lighten the conversation.

"Maybe you don't know this, mister, but me 'n ole Dewey used to ride together. We was pards, you might say."

"I'm sorry to hear that."

"Yeah, well, it's been a while since we've rode together so I can't exactly say we was pards now. Still, I feel bad to see that he's dead. What happened to him?"

Clark put the beer down, then turned to face the man. "I killed him," he said.

Those who were close enough to overhear Clark halted their own conversations and turned their attention toward the two men to see where this would lead.

"Yeah, that's what I thought you might say."

"I didn't have any choice," Clark said. "He drew first."

"Mister, I don't believe he drew first. If he had, you'd be dead now. Mind, I ain't sayin' Dewey ain't the kind who would draw first. I'm just sayin' that he was that good with a gun that iffen he had drawn first, you'd be dead now."

"I'm not goin' to have any trouble with you, am I, friend?" Clark asked. "The reason I ask is, I hadn't planned to kill Gibson, and I don't have any plans to kill you. But if you push this any further, I just may have to."

There was a long silent pause as everyone in the saloon waited to hear the response to Clark's challenge. Then a tall, silver-haired, dignified-looking man stood from one of the tables in the back of the room.

"Jeff, back down," he called to the man who had confronted Clark.

"Mr. Sinclair, I don't think this fella is tellin' the truth," Jeff said. "You know'd Dewey Gibson as well as I did, seein' as he used to ride for you. You know how good with a gun he was, and you know damn well that if he had draw'd first like this here feller is claimin', this feller would be dead."

"You want to kill somebody, or else get yourself killed over someone like Dewey Gibson?" Sinclair asked.

"No, but—"

"There ain't no buts," Sinclair said. He turned to face the others in the saloon. "Gentlemen, I think nearly all of you know me. Some of you, like Jeff here, have ridden for me. But just in case there is someone here who doesn't know me, my name is Martin Sinclair. I own the Bar S Ranch. You may remember that Dewey Gibson used to ride for me, but I fired him, and I want you to know why I fired him. Two years ago, I hired some Mexicans to do some work for me, and one of them had a little twelve-year-old girl. The Mexicans left before the work was done, before I even paid them any money. It was a couple of weeks later that I learned why they left. It was because Gibson raped that little twelve-year-old girl. When I called him on it, he admitted that he had done it, but said he didn't think it mattered none, since she wasn't nothin' but a Mex and would probably grow up to be a whore anyway. As far as I am concerned, Dewey Gibson was nothing but a low-down sorry son of a bitch and if he got himself killed, then I say good riddance."

Sinclair looked back over at the young cowboy who had questioned Clark. "Jeff, you still want to kill someone, or what's more than likely, from the way I gauge this fella, get yourself kilt over Dewey Gibson?"

"No, sir, I don't reckon I do," Jeff replied. "Sorry, mister," he said to Clark. "I reckon I spoke without thinkin'. Hope you don't take no offense to it."

"No offense taken," Clark said.

"Mr. Peterson?" Sinclair called over to the bartender.

"Yes sir, Mr. Sinclair."

"Suppose you give everyone a drink, on me."

"Yes, sir!" the bartender replied enthusiastically. Then, he shouted to the entire saloon. "You heard Mr. Sinclair, boys. Step up and name your poison."

There were fourteen men and three women in the saloon, and all rushed to the bar to get their drink. Clark held his beer out toward Sinclair and nodded his thanks. Sinclair nodded back. The older man had defused a possible situation.

Chapter Nine

The trip from Cheyenne, Wyoming, to Battle Mountain, Nevada, took Smoke seventeen hours. The Pacific Flyer was a premier train, running on the high iron, which required all the other trains on the line, the locals and the freight trains, to move aside to give the right-of-way to the "varnish." Also, because it was a premier train, first-class passengers enjoyed all the comforts of a Pullman Parlor Car, which allowed Smoke to pass a relaxed night, reaching Battle Mountain early morning the next day.

Battle Mountain, located at the junction of Reese River and Humboldt Valley, got its name from a battle that took place between emigrants and Indians some years earlier. In what would otherwise be desert country, the mountain after which the town received its name produced a large, freshwater spring that provided water for the population and the railroad. The town itself was laid out on one street, which ran south of, and perpendicular to, the Central Pacific Railroad and parallel with the Nevada Central.

Smoke spent the day in Battle Mountain. The day was passed pleasantly as he walked around the town, enjoying a flowing fountain, which was the pride of the city, along with the well-tended green grass and colorful flowers, which stood out in strong contrast to the surrounding desert. He took two meals at the hotel restaurant, then at nine-thirty that night, walked down to the depot in time to make certain his horse was loaded onto the stock car for the last leg of his journey. Once his horse and tack had been seen to, he hurried back to the third passenger car to board, being the last passenger to do so.

"Hold on there, mister," the conductor said as Smoke started to board the train. He pointed to Smoke's pistol. "That has to go."

"Go where?"

"Up to the baggage car," the conductor said. "I don't let armed men ride on my train."

"There is no law that says I can't wear a gun," Smoke said.

"If you want to walk around the streets of any town in Nevada carrying a firearm, be my guest," the conductor replied. "But you are about to board my train, and on my train I make the rules. You cannot wear a gun on my train. Take it off, now."

Smoke thought about challenging him further, but needed to get to Cloverdale before it was too late to do anything for Bobby Lee, so he decided it wasn't worth it. He unbuckled his pistol belt and held it out toward the conductor. "Take good care of this," he said. "I will expect it back when I get to Cloverdale."

The conductor took belt, holster, and pistol

with a self-satisfied smirk. "If you ask me, it is all an affectation anyway," he said. "Men like you wear guns for show. Am I supposed to be frightened by it?"

"I reckon not," Smoke replied calmly.

Smoke walked midway through the car, then settled in an unoccupied seat. Shortly after the train got under way, the conductor came through the car, checking everyone's tickets.

"What cretin made out this ticket?" the conductor asked irritably as he examined the ticket Smoke gave him.

"Is there something wrong with it?" Smoke asked.

"We have changed forms. We no longer use this."

"It was issued in Big Rock, Colorado."

The conductor held the ticket for a long moment as he looked at it. "If I had seen this ticket before you boarded, I would not have let you on."

"It was good enough for the Denver and Rio Grande, and the Union Pacific," Smoke said.

"Yes, well, you aren't on the Denver and Rio Grande or the Union Pacific now, are you? This is the Nevada Central," the conductor said with an ill-tempered tone. "Perhaps our standards are a little higher."

"I'm sure they are," Smoke said sarcastically, but the conductor did not pick up on his sarcasm.

"Never mind, I will let you pass, but I intend to send a message to the Denver and Rio Grande, reminding them of the change in forms." With a sigh of disgust, he shook his head, punched a hole in the ticket, then gave it back to Smoke.

At that moment, a small boy came running up the aisle and the conductor reached out to grab hold of his shirt.

"Who is the mother of this child?" he called out.

"I am," a young woman answered from the front of the car.

"Madam, please keep him under control. I will not have urchins running wild on my train."

"Mister, you have about the biggest case of mean I've ever seen," Smoke said. "If you'd ease up just a bit, you might have people thinking better of you."

"I am not concerned about the opinion you or anyone else on this train may have of me," the conductor said haughtily. "I am the conductor and that means I am in charge of this train. Surely even someone like you can understand that. I am concerned only that you obey my rules."

Smoke chuckled. "The Emperor of Lilliput," he said.

"I beg your pardon? Who is the Emperor of Lilliput?"

"Gulliver's Travels?"

"Mr. Gulliver may travel, but as far as I am aware, he has never traveled on my train. And emperor or not, he would still obey my rules."

Turning with a sense of self-importance, the conductor moved on through the car.

After the conductor left, a nice-looking and well-mannered boy came walking up the aisle, balancing himself against the jerk and roll of the train by putting his free hand on the backs of the seats. He was carrying a book.

"Sir, are you Smoke Jensen?"

Smoke was somewhat surprised to be recognized this far from home, and to be recognized by a young boy.

"Yes, I am," he said.

A huge smile spread across the boy's face.

"I knew it! I told Mama that's who you was." He held out the book and a pencil. "Would you please sign this book for me?"

The title of the book was *Smoke Jensen and the Desert Outlaws*. Neither the author nor the publisher had ever acquired Smoke's permission to use his name in their books, and in truth, Smoke was irritated by their very existence. But the boy was genuinely excited, and Smoke didn't want to do anything to disappoint him, so he nodded, then reached for the book.

"None of this is true, you know," Smoke said as he began to sign.

The boy smiled. "I know it isn't," he said. "Heck, I've read enough about you in the newspapers to know that the real things you have done are much better than these stories. But I would like to have your autograph anyway."

"All right," Smoke said, signing the book. "What's your name?"

"Timothy, sir. But ever' one calls me Timmy. How old are you, Tim?"

"Tim, yes, I like that better than Timmy. I think I'll be Tim from now on. I'm fifteen."

Smoke stopped in mid-signing and looked for a long moment at the boy.

"Is something wrong, Mr. Jensen?" Tim asked.

"No, son, nothing is wrong," Smoke said as he completed the signing. He handed the book back. "There you go. Just remember, don't believe everything you read."

"I won't. And thank you, sir," Tim said, holding the book to his chest excitedly as he returned to sit with his mother and younger sister.

Smoke watched as the boy proudly showed the book to his mother and sister. The boy had said he was fifteen. His son, Arthur, would be fifteen now. But Arthur had been murdered along with his mother, Smoke's wife, Nicole.

As Smoke thought of Nicole and young Arthur, he connected them with the mission he was on now, and he remembered what a hard time Nicole's brother had had in dealing with the murder of his sister and nephew.

Young Bobby Lee wiped the tears from his eyes. "My sister never hurt anyone. She was a good person."

"Yes, she was," Smoke answered. He had his arm around the boy's shoulder, and he pulled him closer to him. Although Smoke's own son, Art, was still just a baby, Smoke had become a father figure to Bobby Lee. It wasn't the first time Smoke had ever been a father figure to a young boy. Even before Smoke had married Nicole, he'd rescued a boy who was lost in the mountains, half frozen and half starved. Taking him back to his own cabin, Smoke had raised him until he was an adult. Out of gratitude once the boy was on his own, he'd taken Smoke's last name. He was now known as Matt Jensen, and had established a reputation of his own.

"Why did they kill Nicole? And little Art? He was just a baby. Who could kill a baby?"

"I can't answer that question, Bobby Lee. There are some people who are just too evil to live."

"But these people are evil, and they are alive," Bobby Lee said.

"Yes," Smoke said. *"They are alive now, but they won't be alive much longer."*

"You are going after them, aren't you?"

"I am."

"I want to go with you."

Smoke ran his hand through the boy's hair. *"I know you do, son. And I wish I could let you come with me. But you are still a bit too young, and if I have to worry about you, it will make my job harder to do. You do want to see them pay for what they did, don't you?"*

"Yes," Bobby Lee said resolutely.

"Then you understand why I can't take you with me?"

"Yes," Bobby Lee said again. *"But Smoke?"*

"Yes?"

"When you kill the sons of bitches, kind of think about me while you're doin' it, will you?"

"I promise."

"And I'm sorry I cussed like that. Nicole, she didn't like me saying things like son of a bitch."

"I think, in this case, Nicole would forgive you," Smoke said. *"Sons of bitches is about the only way you can describe these people."*

"Sons of bitches," Bobby Lee said. *"Sons of bitches, sons of bitches, sons of bitches."* He repeated the words, using them as a means of fighting against the sobs that he was trying, not too successfully, to hold back.

A porter came through the car announcing dinner with a three-note chime, thus interrupting

Smoke's reverie. He joined the others in moving toward the dining car.

It was just after midnight and Frank Dodd and the six men with him were waiting alongside the Nevada Central tracks just south of Rock Creek.

"That ain't high enough," Dodd said. He was speaking to Conklin, who was standing on a collapsible ladder. A pyramid of three poles had been erected in the middle of the track, and Conklin was attempting to attach a lantern to the poles.

"That's about as high as I can make it," Conklin said.

"You can get it higher. Put it all the way up on top," Dodd ordered.

"Well, how high does it have to be anyway?"

"It has to be as high as the headlamp on a train," Dodd said. "I want the engineer to think he's about to run smack dab into another train."

"How's that goin' to work?" Stillwater asked. "This here lamp ain't a' goin' to be movin' none. It'll just be sittin' here."

"Believe me, when that engineer sees another headlamp in the middle of the track, he ain't goin' to think about whether it's movin' or not. And so what if it ain't movin'? It would still look like a train is here, even if it's just a' settin' still, and he damn sure ain't goin' to be wantin' to run over it."

"How's this?" Conklin asked after repositioning the lantern, which was an actual lamp taken from the front of an engine.

"Yeah," Dodd said. "Yeah, that's just about

perfect. Come on down now, and get your ladder out of the way."

Wayland Morris laughed. "I have to hand it to you, Frank. When you said you wanted to steal a headlamp off the front of an engine, I thought you was plumb loco. But this here is a good idea."

Phillips and Garrison had joined Dodd, so that there were six men waiting alongside the track for the arrival of the Prospector, which was the name of the train that made this run every night.

"Conklin, as soon as the train stops, I want you and Stillwater to ride up to the cab. Make certain the train stays here. Morris, you and I will hit the express car. Phillips, you and Garrison go through the train and collect whatever money the passengers might have."

"Wait, that ain't fair. Is that all the money we get?" Garrison asked.

"Just do what I tell you, Garrison," Dodd said.

A distant whistle came through the night.

"Get ready," Dodd said. "It won't be long."

When the engineer of the Prospector came around a long, sweeping curve on the Nevada Central, he saw the headlamp of an approaching train.

"Sweet Jesus, Ernie! Look at that!" he shouted, even as he pulled the brake lever to full emergency stop.

"Where'd that come from?" his fireman shouted. "There ain't supposed to be no train a' comin' this a' way now!"

* * *

Smoke was in the bottom berth. He was sound asleep when the train made the abrupt stop. Reaching up, he grabbed the assist strap to keep from being tossed out. Some of the other sleepers were thrown from their berths, and Smoke heard sounds of surprise, pain, and anger.

Having taken off only his boots when he went to sleep, he sat up now and began pulling them on. He had no idea why the train had come to such a sudden stop, but it couldn't be good. He also didn't like the fact that the conductor had taken his pistol and holster when he'd boarded the train earlier that night.

There was a time when Smoke had worn two guns, a .44 on his right hip and a .36 on his left, which he had worn butt-forward. But sometime ago, he had given up that habit, and now wore only one pistol in his gun belt.

There was, however, a habit he had not given up. Smoke had long carried a two-barrel derringer in his boot, and even as he put on his boots, he pulled the derringer out and held it in the palm of his hand. Now, dressed and so armed, he stepped out into aisle of the car.

The car was dimly lit, illuminated by two lanterns that hung from the ceiling. As he started toward the front of the car, he saw the conductor.

The conductor wasn't alone. There was another man with him, and the man with him had one hand on the conductor's shoulder. There was a pistol in his other hand, and that pistol was pointed at the conductor's head. Even in the dim light, Smoke could see the absolute terror in the conductor's face and eyes.

"Mister, just where the hell do you think you're a' goin'?" the man with the gun asked.

"The train came to a sudden stop," Smoke said. "I thought I would investigate the cause."

"Investigate the cause? Haw!" the man laughed. "Mister, you sure talk fancy. But you don't need to do no investigatin'. I'll tell you what's happenin'. We're robbin' the train and I come in here to collect ever'body's money. So you might as well get whatever money you got, and put it there on the floor. All of you folks that's hidin' behind them curtains, drop your money out onto the floor."

"I'll just bet that none of these folks want to give you any of their money," Smoke said calmly. "I know I don't want to give you any of mine."

"Haw!" the man said, laughing again. "You don't want to give me any of your money, eh? Well now, tell me, mister, just how in the hell are you goin' to stop me from takin' it?"

Smoke raised his hand and pointed his derringer at the train robber.

"I'll shoot you if you try," Smoke said.

"Mister, can't you see that I'm pointin' this pistol at the conductor's head?"

"And can't you see that I'm pointing my pistol directly at your head?"

"You don't understand," the train robber said. "If you don't put down that little peashooter of your'n, I'm goin' to blow this little feller's brains out."

"No, *you* don't understand," Smoke said. "I met the conductor earlier today, and I don't like him. In fact, I don't think anyone on this train likes him all that much. So I don't care whether you blow his brains out or not. But just think of this. While you are killing him, I'll be killing you."

"No, my God, no!" the conductor shouted in a high-pitched, panic-stricken voice. He soiled his pants.

"You're—you're crazy!" the train robber shouted. He pushed the conductor out of his way and tried to bring his pistol to bear on Smoke, but it was too late. Smoke pulled the trigger and a black hole appeared in the train robber's forehead. He fell back as women, and the conductor, screamed.

"Where is my gun?" Smoke asked the conductor.

The conductor's eyes were wide open in terror.

"Garrison, what's goin' on in here?" another armed man shouted, coming into the car then. Seeing Garrison dead on the floor, he looked up. "Who did this?"

"I did," Smoke replied.

With an angry bellow, the second train robber raised his pistol, but before he could fire, Smoke pulled the trigger for the second barrel. Like Garrison before him, the train robber went down, this time with a bullet hole in the bridge of his nose.

"Where is my gun?" Smoke asked again.

"I-I had it put into the baggage car," the conductor answered, finally finding his voice.

Moving quickly, Smoke picked up one of the train robbers' pistols, then stepped rapidly to the front door of the car. Standing on the plates between the cars, he looked around and saw two men on horseback alongside the express car. He leaned around the edge of the car and fired. One of the two men went down.

"It's a trick!" one of the men on horseback shouted. "Let's get out of here!"

Smoke saw the robbers turn away from the car. He tried to fire a second time, but the pistol he had taken from the robber misfired and the remaining three men galloped away.

In frustrated anger, Smoke threw the pistol away, then hurried back in to grab the pistol of the other would-be train robber. By the time he got back outside, though, the train robbers had disappeared into the night.

When Smoke returned to the train car, he saw that most of the passengers were out of their berths and were staring with morbid curiosity at the two dead men. The conductor was sitting on the floor of the car, up hard against the front right corner, with his knees drawn up and his arms wrapped around his legs.

The porter now came into the car.

"Anybody kilt in here?" the porter asked.

"Two," Smoke said. "Neither of them passengers."

"Where is Mr. Polosi?"

"Who?"

"The conductor. I been lookin' for him, I ain' found 'im."

"He's up here," Smoke said, stepping to one side and pointing to the figure who sat all drawn up in the corner.

The porter's eyes grew wide in surprise. "Mr. Polosi, you all right?" he asked. "Did you get shot?"

"He's all right."

"You sure?"

"He wasn't shot."

The porter stared at Polosi for a moment longer before speaking again. "Mr. Polosi, don't you think you should tell the engineer to get us goin' again?"

Polosi didn't answer.

"What about these dead folks?" asked the porter. "We can't just leave 'em lyin' here in the car. Don't you think we should move 'em into the baggage car?"

Polosi looked up at the porter, his eyes wide and his lower lip trembling. He tried to speak, but was unable to say anything.

"What's your name?" Smoke asked the porter.

"John, sir. John Ware."

"Any other porters on the train, Mr. Ware?"

"Yes, sir. Two more."

"I expect you're going to need some help getting the bodies out of here."

"Yes, sir, I'll get them to help me. Mr. Polosi, should we put them in the baggage car?"

Polosi stared at the porter, his eyes still wide with terror.

"Mr. Polosi?"

"You'll find another body outside," Smoke said. "You will need to get him picked up as well."

"Yes, sir, we'll do that," the porter said. "Mr. Polosi?" he said again. "Is it all right to put them in the baggage car?"

"I doubt Polosi is going to be much help to you, Mr. Ware," Smoke said. "It looks to me like you're in charge."

"Yes, sir. Well, in that case, I'll move the bodies into the baggage car. Then I'll tell the engineer we can go on. I 'spect we'll get rid of the bodies in Austin."

Chapter Ten

Dodd, Conklin, and Stillwater rode hard for several minutes until the train was far behind them. Finally, Dodd held up his hand, calling them all to a halt.

"Hold it up here. We'll give the horses a blow," Dodd said.

The horses whickered and panted from their recent effort.

"What happened?" Conklin asked. "I thought we had ever'thing set up? Was there law on the train?"

"I only seen one man," Stillwater said.

"You mean one man kilt three of us?"

"We don't know that Morris, Phillips, and Garrison are dead," Dodd said.

"Morris is dead. Did you see the way he fell? He hit his head on the track and it didn't even bother him. He's dead," Stillwater said.

"They was a couple of shots inside the train before that fella stuck his head out," Stillwater said. "So I figure Phillips and Garrison is probably dead too."

"So what if they are?" Dodd replied. "Turns out they wasn't worth much anyway."

"What do we do now?" Conklin asked.

"We're goin' back to Desolation," Dodd said.

"They's only three of us left," Stillwater said. "We're goin' to have to get some new folks to ride with us afore we try this again."

"You let me worry about that," Dodd said. His horse whickered, and Dodd reached down to pat it on the neck. "The mounts has caught their breath. Let's get out of here."

Austin was a silver-mining town, the county seat of Lander County, and with almost ten thousand people, the second largest town in Nevada. The train was no more than an hour late when it rolled into Austin, but because of the attempted train robbery, the sheriff interviewed the train crew and the passengers, so they were delayed in Austin a few hours.

Sheriff Jacobs invited Smoke, who was again wearing his pistol, to his house for breakfast. Breakfast was pancakes, eggs, ham, biscuits, and fried potatoes. Smoke chuckled as he saw all the food being put out on the table.

"Mrs. Jacobs, I do believe that you and my wife, Sally, went to the same school of cooking," he said. "And the first lesson must have been, 'Do not allow a guest to leave the table hungry.'"

"I do like to see a man with a healthy appetite," Mrs. Jacobs replied. The fact that both she and the sheriff were considerably overweight showed that they had healthy appetites.

"The engineer and the firemen said that they

recognized Frank Dodd," Sheriff Jacobs said. "They've mostly stayed down in Nye County. I must say I'm a little surprised to see them up here in Lander County."

"Did you find out the names of the ones I killed?"

The sheriff nodded. "I know two of them. The one with the beard was Cory Garrison, the one with red hair was Jake Phillips. I've had both of them in my jail more than once. I've always thought they were sort of minor crooks, never did anything very big that I know of. I must say, I'm surprised that they were riding with Frank Dodd. I still don't know who the third one is."

"Let me know if you find out who it was," Smoke said. "I've had to kill enough men as it is—I don't ever want to get to the point to where they are just nameless bodies."

"I'm told that you took the two who came into your car out with a derringer. Is that true?" Sheriff Jacobs asked as he spooned a very healthy helping of fried potatoes onto his plate.

"I used a derringer, yes."

"Most people couldn't hit the side of a barn with a derringer, and I hear you did it from at least thirty feet away. That is some shooting for a derringer."

Smoke took a swallow of coffee, primarily to keep from having to respond to the compliment.

"I've heard a lot of stories about you, Smoke Jensen, but I have never heard that you used a derringer."

"The derringer is a backup gun only," Smoke said. "And I had to use it this time because the conductor insisted that I not board the train wearing this." He patted the pistol at his side.

"Ha! I never thought Smoke Jensen would give up his pistol so easily."

"I need to go to Cloverdale and the Nevada Central is the only train that goes where I want to go, so I decided not to make an issue of it."

"Yes, well, I always knew that Barney Polosi was a pain in the ass. But I never knew he was such a weak sister," the sheriff said. "Why are you going to Cloverdale?"

"To see a friend," Smoke replied without specifics.

"Do you know the sheriff there?" Sheriff Jacobs asked.

"No. Do you?"

"His name is Wallace. Herman Wallace. I know him, but I don't trust him."

"Why not?"

"I told you that Frank Dodd and his men work mostly in Nye County?"

"Yes."

"I don't think that is mere coincidence."

"You think Sheriff Wallace is mixed up with Frank Dodd?" Smoke asked.

"I don't have any real reason to think that, so I'm not sayin' it. At least, not officially," Sheriff Jacobs said. "But if I were you, I would sort of watch out for him."

"Sheriff, if you would do me a favor?"

"Sure, just ask."

"Don't put out the word that I had anything to do with foiling the train holdup."

"I'll have to do that if you want to claim the reward," Sheriff Wallace said. "I think there's at least a hundred dollars reward apiece on Phillips and Garrison. And we don't know who the other'n is yet, but once we find out, I wouldn't be surprised but what the reward on him is even bigger."

"Give the reward to the volunteer firemen's fund or something," Smoke said.

"Really? Damn, that's right decent of you, Smoke."

The conversation continued through breakfast. Then, excusing himself, Smoke stood up.

"I'd better get going. I don't want to miss the train."

"Oh, don't worry, you ain't goin' to miss it." Sheriff Jacobs stood up, opened a biscuit, and slid in a piece of ham. "I gave strict orders that the train was not to leave until I got there." He pointed to the pistol that Smoke was now wearing. "And you won't have a problem hanging onto your gun for the rest of the trip either. I've already had a talk with Jenkins, the new conductor. Come on, I'll walk down to the depot with you."

The sheriff took a bite of his biscuit sandwich as he started toward the door.

When they approached the depot, they saw an open coffin standing up against one of the support posts on the roofed depot platform. Inside the coffin was the body of the third train robber. The undertaker had cleaned up his head wound, and crossed his arms across his chest. He was holding a pistol in his right hand. His eyes were open and glazed. On the top of the coffin was a sign that read:

DOES ANYONE KNOW THIS MAN?

At the bottom of the coffin was another sign.

WARNING TO TRAIN ROBBERS
THIS COULD BE YOU

Sheriff Jacobs walked with Smoke to the train, then shook his hand just before he boarded.

"Come back any time, Mr. Jensen," he said. "You will always be welcome."

"Thanks," Smoke said.

The train whistle blew and with a final wave, Smoke stepped up into the car.

As Emmett Clark drew closer to Desolation, he passed through a canyon, on the left side of which rose a high bluff. After passing the bluff, he looked back, and about halfway up the side of the canyon wall, a column could be seen jutting out in front of the bluff, crowned with what looked like the feathers of a war bonnet. This gave the canyon its name, War Bonnet.

Clark was coming to Desolation because he had overheard some saloon conversation back in Geneva that Desolation was not a place anyone would want to visit because of its lack of law.

"*I reckon you could find just about any outlaw in Nevada there if you cared to go look for him,*" one of the speakers suggested.

"*If that's so, why don't the law ever go there to catch 'em?*" another asked.

"*Ha! They ain't no law ever goes there but what*

they don't wind up getting themselves kilt," the first one answered. "They got themselves a boot hill there that ain't for nothin' but law what's come after one or another of them."

Clark wasn't the law per se, but then his occupation of hunting down wanted men and turning them in for the reward wouldn't likely be one that would be welcomed either. He decided, therefore, to pass himself off as someone who was on the dodge from the law.

Black thunderclouds rumbled ominously in the northwest, but held off long enough for Clark to reach the little town of Desolation.

Desolation was laid out along one long street. In the middle of the street on the west side was a railroad depot, complete with a small white sign with the name of the town, and the altitude neatly painted in black letters:

Desolation

ELEVATION: 4,135 FT.

Clark found the presence of a railroad depot to be rather unusual, since there was obviously no railroad. Railroad Avenue continued on as a wagon trail running north and south out of town.

He saw at least two dozen people in town, mostly in little clusters of two or three men. He saw no women and no children, which he took as a good indication that this was the kind of town that had been described to him—an outlaw town.

At intervals all up and down Railroad Avenue,

there were boards stretched across the dirt streets to allow people to cross when the roads were full of mud. There were obviously no street cleaners nor any kind of city sanitation workers for, unlike those towns where the horse droppings were picked up on a regular basis, this street was covered with manure and the stench was almost unbearable.

Clark stopped in front of a saloon that, in keeping with the theme of the town, was called the Railroad Saloon. Dismounting, he tied off his horse, then went inside.

There were several people inside the saloon and here, for the first time, Clark saw women. They were all wearing brightly colored ruffled skirts that came no lower than their knees. Under the bell-shaped skirts could be seen colorfully hued petticoats that barely reached their kid boots, which were adorned with tassels. Their arms and shoulders were bare, their bodices cut low over their bosoms, and their dresses decorated with sequins and fringe. One of them, seeing Clark come in, smiled and came toward him.

"My, what a handsome young man you are," she said flirtatiously. "You don't look anything at all like an outlaw."

"Outlaw?" Clark replied.

For a moment the smile left the woman's face. "Honey, you are an outlaw, aren't you? Because if you aren't, I would advise you to just keep on goin'."

"How did you know I was an outlaw? Does it show in my face?" Clark asked.

The woman laughed at Clark's question.

"Oh, honey, didn't you know? Everybody in Desolation is an outlaw," she said.

"No, I didn't know."

"Hey, you, Cindy," a man called from a table near the back of the saloon. "Get the hell away from him. You are my woman!"

"I ain't nobody's woman, Jules Stillwater," Cindy replied.

"You're my woman until I tell you you ain't my woman no more," Stillwater called back. "Now, get me and my friends a drink."

There were two other men sitting at the table with the one Cindy had called Stillwater.

One of the men sitting with him was a fairly large man with broad shoulders, but what stood out most about him was the disfiguring scar on his face. Half of one eyelid was missing, and part of his lip was cut away so that he couldn't completely close his mouth. This fit exactly the description Clark had heard of Frank Dodd.

"Is that Frank Dodd?" Clark asked.

"Yes. Why do you ask?"

"I'd like to meet him."

"Honey, believe me, you don't want anything to do with him. If you think Stillwater is trouble, you ain't seen nothin' till you cross Frank Dodd."

Clark smiled. "Well, I'll just have to see to it that I don't cross him, won't I?"

Chapter Eleven

The town of Cloverdale was divided into three sections: the American section, the Mexican section, and the Chinese section. The large Chinese section was the result of Chinese having been the principal labor force for the building of the Western railroads. Original plans called for the Nevada Central Railroad to continue south until it connected with the Atlantic and Pacific Railroad at Columbus, but the Nevada Central ran out of money.

The cessation of railroad construction left a lot of Chinese laborers stranded, not only in Cloverdale, but throughout the West. Always an industrious people, the Chinese managed to find other means of employment. In Cloverdale, most sustained themselves by working in the mines, or doing menial labor. But many became merchants, providing unique services, not only to their own race, but to the other residents of the town as well. These services ran the gamut from laundries, to restaurants, to craft shops, to opium dens, to houses of prostitution, to Chinese saloons where specialized Chinese liquor, such as *huangjiu* and *choujiu,* were sold.

Andy Emerson enjoyed spending time in the Chinese section of town because he took pleasure in the game of *fan t'an,* which was a Chinese game of chance. In addition, he felt less intimidated in the Chinese section of town because he was small of stature, as were most of the Chinese. Another advantage to being there was that he was less likely to encounter Sheriff Wallace or any of his deputies.

That was not the case today, though. Sheriff Wallace, who was frequent visitor to the Fangzi Lei Shi, or House of Pleasure, had just finished his visit with one of the whores. The visit had not gone well—he didn't get the whore he wanted, and the one he got would not respond to his specific requests, even when he hit her.

Angry and unfulfilled, he stopped at the Chinese saloon for a glass of *huangjiu,* and was even more irritated when he saw Emerson playing the Chinese gambling game of *fan t'an.* The fact that Emerson not only understood the game, but was good at it, annoyed Wallace, who had never quite caught the hang of it.

"What are you doing here, Emerson?" Wallace asked.

Startled at the unexpected sound of the sheriff's voice, Emerson jumped, knocking the pieces off the board. The *t'an kun,* or operator of the game, called out in angry Chinese.

"Ha!" Wallace said. "You pissed off the Chinaman."

"No, Sheriff, you did," Emerson said.

The game operator said something else in Chinese, and Emerson replied in the same language.

"You can speak that gibberish?" Wallace said, surprised to hear Emerson and the Chinese man in conversation.

"Yes, and it isn't gibberish. It is an ancient and honorable language."

The Chinese man put his hands together and made a slight bow toward Emerson, who returned the salute.

At that moment, another Chinese man showed up, and he began shouting angrily at Wallace.

"What the hell is he jabbering about?" the sheriff asked.

"He says you broke the jaw of the young lady you were with," Emerson said.

"Young lady, hell. She's no lady. She's a whore."

"That doesn't give you the right to beat her," Emerson said.

"Who the hell are you to tell me what rights I have and don't have?" Wallace replied.

"It's just common decency."

"Tell you what, Emerson. Why don't I just throw you in jail again?"

"For what? I haven't done anything. I'm not even drunk."

"You're gamblin', aren't you?"

"So what?"

"You can't gamble in this town unless you are gamblin' at a place that has a license. Woo doesn't have a license. None of the Chinamen do."

"Neither does the Gold Strike Saloon have a gambling license, but folks play poker there."

"That's different. Poker is a private game. The saloon doesn't have anything to do with it. The Chinaman runs this game."

Emerson stood up and shook his head. "You just won't leave me alone, will you?" he asked. "All right, I'll go back to the ranch."

"No, not the ranch," Wallace said. "I told you, you are going to jail."

"I don't think I want to do that," Emerson said.

It was mid-afternoon by the time the train reached Cloverdale. Cloverdale was at the end of the line for the Nevada Central Railroad, and at the far end of the depot there was a round-house that would be used to turn the engine around for its return trip. Smoke Jensen stepped down from the train, then walked up to the attached stock car as his saddle and rifle were off-loaded and his horse led down the car ramp.

"Is this your horse, mister?" the stationmaster asked.

"Yes. I'm Kirby Jensen."

Smoke used his real name because it drew less attention than the sobriquet by which he was more widely known.

"You going to take him now, or do you want to put him up?"

"I would like to put him up for a while, if you can recommend a place."

The stationmaster smiled. "Yes, sir, I certainly

can recommend a place. We have a livery here at the depot if you'd like to leave him here."

"My saddle and my rifle?"

"We can take care of those too."

"Good," Smoke said. He took out two dollars and gave it to the stationmaster. "I'll be back before this runs out."

Smoke's conversation with the stationmaster was interrupted by a loud yell coming from the other side of the train, which was still sitting at the station.

"There he goes, Sheriff!" a man's voice sounded. The shout was followed by the sound of gunshots, and Smoke instinctively drew his pistol, then moved quickly to the rear of the train to see what was going on.

A figure suddenly appeared on the railroad track, having run up the slight grade on the other side. He was a small man, dressed as a cowboy and with a bushy, walrus-type mustache. The young cowboy looked back into the direction from which he had come, and Smoke saw terror in his eyes.

A shot came from the other side of the track, and the cowboy fell, sliding on his back headfirst down the railroad embankment on the near side. Smoke ran over to him and saw bubbles of blood coming from his mouth. He was trying hard to breathe, and Smoke could hear a sucking sound in his chest. He knew then that at least one bullet had penetrated his lungs.

"Oh, damn," the cowboy said. "Oh, damn, I've been kilt, haven't I?"

Smoke looked up to see two men, both wearing

badges, standing on the tracks at the top of the embankment. One of the men was holding a smoking gun in his hand. Putting the pistol in his holster, he came down from the tracks to look at the man he had just shot.

"What about it, Sheriff Wallace? Is he dead?" the other badge-wearing man called from the top of the tracks.

Even as the question was asked, the cowboy drew his last, gasping breath.

"Yeah," the sheriff replied. "He's dead." The sheriff glanced over at Smoke. "Who are you?" he asked.

"I just got off the train," Smoke replied.

"I didn't ask how you got here. I asked who you were, and I expect an answer."

The train whistle blew then and with a rush of steam, a squeak of brakes being released, and a rattling of couplings, it started toward the round-house.

"The name is Kirby," Smoke said. As his name was Kirby Jensen, he wasn't lying, but he did give the sheriff a name by which few knew him, doing so because he thought that, for the time being, it might be best to stay in the shadows.

"Did you know him?" Sheriff Wallace asked, nodding toward the dead man. "Reason I asked, I'm not going to have to deal with you trying to get revenge for him or anything, am I?"

"I've never seen the man before," Smoke said.

"Well, you're lucky," the sheriff said. "His name is Andy Emerson. He rides—that is he rode," Wallace corrected, "for Milt Poindexter. The son of a bitch has been nothing but trouble for the last year. I've had him in jail more often than not."

"Why did you shoot him?"

"Because he ran when I ordered him to stop," Sheriff Wallace said.

"He isn't armed."

"He ran," Wallace repeated, as if that was all the explanation he needed.

"What difference does it make if he ran? It's not like he was going to get away from you, is it? You know his name, you know where he works."

"Mister, you are that close to interfering with the law," Wallace said, obviously irritated by Smoke's comments.

By now, a crowd began to gather around Emerson's body, as many of the people who had been at the depot were drawn to the scene by the excitement. Smoke, not wanting to be a part of the circus, drifted away.

As Smoke walked back to the depot, he saw a paper boy standing at the edge of the platform, selling newspapers.

"Get your *News Leaf* here!" the boy was shouting. "Paper, paper, *Cloverdale News Leaf* here!" The boy looked up at Smoke. "Is Mr. Emerson dead?" the paper boy asked.

"Yes."

"I'd better get back to the newspaper office and tell Mr. Cutler. He'll be a' wantin' to write a story about it, I reckon." Then, reverting to his entrepreneurial spirit, he turned his attention to Smoke, a potential customer. "You just get into town?"

"Yes."

"Then I expect you'll be wantin' a copy of the *News Leaf*. It'll give you all the news of the town, and it'll also tell you all about the hangin'."

"The hanging?"

"Yes, sir, come Friday, there's goin' to be a hangin' right here in town. Why, if you was to walk down the street a bit, you'll see the gallows. It's goin' to be somethin' to see, I'll bet."

"Are you going to watch it?" Smoke asked.

The smile left the boy's face. "No, sir," he said. "I reckon Mr. Cabot done what they said he done. I mean, he was caught red-handed by them folks that was on the train and all. But he was always just real nice to me. Bought a paper from me ever' week. And once he give me a quarter tip for no reason at all. I think watchin' a hangin' might be excitin' and all that, but I ain't in no particular mind to see Mr. Cabot hang."

"I'll take a paper," Smoke said.

"Yes, sir. That'll be five cents."

"Five cents? Most papers cost only two cents."

"Yes, sir, folks keep tellin' Mr. Cutler that, but he says that as long as he's the only newspaper in town, he figures he can charge whatever folks will pay for it."

Smoke chuckled as he handed the boy a nickel. "I guess he has a point," he said.

The boy handed him the paper, which consisted of a single sheet that was printed on both sides. As promised, the lead story concerned Bobby Lee Cabot.

Hanging on Friday

At ten o'clock of the morning on Friday
the 31st instant, Sheriff Herman Wallace,

duly armed with a death warrant signed by His Honor Judge Jeremiah Briggs, will escort Bobby Lee Cabot to the gallows, there to affix a rope around his neck for the purpose of dispatching his soul to eternity.

Cabot is paying the ultimate penalty of death by hanging for his part in the robbery of the Nevada Central Train on the night of 21st ultimate. The robbers, believed to be the Frank Dodd gang, relieved the Nevada Central Messenger of $5,120.00, said money being transferred from the Bank of Reno to the Bank of Cloverdale. Although the messenger, August Fletcher, cooperated in every way, he was shot down in cold blood by the robbers. Mr. Fletcher was married and the father of four. He was a deacon in his church, and it is said of him that no finer man ever walked the streets of Cloverdale. A trial, fairly conducted, and with the verdict delivered by the unanimous vote of twelve men, good and true, has determined that the life of this wonderful man was cut short by the evil doings of Cabot.

The execution of Bobby Lee Cabot is to be publicly conducted with no restrictions applied as to who may attend. All who love justice are invited to be present at the hour appointed. A great crowd present to witness Cabot being delivered into the hands of Satan will send a signal to all who would contemplate duplicating Cabot's foul deed.

After reading the story Smoke perused the advertisements finding one for a hotel.

DEPOT HOTEL

Fremont Street, Cloverdale, Nevada

WILLIAM R. CHAMBERLAIN
Proprietor

*This hotel is situated by the railroad track and it is
but a step from our establishment to the cars
of Nevada Central on one side, and the
Nevada Overland Stage Coach Depot on the other.
All the appointments of a First-Class Hotel
are herein supplied.
Connected to this Hotel is a First-Class Restaurant,
where one might find Pig's Feet, Ham,
and Other Delicacies.*

Folding the paper up and sticking it in his pocket, Smoke left the depot, stepping out onto Fremont Street. Seeing the gallows at the far end of the street, Smoke decided to walk down for a closer inspection.

"You here for the hangin'?" someone asked as he passed one of the business establishments.

Looking toward the sound of the voice, Smoke saw an old, white-haired man sitting on a chair that was tipped back against the front of the apothecary. The man was whittling on a stick.

"Maybe," Smoke said.

"It's goin' to be quite a show," the white-haired man said. He turned his head and expertly spit a stream of tobacco over the boardwalk and into the dirt between the two buildings. "It's a shame they're hangin' the wrong fella, though."

"Why do you say that?"

"Hell, it was Frank Dodd that done the actual shootin'. They was two or three folks that was on the train that night that seen ever'thing. This here fella they're about to hang wasn't doin' nothin' but sort of standin' back. But the judge said that don't matter. He was there so that makes him as guilty as Dodd."

"Do you know the man they are going to hang?" Smoke asked.

"I seen him around a few times," the white-haired man replied. "Always seemed like a decent sort to me. Don't seem to me like he would be the kind to get hisself mixed up with someone like Dodd. Course, you never can tell about some folks. What you see in 'em ain't always what they really are."

"I have to agree with you," Smoke said.

"He tried to say in his trial that he wasn't really ridin' with Dodd, that he was hooked up with him only so he could set a trap for him for the law."

"Do you believe that?" Smoke asked.

The old man spit again. "Don't reckon it makes no never mind what I believe," he said. "I wasn't on the jury, and the jury didn't believe none of it."

"I'd be interested in whether or not you believed him," Smoke said.

"Why? What difference does it make to you?"

"No difference. I was just curious, is all."

"Well, I know what it's like to be curious, so I'll tell you." The old man pulled out a pouch of tobacco and stuck a handful in his mouth. He chewed it a bit to get it to where he wanted it before he spoke again. "I believe him."

"Why?"

"If for no other reason, it's because I don't be-lieve the sheriff," the old man said. "If you ask me, the sheriff is about as crooked as they come. And seein' as Cabot said he was s'posed to be workin' with the sheriff, and the sheriff is sayin' something directly opposite, why, in my book, there ain't no question as to which one of 'em I believe."

As Smoke continued down toward the gallows, he thought of the old man's condemnation of the sheriff. That mirrored the doubt that Sheriff Jacobs had expressed about Sheriff Wallace. And, of course, Smoke's own interaction with Wallace tended to support that idea. From what Smoke could determine about the killing of the young cowboy, it would seem that the sheriff had little justification to shoot.

When Smoke reached the gallows, he saw sev-eral people standing around, their attention drawn not only to the gallows, but to a huge, crudely painted sign. The sign had not been nailed to the gallows, but was on the ground lean-ing up against the platform.

COME ONE COME ALL
WATCH BOBBY LEE FALL
ON FRIDAY THE HANGING WILL BE
WE WELCOME ALL TO COME AND SEE

The reaction to the sign was mixed. There were a few standing around who thought the doggerel funny, and they laughed about it, and pointed it out to others. But there were just as many who thought that writing such bad poetry about someone being hanged was insensitive.

Smoke looked over toward the jail and considered going inside to see Bobby Lee, but decided not to do so yet. He had to figure out some way to help him, so that when he did see him, he would have a plan in place.

A few doors down from the jail, Smoke saw a barbershop and bathhouse, so he decided to stop there before going to the hotel. A little bell attached to the door jingled as he pushed it open. Inside the barbershop, there was a man already in the chair.

"Yes, sir, I'll be right with you," the barber said. "Shave and a haircut?"

"No, I'd like a bath."

"You've come to the right place," the barber responded. "I've got a big tub in the back, lots of hot water, soap, and towels."

He turned his head toward the back of the shop. "Lee!" he shouted, and a Chinese man stuck his head through the curtain that covered a door at the rear.

"Yes, sir?"

"This gentleman wants a bath. Get a tub ready for him."

Lee looked at Smoke, then holding his hand out palm-down, made a couple of downward moves with it. "You come," he said.

Smoke gathered up his saddlebags, then followed the man into the back. Lee pointed to the tub, which, at the moment, was empty. "I fill with warm water," he said.

"Thanks."

Smoke sat down and waited as Lee tossed a few chunks of wood into the stove to build up the fire. Then the small, wiry man began pumping water directly into the tub. After the tub was about one-third full, he scooped out a bucket of water and put it on the stove to heat.

"Soon water be hot enough to make bath good," Lee said.

Smoke nodded, then bent over and started to remove his boots.

"Lee, you no-count Chinaman son of a bitch! Are you back here?" a man yelled, pushing through the curtain.

"Here, Mr. Dawes, what are you doing?" the barber called out from the other side of the curtain. "You can't go barging back there."

"You just stay the hell out of this, Bob. That damn Chinaman owes me five dollars and I aim to collect it."

"I no owe you fi' dollar. You try sell me clock that not work. I give clock back to you."

"Huh-uh. You bought the clock and you're goin' to pay me for it."

"Sir, this gentleman is preparing my bath," Smoke said. "If you have business with him, I would prefer you take care of it at another time."

"I'm about to take me five dollars out of this Chinaman's flesh," Dawes said. "But if you get in my way, it won't bother me to take it out of yours first."

"Oh, I wouldn't like that," Smoke said.

"Ha. I wouldn't think you would. Now you just stay the hell out of my way and let me take care of my business here."

Dawes grabbed a three-legged stool by one of

its legs and lifted it over his head, then started toward Lee, who, with his arms folded across his face, was reacting in horror.

Smoke tapped Dawes on the shoulder, and Dawes turned around with an angry sneer. "I told you to stay the—" That was as far as he got before Smoke took him down with a powerful blow to the chin. The punch knocked Dawes out and, grabbing his feet, Smoke pulled him toward the back door, then motioned for Lee to open it.

"He be very angry when he wake up, I think," Lee said.

"Yes, I expect he will be," Smoke said. With the door opened, Smoke dragged the unconscious man across the alley, then dumped him in the high weeds on the other side.

Earlier, Bobby Lee had been napping on the cot in his jail cell when he heard the shooting, and he sat up, wondering what the shooting was about. Shortly after the shooting, he could hear some commotion out on the street, and though the conversations seemed to be intense, he wasn't able to hear clearly enough to make out what was happening.

"Deputy!" he called. "Deputy Beard! You out there?"

Finally, after several calls, Beard came into the back of the jail.

"What do you want?" he asked.

"What was the shooting?"

"You ain't heard?"

"I heard gunshots. I don't know what it was all about."

"Sheriff Wallace just kilt your friend."

"My friend? Which friend?"

"Ha! Like somebody like you has got so many friends that you don't know who I'm talking about. I'm talking about Andy Emerson, that's who I'm talking about."

"What? Wallace killed him? Why? What did Andy do?"

"You might know that the sheriff told him not to come into the Gold Strike and get drunk no more. So what Emerson done is, he went over into Chinatown and was playin' that gamblin' game them Chinamen like to play. The sheriff seen him there, then told him he was arrestin' him for gamblin' at a place that didn't have no license. Only Emerson said he wasn't goin' to be arrested and he started walkin' away. The sheriff yelled at him, give him a chance to stop, but he didn't. So the sheriff shot up into the air to warn him. Well, when he done that, Emerson commenced to runnin', so the sheriff shot him." Deputy Beard laughed. "Hit him dead center."

"That doesn't seem like much of a reason to be shootin' anybody," Bobby Lee said.

"Ha, that's funny," the deputy replied.

"Funny? What the hell is so funny about that?" Bobby Lee asked, the expression on his face reflecting his confusion over the remark.

"I mean, here you are about to hang, and you're worried about whether or not the sheriff had reason enough to shoot Andy Emerson. Most especial when you consider what kind of a fella Emerson was."

"Emerson was a good man at heart," Bobby Lee said. "I never was able to understand why the sheriff disliked him so. And it surprises me to hear that it went so far as the sheriff actually shooting him."

"He was a damn drunk who didn't know his place," Beard said. "And the only thing that surprises me is that the sheriff didn't shoot the son of a bitch any sooner."

Beard was still chuckling as he went back to the front of the building, closing the door behind him. Bobby Lee returned to his bunk, then lay back down. He thought about dying, and wondered what was just on the other side. Would Emerson be there, waiting for him? Would his ma? Would his sister?

Bobby Lee hadn't been to church in a long time. He wished now that he had paid a little more attention when he had gone.

Chapter Twelve

Feeling much refreshed from his bath, Smoke went to the Depot Hotel.

"Yes, sir, we have the finest rooms in the city," the desk clerk said. "A gentleman of your stature will find nothing better."

"I would like a room overlooking the street," Smoke said as he signed the register.

"I can do that. I do have a drummer who is a regular and who will come in on tonight's train. He normally gets the room overlooking the street, but I'll be glad to let you have it."

"I wouldn't want to put one of your regulars out."

"Oh, don't worry about that, sir. As I said, he is nothing but a traveling salesman. I will accommodate a gentleman over a common drummer any day."

The hotel clerk was a small, unctuous man whose obsequiousness was beginning to get on Smoke's nerves.

"Will you be staying through Friday, sir?"

"I don't know yet."

"You should make it a point to stay through Friday."

"Why? What is so important about Friday?"

"Oh, sir, did you not see the gallows down at the end of the street? We are going to have a hanging here on Friday. It's grisly business to be sure, but it should be a very exciting spectacle nevertheless, and something you will be able to tell your grandchildren about."

"Have you ever seen a hanging?" Smoke asked.

"No, sir. I've never been present when an execution was conducted."

"Conducted?"

"Yes, you know, as the legal extension of a court mandate."

"I see," Smoke said. "Well, I have seen hangings, and it isn't the kind of story you want to tell your grandchildren about." Smoke stopped short of telling the desk clerk that he had not only seen hangings, he had conducted more than one in his mostly violent life.

"Yes, sir, I suppose it could be gruesome, all right. But the man being hanged is a killer after all. And it isn't as if they are lynching him. He was given a fair trial and found guilty by a jury of his peers. We had a judge and lawyers and everything. Besides, the man he killed was a husband and father."

"I heard the man who actually did the killing was Frank Dodd."

"Yes, so they say. But Bobby Lee Cabot was present during the train robbery, and according to the law that makes him as guilty as if he had actually pulled the trigger."

"You have read for the law, have you?"

"No, sir. But I have followed this case with some degree of interest, and I know that the judge instructed the jury to base their decision, not as to whether Cabot actually did the killing, but on the fact that he was there at the time of the killing. That makes him . . ." The desk clerk paused for a moment, looking for the word, then smiled when he thought of it. "That makes him *complicit* in the murder."

"I'm sure," Smoke said. He gave the clerk a dollar. "This will cover my stay for tonight. If I decide to stay longer, I'll give you more money."

"Very good, sir," the clerk said. Reaching up beside him, he pulled down a key and gave it to Smoke. "Your room is two-oh-one. It is at the top of the stairs, the first door on the left. I'm sure you will find it quite satisfactory, but should you have any problems, please don't hesitate to let me know."

Nodding, Smoke picked up his saddlebags and, throwing them over his shoulder, climbed the steps.

The room was typical of many hotel rooms that Smoke had occupied in his life. The bed was high, with a curving iron head and footboards. Sitting beside the bed was a table with a kerosene lantern. On the wall at the foot of the bed was a brown chifforobe upon which set an empty basin and pitcher of water. There was no carpeting on the wide plank floor, and the boards, which had once been painted a deep brown, were now faded in spots. The wallpaper was cream colored, and emblazoned with baskets of purple irises.

Smoke walked over to the window and raised the green shade so he could look out onto Fremont

Street. The window afforded him an excellent view of the gallows that stood in front of the jail, and as he stood at the window, he saw that an arriving stagecoach had to maneuver around the gallows because it took up so much of the street. Once clear of the gallows, the driver snapped his reins against the team, and they broke into a trot so that the coach was moving rather quickly as it passed beneath Smoke.

Hooking his saddlebags over a rung in the chifforobe, Smoke left his room and ambled down the stairs. It was time for him to find the Gold Strike Saloon and talk to Miss Minnie Smith.

Between the hotel and the saloon, he passed the Homestead Hardware Store, and he saw a little knot of people standing on the street just in front of the store, staring in through the window. Curious as to what could be drawing their attention, he made a point to walk close enough by the store to look in the window.

There, lying on a table that was pitched up at about a thirty-degree angle, just high enough to elevate the head, was the body of Andy Emerson. Both of Emerson's eyes were open, though on one, the eyelid was half shut. He had been shot in the back, so there were no visible wounds on the front of his body. His boots had been removed and his toes stuck through one of his socks. There was a hole in the bottom of the other sock. A hastily hand-lettered sign stood up alongside the body.

Andy Emerson
Shot by Sheriff Wallace
In the Line of Duty

The saloon was easy to find. The sign advertising it was a life-sized cut-out and painted figure of a smiling miner. The miner had a pickax slung over his right shoulder, while in his left hand was the reason for the smile. Holding the hand out in front of him, palm up, he was exhibiting a sparkling gold nugget. There was a somewhat smaller sign beside it of a mug of beer, gold at the bottom and white foam at the top.

Smoke pushed his way through the batwing doors, then stepped quickly to one side so that his back was to the wall as he looked the place over. The bar ran perpendicular to the door from the front to the rear of the building along the right side of the room. There were several bottles of spirits sitting on glass shelves behind the bar, their numbers doubled by the mirror at their backs. Nearly a dozen customers stood at the bar, a few of them engaged in animated conversations, but most nursing their own drinks in privacy. Several of the tables had two or more customers, and at least one table had a card game in progress. A group of young women were standing next to the empty piano in the back. One of them was crying, and the others were trying to console her.

"He never did nothin' but get drunk a few times and get into fights. But he never really hurt nobody, he never stole nothin'. He was a good man, a hardworking cowboy," the sobbing woman was saying. The others in the saloon looked toward the girls now and then, the expressions on their faces indicating some sympathy for the plight of the one who was crying.

Smoke selected an empty table near the center of the room.

Seeing him sit down alone, one of the girls who had been standing by the piano came over to talk to him.

"Hi, cowboy," she said. "Something I can get you?"

Smoke nodded toward the weeping young woman. "What's wrong with her?"

"That's Janet Ferrell. Her boyfriend was just killed," the girl said.

"Would her boyfriend be Andy Emerson?"

The girl looked surprised. "Yes. Did you know him?"

Smoke shook his head. "I didn't know him, but I was an accidental witness to the shooting."

"What do you mean you were an accidental witness to the shooting?"

"I had just arrived by train, was seeing to my horse being off loaded from the stock car when it happened. The man Emerson ran up onto the track just behind the train. That's where he was shot."

"Oh, that's right. I heard that the train was still standing in the station when it happened," the girl said. "Tell me this, mister. Was Andy shooting back at the sheriff?"

"No. He didn't have a gun."

"I knew it. Andy never carried a gun. But I know just as sure as God made little green apples that Sheriff Wallace is going to try and claim that he shot Andy in self-defense. Andy wouldn't walk away from a fight. Fact is, he sometimes started them," the girl said. "But not once, in all the time I knew him, did I ever see him with a gun."

"I got the idea from the sheriff that he was always in trouble."

"He was never in any real trouble, and anyone you ask will tell you that. It's just that Sheriff Wallace is a man who likes to boss people around, and Andy didn't take all that kindly to it. The sheriff hated him for that." The girl looked back toward the weeping woman. "Janet is taking this really hard. She blames herself for it."

"Why does she blame herself?"

"Janet was always trying to get Andy to be less belligerent around the sheriff, but Andy wouldn't listen to her."

"She has no reason to blame herself," Smoke said.

"I know it. We all know it, and that's what we've been telling her." The girl looked toward the street. "And now they've got poor Andy trussed up in the window of the hardware store like he's a side of beef or something. If you ask me, what that sheriff did by shooting him when he wasn't even carrying a gun wasn't much more than outright murder."

The girl dabbed her eyes, then added, quietly, so quietly that Smoke barely heard it, "And he is about to do the same thing again, come Friday."

"You are talking about the hanging?" Smoke asked.

"Yes. Bobby Lee Cabot is innocent. And I could have proved it, if the court had let me testify." She wiped her eyes again, then put on a smile for Smoke. "But I know you didn't come in here to listen to me prattle on so," she said. "What can I do for you?"

"I'm new in town," Smoke replied. "And I need a friend."

The girl smiled, then leaned over, putting her hands down on the table in such a way as to afford him a very generous view of the cleavage exposed by her low-cut dress.

"Honey, as I am sure you can tell by the way that I am dressed, that's what I do for a living," she said, now completely back in character. "I am always friendly to handsome men." She laughed, a self-deprecating laugh. "The truth is, they don't even have to be handsome. All they need is money. It just works out nice when they are handsome, like you are."

"Then tell me, my new friend. Where can I find Minnie Smith?"

The smile left the girl's face, and she looked around the saloon anxiously before turning her attention back to Smoke.

"What do you want with her?" she asked.

"I received a message from her," Smoke said without providing any more information.

The girl gasped, then covered her mouth with her hand. "Oh, my God, I didn't think you would come. You are Buck West, aren't you?"

"Yes," Smoke answered. At the moment, he thought it would be easier to say that than to explain who he really was. "Am I correct in assuming that you are Minnie Smith?"

"Yes, I'm Minnie Smith."

"We need to talk."

"All right. Buy me a drink, Mr. West," she said. "That way I can sit and talk with you for a spell without anyone wondering what's going on."

"I'd be glad to. And I'll have a beer," Smoke said. He took a dollar bill from his pocket and handed it to her.

Minnie started to the bar to get the drinks, but on her way she stopped at one of the other tables and spoke to the two men who were there. Smoke saw her nod toward him then, and as she continued on toward the bar, the two men got up and, bringing their mugs with them, came over to Smoke's table.

"You would be Mr. West?" one of them asked.

Smoke nodded, but did not speak.

"May we join you?"

"Yes, please do." He would have said that he wanted no company, had he not seen Minnie talking to them. But he was certain that if she had spoken to them, then she had probably invited them to join in the conversation. And conversation was good, because he needed as much information as he could gather before he made his move. Whatever that move might turn out to be.

The two men sat down as Minnie got a couple of beers at the bar.

"I'm Doc Baker, this is Nate Nabors. He owns this saloon," the older of the two men said.

"Pleased to meet the both of you," Smoke said. He wasn't sure where this was going, so he was keeping his own comments to a minimum.

"I hope you don't mind, Mr. West. I told these two gentlemen that you were here," Minnie said as she returned with the two beers and sat down as well. "They know all about the telegram I sent to you, and they know that you are one of Bobby Lee's friends. They want to help you if they can."

"Help me with what?"

"Whatever it is you plan to do, Mr. West," Nabors said.

"What makes you think I'm going to do anything?"

Minnie had a confused and rather disappointed look on her face.

"I don't know, maybe I misunderstood," she said. "I thought that being one of Bobby Lee's friends you might—uh, well, that is, you did come in response to my telegram, didn't you? The telegram I sent you?"

"I did."

"And you are a friend of Bobby Lee's?"

"I am."

"Here is the thing, Mr. West. You are here, and we don't believe you would have come if you didn't plan to do something," Doc Baker said.

"And if you do have something planned, we want to help, because we don't believe Bobby Lee is guilty," Nabors added.

"Are there many in town like you? By that I mean, people who don't believe Bobby Lee is guilty," Smoke asked. He thought of the old white-haired man he had spoken to in front of the drug store.

The others exchanged glances for a moment. Then Doc Baker answered for all three of them.

"A few more maybe, but I'm afraid there aren't too many of us who feel this way," he said. "The problem is, Bobby Lee was brought in by passengers who were on the train when it was held up and the express man murdered. That means he was obviously there."

"Did anyone testify that he saw Bobby Lee shoot the messenger?" Smoke asked.

"No. Nobody testified to that, because nobody saw him do it," Nabors answered. "And the reason nobody saw him shoot the messenger is because he didn't do it."

"But Bobby Lee was there?"

"Oh, yes, he was there."

Smoke nodded. "Yeah, I was afraid of that. If he was there, then he bears some of the guilt."

"Whose side are you on, Mr. West?" Minnie asked, surprised by the way the conversation was going.

"I'm just trying to find out as much as I can about what happened," Smoke replied.

"What happened is Frank Dodd and the others got away. Someone has to hang, so it's going to be Bobby Lee," Doc Baker said.

"No!" Minnie said, biting her fist as tears sprung to her eyes. "He can't hang."

"He sure as hell can," Doc Baker said. "And if Mr. West here isn't able to do anything about it, Bobby Lee damn well will hang."

"No!" Minnie said again. "No!"

Minnie spoke so loudly that several others in the saloon looked over toward the table she was sharing with the three men, to see what was going on.

"Shh, Minnie, there's no need for everyone in town to know our business," Doc Baker said.

"You're right, I'm sorry," Minnie responded quietly and contritely.

"Did Bobby Lee present any defense?" Smoke asked. "I mean, did he say why he was there?"

"Yes," Nabors replied. "He said he was a railroad detective and he had worked his way into the gang to find out about them."

"And he told the sheriff about the robbery," Minnie added. "The sheriff and his deputies were supposed be waiting in the car when the robbers arrived. That way the sheriff could catch them in the act."

"What went wrong?" Smoke asked.

"He trusted the sheriff. That's what went wrong," Minnie replied.

"The sheriff wasn't in the car," Doc Baker added.

"Did he say why he wasn't in the car?"

"He claims that he never got the letter, and that there was no such plan between him and Bobby Lee," Nabors replied.

"But there was a letter," Minnie insisted.

"How do you know?" Smoke asked.

"Because he told me," she replied. "In fact, he told all of us." She made a circular motion with her hand, which included the other two.

"He told all three of you about the plan?"

"Yes," Doc Baker answered. "He told us before the robbery ever happened what he was planning to do."

"Did you three testify to that in the trial?"

"We tried to," Minnie said. "But they wouldn't let us testify. They said it was hearsay."

"They wouldn't even swear us in as witnesses," Doc Baker said.

"Are you a special friend of Bobby Lee?" Smoke asked Minnie.

"What do you mean by special friend?" Minnie replied.

Smoke looked over toward the woman Minnie

had identified as Janet Ferrell. Janet was still crying about the death of Andy Emerson.

"I mean are you that kind of special friend?" he clarified.

Minnie smiled sheepishly, then nodded. "I am as special a friend as a girl like me can be," she answered. "What about you? How does he know you? He asked me to send the telegram to you, but he wasn't sure it would even get through, and he wasn't sure you would come even if it did. Evidently he hadn't seen you in a while."

"That's right. We haven't seen each other in a very long time," Smoke said, validating her observation. "And the reason I know him is because I was once married to his sister."

"Once married?" Minnie asked.

"She's dead," Smoke said without further elaboration.

"Oh, Mr. West, I'm sorry."

Suddenly, someone barged in through the batwing doors, hitting them so hard that the doors slammed noisily against the walls. Looking toward the disturbance, Smoke recognized Dawes, the man with whom he had had an altercation back at the barbershop.

"There you are!" Dawes shouted angrily. "You're the son of a bitch that hit me from behind!" He had a pistol in his hand and he pointed it toward Smoke, which meant he was also pointing toward the three who were sitting at the table with him.

Reacting very quickly, Smoke turned the table over so that it was between Minnie, Doc Baker, Nabors, and Dawes. He did it just in the nick of time because Dawes fired, wildly as it turned out, his bullet taking a piece out of the top of the table.

Remaining crouched over, Smoke moved quickly away from the table so as not to draw any more fire that could put the others in danger. When he reached the stove, he called out to Dawes.

"I'm over here!"

Dawes' second shot hit the stovepipe, sending out a cloud of black dust, the residue from old fires.

Startled by the unexpected shooting, everyone in the saloon was diving for cover. It was not until then that Smoke drew his own pistol. He shot back, hitting Dawes in the hand, causing him to drop his pistol.

With a cry of pain, Dawes grabbed his hand. Then, shouting out a loud string of curses and his face contorted in rage, he bent over to retrieve his pistol. Smoke fired again, this time hitting the pistol and sending it sliding across the floor.

Dawes started toward it.

"I could have killed you either time, Dawes!" Smoke shouted. "If you touch that gun again, I will kill you. Is that what you want?"

Dawes stopped, then turned back toward Smoke, glaring at him, but saying nothing.

By now, with the shooting stopped, the others in the saloon, some of whom had imitated Minnie, Doc Baker, and Nabors by getting behind overturned tables, began to stand up.

"You were lucky," Dawes said.

"Didn't look like luck to me," Doc Baker said. "Looked to me like he was being generous. Come over here and let me look at that hand."

"It ain't nothin'," Dawes said.

"Maybe it is and maybe it isn't," Doc Baker said. "On the other hand, it could fester and you'd wind up losin' your hand. Or worse. Now get over here and let me look at it, like I said."

Dawes walked over to Doc Baker, holding out his bleeding hand.

"Get me a bottle of whiskey, Minnie," Doc Baker ordered, and within a moment she was back with a bottle. The doctor pulled the cork with his teeth, then poured a generous amount of the whiskey over the wound.

"Ooww, that hurts," Dawes complained.

"Good," Doc Baker said. "It serves you right for doing such a dumb thing. What brought all this on anyway."

Dawes pointed to Smoke. "He hit me from behind for no reason at all."

"Now, Dawes, I just met this man a few moments ago and I already don't believe he would have hit you from behind. And I don't believe he would hit you for no reason," Doc Baker said.

"I didn't hit you from behind, Dawes. I tapped you on the shoulder. You turned around and then I hit you."

"Well, why did you hit me?"

"Because you were about to bring a chair crashing down on the Chinaman's head, that's why."

"That's no reason. The Chinaman deserved it. That Celestial stole five dollars from me," Dawes said angrily.

"And you were going to kill him over five dollars?"

"What if I had killed him? Hell, he ain't nothin'

but a Chinaman anyway," Dawes said, as if that explained everything.

By now, Minnie had torn off part of her under-skirt, and Doc Baker used it to wrap a bandage around Dawes' hand.

"Go home, Dawes. Go home before you get yourself into more trouble," Doc Baker said.

Dawes nodded, then started over to pick up his gun.

"I'll thank you to leave the gun here," Smoke said. He emphasized his comment by waving his gun, indicating that Dawes should stay away.

"Mister, that gun cost me fifteen dollars. There ain't no way I am goin' to just leave it here."

"You are going to leave it until tomorrow," Smoke insisted. "I'm sure the gentleman behind the bar will hold it for you until then."

"How can I trust him?"

"I give you my word, Dawes, that your gun will be here tomorrow," Nabors said. "That's right, isn't it, Paul?" he called out, looking toward the bartender.

Paul, the bartender, was as awed by what he had seen as any of the others. He nodded, but said nothing.

"Yeah, well, it better be," Dawes said. "'Cause if it ain't . . ." He paused, then, with an angry glare, Dawes left the saloon with his gun still lying on the floor behind him.

Chapter Thirteen

With the departure of Dawes, the excitement was over, and everyone in the saloon started talking at the same time, trying to fix in their minds the memory of what they had just seen. The result was a cacophony of excited shouts and conversation.

Smoke walked over to Dawes's pistol, which still lay where it had wound up after being pushed across the floor by Smoke's second shot. Picking it up, he saw that, because of the strike of his bullet, it would need a new handle grip. He gave it to the barkeep. After that, he returned to the table, which had already been righted again, thanks to the efforts of Doc Baker and Nate Nabors.

"Looks like we are going to need new drinks," Doc Baker said.

"Yeah, it looks like it," Nabors said. "Get us another round, would you, Minnie?" Nabors asked. "And tell Paul they are on me."

Minnie nodded, then started toward the bar to carry out the order.

For the moment, Smoke said nothing. He continued to look toward the batwing doors, just to make certain that Dawes didn't suddenly burst back in with a second gun.

"Don't worry about Dawes comin' back," Nabors said, noticing the attention Smoke was giving the door. "I've known him a long time and, believe me, he's too much of a coward to ever try anything against you again."

Minnie returned with new beers for Smoke, Doc Baker, and Nabors. "Now, where were we before all the excitement began?" she asked.

"Mr. West had just told us that he was Bobby Lee's brother-in-law," Nabors said.

"And you said she died?" Minnie asked.

"Yes," Smoke replied. "Actually, she was killed, along with my son."

"Oh. I'm so sorry," Minnie said, reaching out to put her hand on his.

"Did the law ever catch the person who did it?" Doc Baker asked.

"It wasn't a person, it was three persons. And the law didn't catch them. I did."

"You caught them? You mean, by yourself?" Minnie asked.

"Yes."

"With the shooting exhibition you put on here today, I would almost imagine that the odds were on your side, despite the fact that were three of them. I have never seen shooting like that," Doc Baker said. "How come I've never heard of you, Mr. West?"

Smoke took a swallow of his beer, then wiped the back of his hand across his mouth before he spoke again.

"Well, maybe it's because my name isn't Buck West."

"What? I don't understand, if you aren't Buck West, how did you get the telegram?" Minnie asked.

"It is a name that I used once in my past. I believe Bobby Lee used it as sort of a code when he sent the telegram. He knew that I would respond to that name and I suppose he also knew that if he used it, I would realize that the telegram was authentic."

"What is your real name?" Doc Baker asked.

"Jensen. Kirby Jensen, but most folks call me Smoke."

Nate Nabors had just started to take a drink when he heard Smoke give his real name, and he jerked the mug back down so quickly that he spilled some of his beer.

"You are Smoke Jensen?"

"Yes."

Smiling broadly, Nabors extended his hand across the table. "Well, Mr. Jensen, let me tell you it is an honor to meet you. And knowing that you are here, I feel better about this situation already."

"Thank you and it is Smoke, not Mr. Jensen," Smoke replied, taking Nabors's hand.

"Excuse my ignorance here, but is Smoke Jensen a name I should know?" Doc Baker asked.

"You would know it if you ever read anything but those damn medical journals," Nabors replied. "Smoke Jensen is just about the most famous gunman—uh, make that, best-known gunfighter—I mean, well, I don't know what I mean. I know that he isn't a gunfighter who goes around looking for trouble, but he is the kind of man folks turn to when they are in trouble."

Doc Baker nodded. "Mr. Jensen, I'm not one who appreciates guns. I've had to pull out too many bullets from people who were too dumb to reason anything out and wound up letting their guns talk for them. But if you are here to help Bobby Lee, then I say, welcome to Cloverdale."

"How?" Minnie asked.

"How what?" Smoke asked, confused by Minnie's truncated question.

"How are you going to help him?"

Smoke drummed his fingers on the table for a moment before he answered.

"Well, now, to tell you the truth, Minnie, I haven't quite got that figured out yet."

"When you figure it out, if there is anything I can do to help, please let me know."

"I will. And thanks."

"No. Thank you for responding to the telegram."

There is no way I wasn't going to respond," Smoke said. "Like I told you, Bobby Lee is family."

Approximately sixty miles north of Cloverdale, in the small town of Desolation, Emmett Clark was sitting in on a poker game at the New Promise Saloon.

"Deal them," Clark said.

One of the other players was Jules Stillwater, and at this precise moment, he was extremely agitated. The cause of Stillwater's agitation was the attention Cindy was paying to Emmett Clark. She was watching the game from her position behind Clark, and her hand was resting lightly on Clark's shoulder.

"Cindy," Stillwater said. "My neck is stiff. Why don't you come over here in rub it?"

"You willing to pay for it?" Cindy asked.

"Why should I pay for it? Is Clark paying you to put your hand on his shoulder?"

"No."

"Then come over here and rub my neck like I asked. That's what you are supposed to do in here, ain't it? Keep the customers happy?"

"You aren't a customer unless you pay for it," Cindy said. "If I'm not getting paid, then I'll be with who I want to be."

"Ha, Stillwater, I reckon she told you all right," McWorthy said. McWorthy had served ten years in prison for shooting a man back in Wichita. Nobody knew if he was actually wanted now or not, but he had arrived in Desolation a few months earlier, purposely choosing the town because of its reputation as being friendly to outlaws. McWorthy supported himself by petty larceny, which he carried on in surrounding towns, always retreating back to Desolation.

It was McWorthy's deal and his hands moved swiftly as he folded the cards in and out until he was satisfied with the shuffle. He pushed the cards toward Stillwater, who cut them, then pushed them back.

"Is five-card draw all right with everyone?" McWorthy asked.

"Yeah, five-card draw is fine," Stillwater said. "Cindy, let me tell you what I'm going to do. I'm going to win Clark's poke. Then after I take all of his money, I'm going to spend every cent of it on you. What do you think about that?"

"If you've got the money, I'll be your honey," Cindy replied, and the others around the table, including Clark, laughed.

Clark lost fifteen dollars on the first hand after having folded cautiously with a hand that would have been good enough to win, had he stayed in the game.

Stillwater won the hand, and he cackled as he dragged in the pot.

"If you ain't got the guts to play the game, you might want to sit out the next hand," he said to Clark. "You should've bet them cards."

Clark gave up the next hand as well, even though it was strong enough to have at least bet the first round.

"Damn," Stillwater said as he raked in his winnings. "Dodd don't need to come up with no more jobs. Not as long as I can win money from you."

This time, Stillwater got a laugh.

Clark was down thirty dollars by the third hand, but there was over sixty dollars in the pot, and he had drawn two cards to complete a full house. When the bet came to him, he put his hand on the money, pushed it out, then drew it back, thought about it for a moment, then pushed it back out.

"What? You mean you are going to bet this time?" Stillwater teased. "Better be careful now, you might want to think about that. You don't want to get too brave. I'll see your five, and raise you five."

Clark studied his hand for a long moment before, and with some hesitation, he called.

"All right, Clark, let's see your cards," Stillwater said. Stillwater was holding three jacks, and he laughed when he saw Clark's hand.

"You were holding a full house and you didn't raise?"

"You might've had a stronger hand. I like to be certain about things. And as you can see, prudence was a good choice," Clark said as he raked in the pot. "I am now forty dollars ahead."

"You don't know much about cards, do you?" Stillwater said. "Hell, iffen I'd had that hand, I would'a won eighty, maybe a hunnert dollars with it."

"But, you didn't have that hand, did you?" Clark asked.

"Tell you what, kid. Why don't I just show you what this game is all about. I've been layin' off you a bit because I can see that you don't have no idea at all about playin' cards. Well, I'm about to teach you how to play, and it's goin' to cost you some money."

"You mean you want me to pay you for lessons?" Clark asked.

"You don't have to pay me. I'll just take the money from you, and that'll be lesson enough for you," Stillwater said. "All you got to do is pay attention while you're losin'. I'm going to take every dollar you have, and spend it all on Cindy."

"Oh, well, then Cindy can't lose, can she?" Clark said.

"What are you? Some kind of a wise guy?" Stillwater asked.

Though Clark gave no outward sign, inwardly

he smiled. Stillwater was extremely agitated now, and the more agitated he became, the more injudicious would be his decisions. This was going to be an interesting game.

"I'm going to ante the limit this time," Clark said hesitantly. He put his hand on the money and held it for a moment, as if thinking about it, then, with a sigh, pushed the money forward. "Ten dollars."

"Oh, ten dollars?" Stillwater said. "That's a little steep for you, ain't it?"

"Not too bad. I'm forty dollars ahead, so I'm not actually betting with my own money," Clark replied.

"Ahh, not betting with your own money. That's just real smart now. I tell you what. How about we up the ante a little?"

"Up the ante?"

"Sure, why not? Like you say, you aren't playing with your own money. What will it hurt if you lose a little?"

"I don't know. If we raise the ante, it wouldn't take too long before I would be playing with my own money again."

"So what you are saying is, you are afraid to raise the ante."

"I wouldn't say I am afraid."

"You wouldn't, eh? What would you say?" Stillwater teased.

"I think I would rather say that I am cautious," Clark replied.

Stillwater laughed. "Did you hear that, boys? I say he's afraid, but he says he's cautious."

The others around the table laughed.

"What do you say, Cindy? Is he cautious? Or is he afraid?"

"Jules, why don't you quit picking on him?" Cindy asked.

"No, I ain't goin' to quit pickin' on him," Stillwater said. "He sat down to play a man's game with men, so let him be a man. Now what do you say, boy? Are you going raise the ante? Or are you too scared?"

"I suppose I'll go along with raising the ante," Clark said, continuing the illusion that he was not real comfortable with the situation.

"Ha!" Stillwater said. He shoved the cards across the table to Clark. "It's your deal. You do know how to deal, don't you?"

"Yes, I know how to deal. Everyone knows how to deal," Clark replied, as if he had been offended by Stillwater's comment.

Clark picked up the cards, then skillfully, and without being detected, felt them as he began shuffling, checking for pinpricks and uneven corners. He was satisfied that they were playing with an honest deck.

In truth, Clark was exceptionally skilled at cards, but had purposely passed himself off as a novice. Evidently, his ruse had worked, because Stillwater was sure of himself to the point of overconfidence. And that, Stillwater's overconfidence, was the only edge Clark needed in the game.

Clark dealt the cards. The other players, perhaps motivated by the supposed recklessness of Clark and Stillwater, bet briskly so that, within a few moments, the pot was over two hundred dollars.

"Wait a minute," Conklin said. "What am I doing

here? I'm forty dollars into this pot. How did it get so big? I can't afford to stay in this game."

Well, you have this fella to thank for that," Stillwater said. "He's all full of himself because he won the last hand."

"I haven't been raising the bets, I have just been matching them," Clark said. "And I think Conklin is right, it has gotten too high, but I am almost too afraid to drop out now. I wish I had been more prudent. I fear that I have too much invested."

"Hah! Now, sonny, you are in a man's game," Stillwater said. "Let's just see how much of a man you are. It's going to cost you one hundred dollars to stay in."

"That's it, I'm out also," McWorthy said. "Stillwater, you ain't got no right to just up and buy a pot like that."

"Same rules goes for you as goes for the kid here," Stillwater said. "If you ain't man enough to stay in the game, you shouldn't of got into it in the first place. I guess that means I won." Stillwater chuckled, then reached for the pot and started to pull it toward him. "And now, kid, this is what I mean about teaching you a lesson."

"Wait a minute," Clark said. "Don't I get a chance to bet?"

"You want to bet? Sure, go ahead. Me an' Cindy can have us a fine old time on your money. The bet to you is one hundred dollars."

The hesitancy and confusion left Clark's face, and he stared across the table at Stillwater and smiled. Then the smile turned to a quiet, confident chuckle.

"I'll see your one hundred, and two hundred more to you," he said.

"What?" Stillwater gasped.

Clark laid his hand down, putting four cards to one side, and one card separated from the others.

"If you want to see my hand, it's going to cost you two hundred dollars."

"I ain't got that much money. Conklin, lend me two hunnert dollars."

"Now, tell me, Jules. If I ain't goin' to put up the money to stay in the game myself, why should I back you?" Conklin asked.

"McWorthy?"

"I ain't got two hunnert dollars, Stillwater. I ain't even got one hunnert dollars. And I wouldn't lend it to you if I did have it," McWorthy answered. "Look at the way he laid them cards down. Hell, he's got four of a kind, and I wouldn't be surprised if it wasn't four aces. I mean, you seen how slow he's been to bet. You know damn well he wouldn't be bettin' no two hunnert dollars if he didn't have hisself a winnin' hand."

By now, the stakes of the game had grown high enough to attract the attention of everyone else in the saloon, and there were several men standing around the table, watching the game with intense interest.

"He's bluffin', Stillwater," one of the onlookers said. "Hell, I can tell by lookin' at him that he's bluffin'. Call his hand."

"You got two hunnert dollars?" Stillwater asked.

The man shook his head. "This ain't my game," he said. "But if it was my game, I'd call him."

"Really? Don't forget, this is the fella who

wouldn't even raise a full house. Is that what you've got, Clark? A full house?"

"It can't be a full house," Conklin said. "Look at the way he has them cards lyin' there. Four to one side, and one to the other."

"It's like I said," McWorthy said. "He's got four of a kind."

"What are you going to do, Stillwater?" one of the bystanders asked. "You can't just sit there all night."

"Will somebody lend me two hunnert dollars?" Stillwater called out. "Anybody?"

The room was quiet for a long moment.

"I will," Cindy said.

A huge smile spread across Stillwater's face. "Ha! I know'd that when it come right down to it, you would come back over to my side."

"If you win, I'll take the money right now," Cindy said. "But if you lose, then I'm going to want to be repaid four hundred dollars."

"What makes you think I have four hundred dollars?"

"Maybe you don't have it right now, but you'll be doing another job with Frank Dodd soon, and when you do, I'll expect my four hundred."

"All right," Stillwater said. "It's a deal."

"Jules, you might want to think about this for a bit," Conklin cautioned.

"What do you mean?"

"Look at where she has been standin'," Conklin said. "You think she don't know what his hand is? Now, you got to ask yourself, is she doin' this just so she can get a cut of your money next time we do a job? She might just be tryin' to sucker you in."

"Yeah," Stillwater said. He stroked his chin and stared across the table at Clark. "You think you've got me in your sights, don't you?"

"I'm just trying to learn the game," Clark answered innocently.

"All right, all right, the pot's yours," Stillwater said, turning his cards up on the table. He had a full house, aces over jacks. "What have you got?"

Clark's cards stayed facedown on the table just the way he left them, four in one pile, one in another. He reached out to rake in his pot.

"I asked you a question, mister. What have you got?" Stillwater asked again. He reached for Clark's cards, but Clark caught him around the wrist with a vise grip.

"Huh-uh. I don't know all that much about this game, but I know that if you don't pay, you don't see. You didn't pay, so you don't see them," Clark said easily.

With his other hand, Stillwater slid a twenty-dollar bill across the table.

"Is that enough to let me see?"

"I reckon so. Like I said, if you're willing to pay for it." Clark turned up his cards. Instead of four of a kind, there were two small pairs.

"What? I had a full house! You didn't have me beat!" Stillwater said angrily.

"Well, now, let's think about that, Stillwater," Clark said. "You are right, my cards didn't beat your cards but I did beat you," Clark said. "It's called running a bluff." He smiled up at Cindy. "What do you think, Cindy? It looks like he won't be spending any of my money on you after all. But that's all right. I'll spend some of his money on you."

"Mister, I ain't goin' to forget this," Stillwater said angrily. He stood up, then walked quickly, and angrily, out of the saloon.

Everyone in the saloon was quiet as Stillwater left. Then Conklin looked over at Clark.

"Kid, he's my pard, and I ride with him," Conklin said. "But I got to tell you, he ain't the kind you want on your bad side. If I was you, I'd be mighty careful around him from now on."

"Thanks," Clark said. "I'll heed your advice."

Chapter Fourteen

"Cloverdale is a nice town," Doc Baker was saying. "That's why I moved my practice here. Right now we are at end-of-track, but if they ever continue it on into California, as I believe they will, it will be an even nicer town."

"It would be nicer now if it weren't for Wallace," Nabors said.

"Tell me about this sheriff," Smoke said.

"I saw a word one time that fits this sheriff," Nabors said. "The word was potentate. That's what this sheriff thinks he is."

"But he was elected, wasn't he?"

"Oh, yes, he was elected all right," Doc Baker said. "And if you would ask the average person on the street what kind of job they think he is doing, they would probably say he is doing a good job. He keeps his jail full of drunks, people who spit on the street, deadbeats, and the like. But all the time he is doing that, people like Frank Dodd and his gang operate with impunity."

"Impunity," Nabors said, laughing. "Now, you see here, Smoke? That's why I like to keep the doc on as my friend. How many people do you know who can use a word like impunity?"

Smoke thought of his wife, Sally, back at Sugar-loaf. A former schoolteacher, and the smartest person he had ever known. Impunity would be one of her words. He smiled.

"It's a good word all right," he agreed.

"That's him," someone suddenly yelled, his shout having the effect of bringing all other conversation to a halt.

Looking toward the sound of the shout, Smoke saw Dawes standing just inside the saloon, holding his bandaged hand. He let go of it long enough to point Smoke out to a man wearing a badge. Smoke recognized him as the same man he had seen on the railroad track, shortly after the cowboy, Andy Emerson, had been killed. It was Sheriff Wallace.

"That's the man who shot me."

"Is that true, mister?" Wallace asked. "Did you shoot Mr. Dawes?"

"I did."

"Wait a minute, I know you. You're the fella I met who had just came in on the train after the little ruckus with Andy Emerson, aren't you? You're the one who was interfering with the law."

"We've met," Smoke said.

"Well, I don't know where you came from, mister. But in Nye County, we got us a law against shootin' folks."

"Yes, that's been my observation in most places I've been," Smoke replied. "But from what I have seen here, it evidently does not apply to people who are wearing a badge. I notice that you had no compunctions about killing that unarmed cowboy."

The sheriff, who was probably three inches taller and eighty pounds heavier than Smoke, got an irritated look on his face.

"Mister, I've only met you twice, and you've put a burr under my saddle both times."

"What do you mean, Sheriff? I haven't been belligerent."

"No, but you always seem to have something smart to say."

"I'm sorry if I've been too smart. I know how difficult it can be for someone like you to have to deal with intelligent comments. I'll try and bring it down," Smoke said.

Minnie, Doc, and Nabors tried hard to smother their smiles.

"Just as long as you understand," the sheriff said, totally unaware that he just been mocked. "Why did you shoot Dawes?"

"Because he was shooting at me," Smoke replied.

"He's tellin' the truth, Sheriff Wallace," Doc Baker said. "Dawes came in here shooting."

"That's right, Sheriff," Nabors added. "And I aim to sue him for a new table and a new stovepipe. Look here what he did." Nabors pointed to the hole in the tabletop, and another in the stovepipe.

"Can anyone else back that up?" Sheriff Wallace asked.

"I can back it up, Sheriff," the bartender said. He pointed to Dawes. "Truth to tell, it's a plumb wonder Dawes didn't get hisself shot dead. Most anyone else would have kilt him. But this feller, just as calm as a summer day, shot the gun right out of his hand. Then, when Dawes tried to pick it up, this feller shot again, only this time what he done was, his bullet pushed the gun all the way across the floor."

Sheriff Wallace squinted as he looked back at Smoke. "Do you mean to tell me you wasn't shootin' at him and just missed? You was *tryin'* to shoot the gun out of his hand?"

"I wasn't *trying* to do it, Sheriff. I did it," Smoke said.

"You are either one hell of a good shot, or a damn fool," Sheriff Wallace said. He looked at Dawes. "Did you shoot first?"

"I told you, Sheriff, he hit me from behind."

"Get on out of here," the sheriff growled. "If what these folks are saying is true, then you are the one I should put in jail."

"It ain't right, Sheriff, he had no call to—"

"I said get out of here," Sheriff Wallace repeated, more forcefully this time.

Glaring at the sheriff and the others in the saloon, Dawes left. Sheriff Wallace walked over to the door and watched for a moment to make certain that Dawes left as ordered. Then he turned back toward Smoke.

"What did you say your name was, back at the depot?"

"Jensen."

The sheriff squinted at Smoke. "Wait a minute, I thought you said your name was Cody, or Kirby, or something like that."

"Kirby," Smoke said. "Kirby is my first name. Kirby Jensen."

"Well, Mr. Jensen, here is a word of advice. Next time someone points a gun at you, I wouldn't recommend you trying to shoot the gun out of their hand. If you are going to shoot, shoot to kill. You might not be so lucky the next time."

"Thanks," Smoke said. "I'll keep that in mind."

"Minnie," the sheriff said. "Have you heard anything back from that telegram you sent to Buck West?"

Minnie gasped. "What? How did you know I sent a telegram?"

"I'm the sheriff. It's my business to know."

Minnie looked over toward Smoke, who, with a barely perceptible shake of his head, cautioned her to say nothing about it.

"Well, if it's your business to know, then you probably already know that I didn't hear anything back from him."

"It's just as well," Sheriff Wallace said. "I don't know what Cabot had in mind when he had you send that telegram, but I plan to keep a close eye on him."

"Sheriff, I don't know what happened to that letter he sent you, but if you had gotten it, you would know that he really didn't have anything to do with that holdup," Minnie said.

"There was no letter," Sheriff Wallace said.

"There was too," Minnie insisted. "I don't know why you never received it, but there was a letter.

"Even if there had been no letter, he talked to you about it," Minnie added. "He made plans for you to be waiting for him in the express car."

"And you know this because?"

"I know this because he told me about it before the robbery took place. He told all three of us." Minnie took in Doc Baker and Nate Nabors with a wave of her hand. "And we were ready to testify about it too, but the judge wouldn't allow it."

"The judge said that we could not testify, because it would not be direct information. It would be considered hearsay," Nabors said.

"Only you could have testified that he set up an arrangement with you," Doc Baker said.

"But you didn't do it," Minnie added angrily.

Sheriff Wallace chuckled. "I didn't do it because there was no letter, and he didn't talk to me. Don't you understand what he was doing? He was setting up his alibi with you. I'll give him this. For all that he is a train robber and murderer, he's smart. It takes someone smart to set up something like that. But what it all comes down to is his word against mine. The jury believed me. They didn't believe Cabot."

"I believe him," Doc Baker said.

"Why should you believe him? You were in the courtroom, Doc. You heard the letter they read from the WCSA. They said no such investigation had been authorized. No, sir, Bobby Lee Cabot is as guilty as sin."

"And because the judge wouldn't agree to let us testify, he is going to hang," Minnie said.

Sheriff Wallace chuckled. "Yes, ma'am, he is going to hang, all right. We are goin' to have us one Jim Dandy of a hangin'. We'll have folks comin' in from all over the county this Friday mornin' to watch it, and I don't plan to let 'em be disappointed by anything this Buck West fella might have in mind. I reckon this is goin' to be about one of the best days for business we've ever had. If it goes over as well as I think it will, why, I just might see if I can't arrange a hangin' about ever' month or so. It'll bring so much business into town that I'll have ever' storekeep in town votin' for me."

"You murderer!" Janet suddenly yelled. She was coming from the kitchen, moving quickly toward the sheriff with a butcher knife her hand. "You killed Andy!"

"What the hell?" Sheriff Wallace shouted. He started to draw his gun but before he could, Smoke reached out and grabbed Janet's wrist, forcing her to drop the knife.

"Janet, you don't want to do this," Smoke said.

Janet put both her hands to her face and began crying.

Looking back toward Wallace, Smoke saw that he was still holding his gun, though he wasn't pointing it at anyone.

"Put your gun away, Sheriff," Smoke said.

"Did you see that crazy bitch? She tried to kill me!"

"You were never in any real danger. Now, put your gun away, unless you plan to kill an un-armed woman in front of all these witnesses."

Wallace hesitated for a moment, then returned his pistol to his holster. He pointed at Nabors. "She works for you," he said angrily. "And I'm telling you right now that you had better keep her under control."

"You aren't going to try anything like that again, are you, Janet?" Nabors asked.

Still sobbing, and with her hands covering her face, Janet shook her head no.

"You won't have any more trouble with her, Sheriff," Nabors said.

"Yeah, well, like I say, you just damn well better keep her under control," the sheriff said.

There was a long moment of silence after the sheriff left. Then a couple of the other saloon girls went over to comfort Janet and general conversation in the saloon resumed.

"It looks bad for Bobby Lee, doesn't it?" Doc Baker asked.

"I'm afraid so," Smoke agreed.

"So, what you are saying is, there is no way we can stop the hanging this Friday?" Minnie asked.

"No, I didn't say that. He's not going to hang this Friday," Smoke said.

"But you said that it looks bad for him."

"I can stop the hanging."

"How?"

"If he's not in jail, they can't hang him. And I intend to get him out of jail," Smoke said. "But that isn't enough. We are also going to have to prove his innocence. If we don't do that, he'll just be an escaped prisoner with wanted posters plastered in just about every state and territory west of the Mississippi."

"Do you think you can prove his innocence?" Doc Baker asked.

"Let me ask you this," Smoke replied. "Do you believe he is innocent?"

"Yes, of course I do. Don't you believe he is innocent?" Doc Baker replied.

"I don't know, it's been a long time since I last saw Bobby Lee," Smoke said. "But it doesn't matter to me whether he is innocent or not. I don't intend to let him hang."

"If he is innocent, and I believe with all my heart that he is, will you be able to prove it?" Minnie asked.

"Yes. If he is innocent, I will prove it."

"How?"

"We'll start by finding the man who actually did kill the express messenger," Smoke said.

"That would be Frank Dodd," Nabors said.

"Yes."

"That's quite an order," Doc Baker said. "There is a rather significant reward out for him, and people have been after him for at least three years now."

"And they say he got over five thousand dollars from that last robbery. With that much money, there's no tellin' where he is by now."

"We'll find him," Smoke said.

"You said you were going to get Bobby Lee out of jail," Doc Baker said.

"That's right."

"How are you going to do that?"

Smoke shook his head. "If you know beforehand how I'm going to do it, then you would be a co-conspirator. It's better that you don't know. All I can say is, when it happens, you'll know."

Back in Desolation, everyone was still talking and laughing about the bluff Emmett Clark had run on Jules Stillwater. There was some concern as to how Stillwater would handle it, but most thought he would do nothing more than sulk around for a few days.

But Stillwater had something else in mind, and the first indication Emmett Clark had of Stillwater's sudden intrusion into the saloon was when a bullet from Stillwater's gun smashed the glass that was sitting on the table between Clark and Cindy. Glass and whiskey flew from the impact of the bullet. Even before the second bullet plowed into the table, Clark leaped up from his chair, but to his shocked surprise, the back of the chair caught the handle of his pistol and jerked it out of his holster. He was now unarmed!

"You son of a bitch!" Stillwater shouted. "Cindy is my woman! You stay the hell away from her!"

"Jules! Have you gone crazy?" Cindy shouted. "I'm anyone's woman who will buy me a drink! You know that!"

Stillwater fired again as Clark dashed across the saloon toward the bar. The bullet crashed into the mirror behind the bar, bringing it crashing down in great jagged shards of glass.

With angry shouts and screams of terror, every customer in the saloon, men and women alike, hurried to get out of the way of the mad gunman's wild shooting.

Stillwater's third shot was fired as Clark rolled across the bar and onto the floor behind. Clark lay on the floor for a moment, breathing a sigh of relief that Stillwater had missed. Then, even as he spied the double-barreled ten-gauge shotgun the bartender kept behind the bar, he heard a low, evil laughter. Clark reached over and pulled the shotgun toward him, cocking both barrels.

"You think you can hide behind the bar?" Stillwater said.

Looking toward the sound of the voice, Clark saw that Stillwater had come to the open end of the bar and was now looking down at Clark, an evil smile displaying his pleasure at now having the advantage. "You took the wrong man's woman, you snot-nosed kid."

Stillwater was holding a smoking pistol, which

Clark knew held three more shots. Stillwater smiled triumphantly. Then he saw the shotgun in Clark's hands and the smile of triumph changed quickly to an expression of horror. He tried to pull back the hammer of his pistol, but it was too late. Clark pulled both triggers.

The roar of the two shells discharging at the same time sounded like a cannon, compared to the pop of the pistol shots. The twin loads of ten-gauge double-aught buckshot opened up Stillwater's chest and he fell back through the window, crashing onto the porch in front of the saloon.

Clark put the gun down, then lay still on his back for a long moment, relieved that he was still alive. Gun smoke was swirling about, now permeating the room with its nostril-burning, acrid smell. Finally, he stood up, and walked over to the window to look through the smashed glass of the front window.

"What happened?" someone shouted from the street.

"What was that?" another called.

The shouts were all coming from outside, as nobody in the saloon had yet recovered from the shock of what they had just witnessed.

Stillwater had one foot up on the windowsill, the other had somehow folded up underneath him in a way that would have been impossible if he were still alive. His chest had been carved open by the heavy load of buckshot.

"Damn, I ain't never seen nothin' like that," someone said, and looking around, Clark saw that the others were beginning to reemerge. Walking back over to the table, Clark picked up his pistol, which was still lying on the floor.

"Cindy?" Clark called out as he put the pistol back in his holster. "Cindy, are you all right?"

"I'm fine," a woman's voice replied. Like the others, Cindy had regained her feet and was now walking toward Clark.

"What was this all about?" Clark said. "Why did he come after me like that?"

Cindy shook her head. "I don't know why," she answered. "I mean, he always hung around me anytime him and his friends were here, but there was never no words spoke or nothin' to make him think we was anything but just friends. I mean, he know'd what I done for a livin'."

"Who the hell just killed Stillwater?" a gruff voice asked, and looking toward the door, Clark saw Frank Dodd coming in. Almost imperceptibly, Clark moved his hand closer to his pistol, not knowing how Dodd was going to react to losing one of his men.

"I killed him," Clark said.

"Stillwater's the one that started it. He come in here a' blazin' away," one of the other men said.

Dodd walked over to the shattered window to look out at the body. Stillwater's eyes were open and opaque, his mouth was set in a sneer.

"You carry a shotgun, do you?" Dodd asked.

Clark shook his head. "Not normally. But I just happened to have one handy when I needed it." he said.

Suddenly, and inexplicably, Dodd laughed out loud. "You just had one handy, did you?"

"Yeah."

"Stillwater needed killin', Frank," Conklin said. "Hell, the way that dumb sumbitch was blastin' away, he could of kilt any of us."

"That's the truth," one of the others said.

Dodd stroked his chin and nodded as he stood there, looking down at Stillwater's body.

"The only thing is, that makes four good men I've lost in the last week," Dodd said.

Suddenly, Emmett Clark saw this as his opportunity to join Dodd's gang.

"You lost four men," Clark said. "But you didn't lose four good men. Not if Stillwater was any indication."

"I suppose you think you are better than they were?" Dodd asked, showing a little irritation as Clark's comment.

"Hell, yes, I'm better," Clark said. "I'm better than all four of them combined."

"What do you think, Conklin?" Dodd said. "Sounds to me like this boy is applyin' for a job."

"Sounds like that to me too," Conklin said.

"What about it, boy? You want to ride with me?"

"Yeah, I do," Clark said. "If truth be told, that's why I came here in the first place."

"What do you say, Conklin? Is he as good as Stillwater was?"

"Look at it this way, Frank. Stillwater and this boy had a face-to-face showdown, and the boy won."

"All right, boy, you can ride with us," Dodd said.

Clark held up his hand. "Not so fast."

"What do you mean, not so fast? I thought you wanted to ride with me.

"I do, but not if you are going to keep calling me boy," Clark said.

Dodd laughed out loud. "So, you don't want to be called boy, do you?"

"My name is Clark. Emmett Clark."

Dodd nodded, and laughed again. "All right, Mr. Emmett Clark, I reckon anyone who can come out on top of a fight with Stillwater has earned the right to be called by his name."

"In that case, Mr. Dodd, I'd be just real happy to ride with you."

Chapter Fifteen

Back in Clovedale, Smoke decided to take a walking tour of the town, figuring that if he was going to break Bobby Lee out of jail, it would be to his advantage to have a feel of the place. Fremont Street was the main street of town, running north and south on the east side of and parallel to the railroad. West of the railroad, and running parallel to it, was the Reese River, a rocky stream that was so narrow and shallow that no bridge was required for a horse or wagon, and only a couple of boards were in place for foot traffic. The river was bordered on both sides by aspen and cottonwood trees. First Street crossed Fremont, the railroad, and the Reese River at a right angle, just south of the depot between the train station and the roundhouse. The railroad divided First Street into West First and East First. The houses and business establishments along West First were all Chinese.

Second Street was also divided into West and East Second, and West Second Street was primarily Mexican. Americans made up the entire population east of the railroad, along Fremont, as well as up and down East First and East Second Streets.

An alley that ran behind all the businesses separated Fremont Street from Vaughan Lane which ran behind, and parallel to Freemont. There were no businesses on Vaughan Lane, just private residences.

Smoke walked up Fremont from First to Second Streets, then east on Second Street to the alley. He came back down the alley to First Street, then went back up Vaughan Lane to Second Street again. Looking east beyond Vaughan Lane, he saw a long snaking ravine that ran toward the Toiyabe Mountain Range.

Although there were ranches around Cloverdale, the most important industry to the town were the nearby mines. To that end, there were several business in town that provided material and equipment for mining. Smoke went into one of the mining stores to make a purchase. Leaving with his acquisition securely wrapped in paper, he returned to the Depot Hotel, then took it upstairs to his room.

"I see that you have taken advantage of some of our stores and shops," the hotel clerk said when he saw Smoke going up the stairs carrying his package.

"Yes, I found a bargain," Smoke called back. He wondered what the clerk would think if he knew what was really in the package.

When Smoke stepped into the jail a few minutes later he saw Sheriff Wallace sitting at his desk while one of his deputies was over by the stove, pouring himself a cup of coffee.

"Well now, Harley, lookie here," the sheriff said as Smoke stepped inside. "This is the fella I was tellin' you about, the one that shot the gun out of Dawes' hand."

Deputy Harley Beard looked up from the coffeepot. "Is that true? Did you really intend to shoot the gun out of Dawes' hand? Or is that just the way it happened?"

"Both," Smoke answered.

"What do you mean, both?"

"I intended to shoot the gun out of his hand, and that's the way it happened."

Harley laughed.

"What can I do for you, Jensen?" Sheriff Wallace asked.

"I'd like to see the prisoner you are planning on hanging," Smoke said.

Wallace shook his head. "Ain't no need for you to do that. You want to see him, you can see him Friday mornin', same as ever' one else."

"I need to see him now," Smoke said. "That is, if the reward is going to be paid."

"What reward are you talking about?" Wallace asked.

Smoke pulled an envelope from his pocket. Inside the envelope was the document he had asked Curly Latham to print for him.

$5,000.00 REWARD
Bobby Lee Cabot
DEAD OR ALIVE

Contact: Sheriff Monte Carson
Big Rock, Colorado

"I'm talking about this reward," Smoke said, showing the document to Sheriff Wallace. "If I wait until Friday, it'll be too late to collect."

Wallace chuckled. "Seems to me that's your worry, not mine. Why should I care whether or not you collect a reward?"

"You don't understand, Sheriff," Smoke said. "I can't collect the reward anyway." Smoke showed Wallace the deputy sheriff's badge he was carrying. "In Colorado, law officers can't accept a reward. You are the one who will be missing out on the reward."

"What do you mean? You just said that law officers can't collect a reward."

"Colorado law officers can't collect a reward. But you aren't a Colorado law officer. You are a sheriff in Nevada."

"Hmm," Wallace said, stroking his chin. "You may have a point there."

"Sheriff, what about them three passengers that actually brought him in?" Harley asked.

"What about 'em?" Wallace asked.

"Ain't they the ones that should be gettin' the reward if there is one?"

"Harley, have you ever heard the sayin', 'Possession is nine tenths of the law'?"

"No. What's that mean?"

"That means Bobby Lee Cabot is a prisoner in my jail and them passengers ain't got nothin' to do with it. Ain't that the way you look at it, Jensen?"

"That's right," Smoke said. "It all depends on where the prisoner is."

Sheriff Wallace smiled. Then the expression changed to one of concern. "Look here, Jensen, you ain't tryin' to tell me that I have to turn this fella over to you in order to get the reward, are you? 'Cause what with him already bein' found guilty and sentenced an' all, I don't think I can do that."

"No, I'm not saying you have to turn him over to me," Smoke said. "You can go ahead and hang him as far as I'm concerned. But you do have to let me see him. I have to make certain that the prisoner you have here is really Bobby Lee Cabot."

"Oh, it's Bobby Lee Cabot all right," Sheriff Wallace said. "You can take my word on that."

"Sorry, Sheriff, I wish I could," Smoke said. "But if I'm going to have Sheriff Carson back in Colorado authorize the reward payment, I'm going to have to see the prisoner for myself."

"So he's wanted in Colorado, is he? I knew it," Wallace said. "And here he was trying to make arrangements with me to trap Frank Dodd."

"Wait a minute. Are you saying that he was trying to make arrangements with you? I heard you tell Doc Baker and the others that there were no arrangements discussed."

"Yeah, well, why complicate things?" Sheriff Wallace asked. "If Baker, Nabors, and the whore knew he actually had talked to me, they never would believe that he is guilty. He did try and tell me something about me being in the express car, but I knew all along that something was wrong. For all I knew, he might have been trying to set a trap for me. Anyway, you just proved my point by showing me this dodger sayin' he's wanted in Colorado." Wallace stroked his chin as he looked at the reward poster. Then he nodded, and handed the reward poster back to Smoke. "All right, you can see him."

"Thanks."

"Take Deputy Jensen back to the jail cells, Harley."

Harley nodded, then opened a door that led into the back of the building. He motioned for Smoke to follow him.

"Cabot!" Harley shouted as they stepped into the back where there were two cells. Only one of the cells was occupied, and Bobby Lee was the only person in that cell.

Bobby Lee had been lying on his bunk, and he got up and moved to the front of the cell.

"You've got a visitor!" Harley said.

Smoke was walking behind Harley, so that Harley could not see his face. Smoke shook his head, and held up his hand to caution Bobby Lee not to give any reaction.

"There you are, Cabot!" Smoke said gruffly. "I'll just bet you never thought you would see me again."

"What are you doing here?" Cabot asked. He wasn't sure what Smoke had in mind, but whatever it was, he was going to play along with it.

"What am I doing here? I'm here to watch justice be done," Smoke said. "I'm going to send a telegram to Sheriff Carson back in Colorado, telling him that you have been captured. Then I'm going to watch you hang so I can report on that too."

"You can tell Sheriff Carson that I told him to go to hell."

"Deputy, let me have a few minutes alone with this man, will you? I need some information, and I think I can get it out of him if I can talk to him alone."

"I'll leave you back here with him, but I'll have to take your gun," Harley said.

"Makes sense," Smoke replied. He pulled his pistol from his holster, handed it over to the deputy, then turned back to Bobby Lee.

"What did you do with the money you took from the stagecoach robbery?" Smoke asked gruffly.

"Why should I tell you anything? I'm going to hang in a couple of days anyway."

"I would think you would want to unburden your soul," Smoke said.

"Ha! Unburden his soul," Harley said. "That's a good one." The deputy was still laughing as he stepped through the door and closed it behind him.

Smoke heard the door close behind him, and he looked around to make sure Harley was gone. Then, and only then, did he stick his hand through the bars.

"Bobby Lee, it is good to see you again after all these years," Smoke said quietly.

"You don't know how good it is to see you," Bobby Lee said. "I'm not guilty, by the way."

"I didn't think you were," Smoke said. "And what the sheriff said a moment ago about you trying to make arrangements with him to trap Dodd just verified it."

"Damn, you mean he admitted it? During the

trial, he said there were no such arrangements being made, the lying son of a bitch."

"Yes, he admitted it. But to tell you the truth, Bobby Lee, I really don't care whether you actually did it or not. You are family, so there is no way I wasn't going to be here."

"Yes, well, I wasn't sure you would come but I'm thankful for it, even if it is only to make certain I have a friendly face in the crowd come Friday."

"Oh, I don't plan on being in the crowd on Friday. In fact, I don't plan on there being a crowd Friday, seeing as there won't be any hanging for them to watch. You and I will both be gone by then."

"How? Do you have a plan of some sort?"

Smoke looked around and saw a clock on the wall just outside the two cells.

"Can you see that clock?" he asked.

"Yes, I can see it clearly."

"What about at night? Can you see it at night?"

"Yes. You see the lantern close to it? The sheriff keeps it lit all night. That's so they can look in on me from time to time."

"Good," Smoke said. Pulling out his pocket watch, he synchronized the time on his watch with the time on the clock. "Now, this is what I want you to do. At exactly five minutes after eleven o'clock tonight, I want you to take the mattress off your bunk, come over here to this side of the cell, lie down, and cover yourself with the mattress."

Bobby Lee smiled. "Sounds like you have a plan," he said.

"I do," Smoke replied. "If it doesn't kill us both."

"You want to know where the money is!" Bobby Lee said, suddenly changing his expression to one of anger. "You can tell the people back in Colorado that I'll tell them when I meet them in hell!"

Smoke didn't have to look around. He knew that either Sheriff Wallace or Harley had just opened the door.

"Have it your way, Cabot," Smoke said, mirroring Bobby Lee's tone of voice. "In the meantime, I will take great pleasure in telling them that I watched you hang."

Smoke heard a chuckling behind him. Then he turned to see the sheriff standing in the open door.

"I take it you are satisfied this is your man?" Wallace said.

Smoke nodded. "It's him, all right. But I didn't get much out of him."

"I didn't think you would. How long before I get the reward money?"

"It shouldn't be too long, Sheriff. All I have to do now is telegraph the information back to Colorado."

"Come on back out front," the sheriff invited. "I'll give you your gun back. Would you like a cup of coffee?"

"A cup of coffee would be good," Smoke said.

"How about a cup of coffee for me?" Bobby Lee called out.

"Sure, I'm a good sort," Wallace said. "I'll have Harley bring you a cup."

Smoke followed Wallace back to the front of the jailhouse building. "Harley, take the prisoner a cup of coffee," he ordered.

Harley poured a cup, then took it back to Bobby Lee.

Smoke walked over to a wall festooned with reward dodgers. There, he saw a wanted poster for Frank Dodd.

"I understand this is the man Cabot was mixed up with," Smoke said, pointing toward the poster.

"That's him, all right."

"Tell me about Dodd."

"He's a robber, and some say a murderer."

"Is it true that he is the one who actually shot the railroad messenger?"

"Where did you hear that?"

"Some folks down at the saloon were talking about it."

"Yes, well, I wouldn't pay too much attention to what anyone down at the Gold Strike has to say. Cabot used to hang around down there quite a bit and evidently, he made a lot of friends. If they thought lyin' to you would help him out, they would likely tell you anything."

"You mean like them telling me that Cabot sent you a letter before the holdup, asking you to be waiting with some deputies in the express car?"

"Yeah, like that," Wallace said gruffly. "Look, I don't care what they said, there wasn't no letter from Cabot tellin' me to be waitin' in the express car," Wallace said angrily. "If there had been, don't you think I would have been there? I'd like nothing better than to round up Frank Dodd and his gang. Cabot tried to tell that story in court, but there didn't nobody buy it."

"But you said while ago that he was trying to set up a deal with you to trap Dodd. Isn't this what you were talking about?"

"Yeah, but like I said, I knew he was lying even then. People like Bobby Lee Cabot will say anything if they think it will get them out of trouble."

"I suppose so," Smoke agreed. "But as far as the good people of Colorado are concerned, it all works out in the end. He was found guilty and he was sentenced to hang."

"That's right. He was found guilty and he will be hung," Wallace said, as if his point had been made.

"I'd like to ask you about his horse."

"His horse? What about his horse?"

"Where is it now?"

Sheriff Wallace chuckled. "Funny thing about that horse. When the train passengers took Cabot prisoner, they left the horse out there. But by the middle of the next day, he came back to town. We got him, and put him in the barn out behind the jail."

"I'd like to see it."

"Why?"

"The story is that he stole the horse from the man he shot," Smoke said. "If I see the horse, I can take the description of it back with me. That will help close out this case."

"I don't care where he got the horse, it belongs to me now. That is, it belongs to Nye County," Wallace said. "I intend to sell that horse for enough money to pay for the expense of hanging him."

"Don't get me wrong, Sheriff. I have no intention of trying to take the horse back with me. All I need to do is look at it so I can describe it when I get back."

At that moment, Harley returned from having delivered the coffee to the prisoner.

"Harley, take Deputy Jensen out to the barn and show him Cabot's horse and saddle."

Harley nodded, and again motioned for Smoke to follow him. The barn was behind, and across the alley from, the jail. There were three horses in the stable, two roans and a gray. The gray was so light as to be almost white.

"The gray is his," Harley said.

"And his saddle?"

"It's in here." Harley led Smoke into the tack room and pointed to a saddle that was straddling a waist-high wall. "That's it."

"What kind of sheriff is Wallace?" Smoke asked.

"He's all right, I guess," Harley replied hesitantly. "Why do you ask?"

"No reason. I'm sure he'll share the reward money with you."

"Yeah, I-I guess so," Harley replied hesitantly.

"Especially since you know that, by rights, it should go to the three railroad passengers who actually brought Cabot in," Smoke said.

"Yes," Harley said. Then he made a dismissive motion with his hand. "They are going to wind up with it anyway, soon as they find out it's being paid."

"How are they going to find out?" Smoke asked. "Nobody knows about the reward but us, and I'm under no obligation to pay it to the train passengers."

"Yeah, that's right, isn't it? If nobody but us knows, then they won't get a cent," Harley said.

"On the other hand, Sheriff Wallace now knows that you know about the reward. And I would think that your keeping it secret about the reward should be worth something to the sheriff. Don't you?"

Harley smiled broadly and shook his head. "Damn right," he said.

"We can go back in now," Smoke said. "I'm satisfied that I've seen his horse and his saddle."

"What do you think?" Sheriff Wallace asked when the two of them returned to the jailhouse.

"Yes, that's the horse all right. I'll be able to report that as well, and we can finally close the books on this case. All that is left to be done now is pay out the reward money to the two of you," Smoke said.

Sheriff Wallace looked over at his deputy, then back at Smoke. "What do you mean pay the reward to the two of us? I'm the one that made the arrest. I thought—that is, when we were talking— I thought you said that I would be getting the reward money."

"Yes, but that was before I learned that there were some railroad passengers involved. By rights, the reward money should go to them. But that could get very complicated. The best thing to do is keep the news about the reward quiet. And as of right now, only the two of you know about the reward. So the easiest way to keep it quiet is to just pay the two of you off and forget about it. Do you understand?"

Wallace glared at Harley for a moment, then he nodded. "Yes," he said without enthusiasm. "I understand."

"I thought you might," Smoke replied.

Chapter Sixteen

"Ha," Conklin said. "Look at that! I just pissed that grasshopper offen that branch."

"Now, why the hell would either one of us want to know what you do when you take a piss?" Dodd asked.

"I just thought it was funny, that's all," Conklin said as he rebuttoned his trousers.

"When is the stage coming?" Clark asked.

Emmett Clark had accepted Dodd's invitation to join his gang and this, a planned stagecoach holdup, would be his first job. He'd wondered about it when Dodd invited him along. Should he join him? He'd considered all of the ramifications.

On the one hand, if he joined and actually participated in the coach robbery, then he would be as guilty as Dodd and Conklin. But it would also give him a position of trust with the two of them, which he could use to bring them both in and collect the reward. If, in fact, that was still his purpose. The truth was, the more he associated with the friends he had made in Desolation, the less appeal the idea of being a bounty hunter held for him.

"It'll be here soon," Dodd said.

"How much money is it carryin'?" Conklin asked.

"It will be carrying some of the money that was on the train," Dodd responded. "You know, the money we didn't get?"

"So if all the money is on the stage, why didn't we rob the stage in the first place, instead of tryin' to hold up the train?"

"The money comes down from Battle Mountain to Austin, where it's divided up, then put on stages and sent out to other banks all over the county," Dodd explained. "That means there won't be as much money on the stage as there would have been on the train."

"How much will there be?" Clark asked.

"How am I supposed to know?"

"Well you been gettin' all your information from somewhere," Conklin said. "I figured you would know."

"Where do you get your information?" Clark asked.

Dodd stared at Clark for a long moment. "You ain't been ridin' with me long enough for me to answer that."

"Sorry," Clark said. "I didn't mean anything by it. I was just curious, is all."

"Yeah, well, no need in your being curious, because you don't need to know."

"What if you was to get kilt?" Conklin asked. "If that was to happen, we wouldn't know where to go to get the information so's we could keep on a' doin' this."

Clark was glad that Conklin was also showing some curiosity about Dodd's source of information. That would lessen any suspicion that Dodd might have about Clark's inquiry.

"What difference does that make to me?" Dodd asked. "If I get myself kilt, then I don't care whether you keep on doin' this or not. Seems like to me, the best thing you could do is just make sure I don't get kilt."

"Ha. I'd call that pretty good insurance," Clark said. "You got it fixed so that Conklin and I don't have any choice but to keep you alive."

"Yeah," Dodd said with an evil grin. "That's exactly the way I got it planned."

"Shh!" Conklin hissed. "I think I hear it."

The three men fell silent and listened.

Then they heard the driver's whistle, followed by the crack of a whip.

"Hyar, hyar, giddap there, giddap!" the driver shouted at his team. His voice was tinny in the distance.

"Remember, we don't do nothin' till he gets to the top of the grade and stops to give the horses a blow," Dodd said. "Now, get out of sight."

The three men got back off the road, taking concealment behind rocks and low-lying bushes. The coach continued its slow and laborious climb up the long, winding grade, sometimes visible and sometimes not. Finally it made the last switchback, then reached the crest.

"Whoa!" the driver called to his team. The six horses were breathing hard and the driver set the brake, then called down to his passengers.

"Folks, we're goin' to be here for a few minutes

to let the horses get their breath. May as well climb down and stretch your legs a bit, and enjoy the view."

Three men and a boy climbed out of the coach. Since there were no women, two of the men began relieving themselves, one on the front wheel, the other on the back wheel.

The driver climbed down and began checking the harnesses on his team. The guard left his shotgun up on the seat and he began climbing down as well.

"What are you doin', Tony?" the driver asked.

"I'm goin' take a leak."

"We ought not both of us be down at the same time," the driver said.

"Hell, Ralph, you can see for yourself there ain't nobody around," Tony said. "But if you want me back up there, I'll—"

The sound of a gunshot interrupted Tony in mid-sentence. He was at the top of the wheel, nearly ready to get back into the box, when he suddenly threw both arms up, then fell, landing hard on his back.

"Tony!" the driver shouted, running over to him.

Emmett Clark gasped out loud when Dodd shot the guard. Fortunately, his gasp of surprise and disapproval was covered by the sound of the rifle shot.

My God, he was now a party to murder!

He hadn't planned on taking part in a murder.

What had he planned? He was taking part in a felony, the robbing of a stagecoach. Did he think it would be a walk in the park?

"All you fellas get your hands up," Dodd yelled

as he, Conklin, and Clark moved quickly out into the road.

The driver and his passengers complied and five sets of arms went into the air.

"Can I take a look at my friend?" the driver asked.

"No, what I want you to do is climb up there and throw down the express pouch."

"But he might still be alive," Andy insisted.

Dodd walked over to the prostrate form of the stage guard and, at point-blank range, shot him in the head.

"Tony!" Ralph shouted in shock and sorrow.

"He ain't alive no more," Dodd said. "Now throw me down that pouch like I asked."

Ralph climbed back up into the driver's box, then leaned over to reach under the seat. Dodd moved closer and pointed his pistol at the driver.

"Mister, if you have anything in your hand other than what I asked for when you raise up, you are going to be as dead as your friend."

"No, no!" Ralph said, holding up his hands. "I'm just going to get the pouch, that's all."

Ralph got the pouch, then threw it down.

"That's a good man," Dodd said. Dodd walked up to the off-side lead horse, put his gun to the horse's head, then pulled the trigger. The horse dropped in his traces, and the other horses jerked back and whinnied in fear and confusion.

"Why did you do that?" Ralph asked angrily. "You had no call to kill an innocent horse." He climbed back down from the driver's box, then put his hand out to calm the rest of the team.

"I did it for your own good," Dodd said. "By the time you get this horse out of harness, we'll be well out of here and you won't have any notion to try and come after me."

"Mister, you are a mean man," the boy shouted.

Dodd backhanded the boy, sending him careening against the side of the coach. His mouth started bleeding.

"You son of a bitch!" the boy's father said. Suddenly and totally unexpectedly, the boy's father hit Dodd with his fist, knocking the outlaw down. Dodd dropped his pistol and the man started to reach for it, but Clark cocked his own pistol and shoved it in the man's face.

"Don't even think about touching it," he said. He was trying to make himself as menacing as he could, but in fact what he was doing was saving the man's life.

At least, he thought he was. But an angry Dodd regained his feet and recovered his pistol.

"I'm going to kill you, mister," Dodd said. "Nobody does that to me and gets away with it."

"No!" Clark shouted.

"What do you mean no? You tellin' me how to run this operation, are you?" Dodd asked, his voice showing his displeasure over being challenged.

"I mean no, let me do it," Clark said.

"Why would you want to do it? I'm the one he hit."

Clark smiled at Dodd. "I'm new with this outfit," he said. "Maybe I'm just trying to make a good impression on you."

Dodd laughed out loud. "All right," he said. "If you want to kill him, be my guest."

Clark pointed his pistol at the boy's father.

"Come along, you," he said. "Over here, behind these rocks."

"Wait a minute, what are you doing? Where are you going with him?" Dodd asked. "I thought you were going to shoot him."

"Oh, I'm going to shoot him, all right," Clark said. "But I don't want to do it in front of the boy."

"Softhearted, are you? Well, let me tell you somethin'. In this business, it don't pay to be soft-hearted. Ever," Dodd said. "But it don't bother me none where you do it, as long as you do it, so have it your way. Take him over there and shoot him."

"Pa!" the boy shouted. He wrapped his arms around his father's legs.

"Better make the boy stay back, or I'll shoot him too," Clark said.

"Stay here, Kenny," the father said.

"No!"

"Stay here, Kenny!" the father said more force-fully this time.

"Come here, boy, stay with me," Ralph, the driver, said.

Clark made a motion with his pistol. "Let's go," he said.

"Don't take all day with it!" Dodd called out.

Clark led the boy's father around to the other side of the rocks. Then he pulled his knife.

"What are you going to do?" the man asked, seeing the knife.

"Cut your hand, then squeeze out some blood," Clark replied speaking quietly.

"What? Why should I do that?"

"If you want to live, do what I say," Clark said.

"Please," he added, the tone of his voice more pleading than demanding.

The expression on the man's face turned from fear to confusion, then from confusion to a glimmer of hope. He cut his hand, then squeezed the wound to get a lot of blood.

"Put it on the back of your head," Clark said.

The man complied.

"Turn around, let me see."

"You want me to turn around?" Fear returned to the man's eyes. Had this all been a ruse?

"Turn around," Clark said again.

"Clark! What's taking you so long?" Dodd shouted.

"I'm just having a little fun with him is all," Clark called, looking back toward Dodd.

"Well, do it and be done with it," Dodd ordered.

When Clark turned back toward the stage passenger, he was shocked to see the passenger holding a pistol in his hand.

"You didn't know I had this, did you?" he said with a triumphant grin.

"No, don't do this!" Clark shouted as he saw the man thumb back the hammer. Clark had no choice but to shoot, his bullet hitting the stage passenger between the eyes.

"Pa!" the boy shouted, his shout followed immediately by wailing sobs.

Clark walked back to join the others. Dodd and Conklin were already mounted, and Conklin was holding the reins to Clark's horse.

Without speaking, Dodd rode over to the edge of the rocks, then looked around behind them. Seeing the man lying on his back with a bullet hole between his eyes, Dodd nodded.

"Good job," he said. "Come on, let's go."

Again the boy cried out, and tried to go to his father, but the driver held him more tightly.

"You son of a bitch!" the boy shouted at Clark. "I'll kill you for this some day!"

"You might at that, boy. You might at that," Clark said, fighting the bile in his throat over having killed an innocent man.

Innocent? What is innocent? he wondered. That was certainly no longer a word he could use when thinking of himself. How easily he had slipped over the line onto the outlaw trail. He had started out to do good, to bring evil men to justice. Now, he was as evil as anyone he sought.

After holding up the stagecoach, Dodd, Conklin, and Clark rode hard for the rest of the day, stopping only occasionally to give the horses a breather. Even then, they didn't stop, but continued to walk, always putting distance behind them. They did pause briefly just before nightfall in order to eat a few bites of jerky and to take a few swallows of water.

"Hey, Dodd, don't you think it's about time we seen what we took offen the stage?" Conklin asked.

"Yeah," Clark said. "Why don't you cut open that pouch and let's have a look."

"All right," Dodd agreed. Pulling his knife from its holster he ripped a tear in the canvas, then reached in to pull out several letters, newspapers, flyers, and finally, two packets of money.

"Two little packages?" Conklin said, obviously disappointed. "That's all we got is two packages?"

Dodd divided one of the packages in half, giving half to Conklin and half to Clark. He took the other packet for himself.

"I thought we divided equally," Clark said.

"You thought wrong," Dodd said. "I get half, everyone else divides what is left."

Clark counted the money in his share. It came to five hundred dollars.

"Not bad for three minutes of work, is it?" Dodd asked.

"I guess not," Clark agreed.

"We got five thousand off a train oncet," Conklin said.

"Five thousand?" Clark said. "Damn, why couldn't we pull a job like that?"

"We'll get another one like that," Dodd said. "Don't worry."

"When?" Clark asked.

"Damn, Clark, you just joined up with us. You're gettin' a bit anxious, aren't you?"

"In for a penny, in for a pound," Clark said. "I just see no sense in fooling around with little jobs."

"In for a penny, in for a pound," Conklin said. He laughed. "I like that. Where did you hear something like that?"

"I don't know," Clark answered. "I've always heard it."

Conklin was chewing on a piece of leathery jerky. He took a drink of tepid water from his canteen, then spit some out in disgust and wiped his mouth with the back of his hand.

"Hell, we might as well be drinkin' piss as drinkin' this," he complained. "And why are we eatin' jerky? We ought to be eatin' ham, or pork chops or fried chicken and drinkin' beer, instead of jerky and water. Ain't there a town somewhere near here?"

"What if there is?" Dodd answered.

"Well, if there is, we could go in an' get somethin' fit to eat an' decent to drink," Conklin said. "We got money now. We got lots of money. Leastwise, that's what I'm a' thinkin'."

"Do me a favor, Conklin, and don't do no thinkin'," Dodd said. "You ain't got enough brains to think."

"You got no right to talk to me like that, Dodd."

"You don't like ridin' with me, you can always go out on your own," Dodd said. "Is that what you want to do?"

"No, I'm satisfied with the way things is goin'. I was just thinkin' it would be nice to spend some of this money we've got, is all."

"We'll spend it when the time is right. But we can't spend none of it around here. There's too many folks that know who we are, and this is too close to where we've been workin'."

"It just don't sit well with me, havin' money and not bein' able to spend none of it," Conklin said.

"Dodd is right," Clark said. "It would be foolish to get careless now."

"What the hell do you have to say about it anyway?" Conklin asked. "You just joined up with us. Hell, I been ridin' with him for more than a year."

"I'd like to ride with him for more than a year too," Clark said. "But if we do something dumb like going out and spending all this money now, would be the same thing as wearing a sign around our necks that said, 'We just robbed a stagecoach.'"

"What? Who would wear a sign like that?" Conklin asked, totally missing the point.

Dodd laughed out loud. "Conklin, you sure are one dumb son of a bitch, do you know that? I swear, it's good to have Clark along if for no other reason than to have someone else smart to talk to."

"Yeah, well, just remember who your real pard is," Conklin said, glaring at Clark.

"We're still pards, Conklin," Dodd said. "As long as you do what I tell you to do. And I'm tellin' you that we ain't goin' to be spendin' any of this money anytime soon."

"Yeah, I guess you are right," Conklin said. "But I don't mind tellin' you, it sure don't set right in my craw knowin' how much money we got and all, but not bein' able to even go into town an' buy us a decent meal."

Chapter Seventeen

As Clark, Conklin, and Dodd were discussing their take from the stagecoach, Smoke was in the Gold Strike Saloon, just finishing his supper.

"That was a good meal." He pushed his empty plate to one side and picked up his cup of coffee.

"I'll tell Mrs. Allen," Minnie said. "She works so hard in the kitchen all the time and she never gets any recognition."

"Mrs. Allen, you say?"

"Yes."

Smoke set his cup down, then walked to the door that led to the kitchen and pushed it open. It was very hot in the kitchen, the heat coming from the huge cookstove that sat on the side wall. An older woman was bent over at the waist, looking into the oven. Smoke waited until she closed the oven door, then turned around. Her eyes were tired, and there was a patina of sweat on her face.

"Mrs. Allen?"

Mrs. Allen looked up. "Yes, sir?"

"I just wanted to tell you how much I enjoyed

my supper. The biscuits were so light they nearly floated off my plate. The ham was delicious, and the potatoes were just right."

The cook smiled and, for a moment, the tiredness left her eyes. "Why, I thank you, sir," she said.

"But if you ever meet my wife, don't tell her I told you this. I'm afraid she would be very jealous of you."

Mrs. Allen laughed out loud as she pushed an errant fall of white hair back from her forehead. "I hardly think, sir, that your wife could ever be jealous of me."

Smoke nodded, then returned to his table.

"That was nice of you to do that," Minnie said.

"It is easy to be nice to nice people," Smoke replied. He picked up his cup and saw that it had been refreshed with hot coffee.

"I thought it might get cold while you were talking to Mrs. Allen."

"Thanks."

"You spoke to Bobby Lee today, didn't you?"

"Yes, I did."

"What did you tell him?"

"I told him to be ready."

"Be ready for what?"

"Just be ready," Smoke said.

"Tonight?" she asked.

Smoke took a swallow of his coffee and looked at Minnie over the rim. Girls like Minnie referred to their profession as being "on the line." Minnie had been on the line for two years, but dissipation had not yet set in, and she was still very pretty. She had long blond hair, deep blue eyes, high cheekbones, and unblemished skin. The clothes she wore while working displayed smooth shoulders and the creamy tops of well-formed breasts.

She didn't look anything at all like most of the soiled doves one found working in saloons and cribs across the West. She looked as if she could have been a next-door neighbor back at Sugarloaf Ranch, someone who would visit with Sally and swap recipes or join other women in a quilting bee. She could be any young rancher's wife, raising children and helping her husband build a life for their family.

But she wasn't some young rancher's wife. Minnie Smith was a whore.

Smoke wanted to ask her how she ever got into the business in the first place, but he thought the question might offend her, so he held his tongue.

"It is tonight, isn't it?" Minnie asked again after the long silence.

"I can't tell you that," Smoke said.

"How are you going to do it?"

"Minnie, don't ask me any more questions," Smoke said. "Get too closely involved, even if it is only by prior knowledge, and you can be charged with complicity."

"All right," Minnie said with a nod of her head. "I understand." She put her hand across the table to rest it on Smoke's hand. "Bobby Lee is lucky to have a friend like you," she said.

It was much later that same night when Smoke rode his horse down to the far end of Fremont Street. Because of the lateness of the hour, most of the town was asleep, though the sound of the piano could be heard spilling out onto the street from the Gold Strike Saloon. As far as Smoke could tell, he was the only one outside, and almost every building was dark, though from a few houses that sat back off the main street, there could be seen the dim glow of a lantern or candle.

Smoke rode by the gallows, looming large and ominous in the night. The sign containing the doggerel about the hanging, written by some clever, if morose, bard, was still in place. Fortunately, it was unreadable now because of the darkness.

Looking around to make certain he wasn't being observed, Smoke removed a small piece of cardboard from under his shirt. On one side the cardboard read: PEAR'S SOAP.

On the other side, Smoke had hand-lettered a sign of his own. Using his knife, he pried a nail out from the gallows, just far enough to allow him to attach the sign.

Come one, come all
Nobody is going to fall.
On Friday there will be nothing to see,
'Cause Bobby Lee will be with me.

Smoke chuckled. All right, he conceded, it wasn't up to the level of Longfellow, but it was certainly appropriate for the occasion.

Somewhere, a dog began yapping, and a bit closer, he could hear a baby crying. A cat jumped down off the porch from Tilghman's Apothecary, and ran quickly and silently across the street in front of Smoke, bounding gracefully onto the front porch of Goldstein's Feed and Seed. If anyone was watching through a window of one of the dark buildings, they would assume Smoke was riding out of town, which is exactly what he wanted them to think.

Smoke rode between the track and the river for about a mile beyond the edge of town. Just to the left of him, the river was a narrow, babbling ribbon of black, with silver highlights from the three-quarter moon that hung overhead. Out here he heard the yipping and yowling of a coyote, and the quieter, but closer hoot of an owl.

Once he had ridden far enough into the dark to be absolutely certain that he could no longer be seen by anyone who might have been watching him, he made a very big U, then came back into the town, only this time he entered Cloverdale, not on Freemont Street, which was the main street, but through the alley that ran between Freemont Street and Vaughan Lane. There was no ambient light back here, and the adjacent buildings cast shadows over the moon glow so that the alley was exceptionally dark. Smoke rode very slowly, trusting his horse, Seven, to find its way.

"There are other names for horses, you know," Sally had told him when he bought the horse and announced its name.

"I know."

"This is your third horse named Seven. And you've had three named Drifter."

"I like the names."

"Evidently. But you can't just keep naming every horse the same thing."

"Why not? Didn't you tell me that England had eight kings named Henry?"

Sally started to respond, then shook her head and laughed. "You win," she said. "How can I argue with that?"

Smoke stopped behind Bloomberg's Mercantile, then tied off his horse.

"Wait here, Seven, I'm about to bring you some company," he said. Seven snorted and shook his head as if he had understood every word, and Smoke picked his way carefully through the bottle-strewn alley as he moved toward the jailhouse. When he reached the jail, he crossed the alley and stepped into a barn that was just behind the jail. It was very dark inside the barn, but he could hear, as well as smell, the horses. Removing a small candle from his pocket, he popped a match with his fingernail, then lit the candle. Wedging the candle between two boards, he used the wavering light to pick out the gray. He saw too that the saddle was still in place on the half wall.

Once he had everything located, he extinguished the candle lest someone see a light in the barn and wonder how it got there. Walking over to where he had seen the saddle, he picked it up, then felt his way into the gray's stall. Working in the dark, he put the saddle on the horse's back and it whickered, shook, and stomped its left front foot.

"Easy, boy," Smoke said soothingly. He cupped

the gray's ear in his hand. "I'm a friend of Bobby Lee's. I'm taking you to him."

Smoke's soothing voice had the effect of calming the horse. He cinched the saddle down, then led the gray out of the barn, and then three buildings up the alley, where he tied it off alongside Seven.

"See here, Seven, I told you I was going to bring you some company. Now you two get acquainted," he said easily. "I want the two of you to get to know each other because if everything goes right, you'll be spending a lot of time together.

"That is, if everything goes right," he repeated under his breath.

From Seven's saddlebags, he pulled out the package he had bought at the mining supply store earlier in the day, then removed the wrapper, exposing two sticks of dynamite. With dynamite in hand, he started back toward the jailhouse, leaving the horses behind him. He had tied the horses behind the Mercantile store rather than the jail because he wanted to make certain the animals were far enough away not to be hurt by the detonation of the dynamite.

There was definitely going to be an explosion, and it was going to be a big one, because Smoke planned to blow a hole in the back of the cell that Bobby Lee was occupying. The challenge would be in getting an explosion of sufficient force to blast a hole large enough for Bobby Lee to crawl through, without making it so big that it brought down the entire building and injured, or even killed, Bobby Lee. But though that might challenge most, it wouldn't be a particular challenge to Smoke. He had done a lot of exploring, prospecting, and even mining in his young life, and he had, long ago, become an expert in the use of explosives such as nitroglycerine and dynamite.

When Smoke reached the back of the jailhouse, he stopped and listened very closely. Though muffled, he could still hear sounds from the saloon at the far end of the street, the tinkling of the piano, augmented now by the high-pitched laughter of one of the women, as well as the loud guffaws of more than one man. He could also hear crickets and other night insects. From the corral of the freight wagon company came the bray of a mule.

So far, not one person had seen him, and that was very good. He didn't need to be arousing any suspicions now.

Smoke got down on his knees and studied the brick wall. He found one brick that was cracked all the way through. Pulling his knife from its rawhide scabbard, Smoke began working at the mortar around the brick until all of it was chipped away. With the mortar gone, it was easy to pull out the broken half of the brick. That gave Smoke a hole into which he could place the two sticks of dynamite.

Smoke put the two sticks of dynamite in the hole, wedging them back in place with the broken pieces of brick. Then he pulled the small piece of candle from his pocket again and, once more popping the match head with his thumbnail, lit the wick. Using his hat to shield the light of the candle from unwanted view, he checked the time on his pocket watch.

It was four minutes after eleven.

Inside the jail cell, Bobby Lee wondered what was going on. He had heard nothing from Smoke since the quick meeting he'd had with him earlier today.

That made him feel a bit uneasy. He wished he would have heard from him again, at least one more time, just to reassure him that everything was still in place. But as his cell had no rear window, there was no easy way Smoke could have made contact with him. He just had to assume that Smoke would keep his word, and from what he remembered of the man who had once been married to his sister, Smoke Jensen was a man of his word.

Bobby Lee checked the clock on the wall for at least the tenth time in the last four minutes. When it reached four minutes after eleven, he pulled the mattress from his bunk, then moved to the front of the cell and lay as close to the cell bars as he could. Smoke had told him only to be here at five after, but Bobby Lee was taking no chances on the clock having lost time during the day.

Holding the mattress over him securely, he waited.

The clock was ticking loudly, but not as loudly as the snores of Deputy Jackson, who had the night duty, and who was sleeping in his chair in the front office.

He wanted to look at the clock again, but he

couldn't do so without raising his head up from under the mattress, and he was afraid to do that. Smoke had said specifically, "If it doesn't kill us both." Bobby Lee was sure he intended to blast out the back wall, and he didn't want to take a chance on sticking his head out at the exact moment of the blast.

How long should he stay here?

What if Smoke was five minutes late? An hour late? What if he didn't show up at all?

He would show up. Bobby Lee was sure he would show up and if he had to, he would lay right here, on the floor, until daylight tomorrow morning.

The steady ticking of the clock and the loud, ripping snores of the deputy continued.

Chapter Eighteen

The Gold Strike normally did a very brisk business between ten p.m. and midnight, and it being nearly five after eleven, the saloon was filled with customers. Arnie Sage was grinding away at the piano, a couple of the girls were dancing with the customers, and the other three were moving around the room smiling and serving drinks.

Doc Baker was playing a game of chess with Byron Hughes, the pharmacist. Paul, the bartender, was busier than he had been all night, and Nabors, who, for much of the night had been helping out behind the bar, had just walked away to take a break. He saw Minnie sitting alone and he crossed over to join her.

"What's wrong with all the men in here that not one of them will sit with a pretty girl?" Nabors asked. "I can't believe you are all alone."

"Several have come over, but I've sent them away. I'm sorry, Nate, I know I should be more friendly, I mean it's your business and all," Minnie said, "but I'm just too nervous right now."

"I know you are nervous, and I don't blame you. But don't worry about it," Nabors said with a dismissive wave of his hand. "There's nobody in town who didn't know about you and Bobby Lee, and they know he's going to be hung on Friday, so nobody is going to hold it against you."

"You mean he is scheduled to be hanged on Friday," Minnie said.

"Yes, scheduled."

"I'm hoping that Mr. Jensen will be able to change that," Minnie said.

"Well, don't get your hopes up too high," Nabors warned. "I'm sure he means well, but to be honest, I don't have any idea of what he could possibly do to get Bobby Lee out."

"I know it seems impossible, but I have a feeling about this man Smoke Jensen. I have a very good feeling about him," Minnie said.

"How is Janet doing?" Nabors asked, turning in his chair to look at the young woman who had been special friends with Andy Emerson. "It looks like she is doing all right."

Janet was laughing and flirting with all the men.

"Not really," Minnie said. "If you ask me, it looks like she's trying just a little too hard."

"Yeah, you may be right," Nabors said. He nodded toward a group of cowboys who were standing at the end of the bar. "Those boys all rode with Andy, and they seem to be taking it all right," he said. "They've been telling 'remember when' stories about him all night."

Minnie smiled. "From what I knew of Andy Emerson, there are probably quite a few stories to be told."

She and Nabors grew quiet so they could listen in to the latest story.

"Remember when Mr. Poindexter was going to sell that horse that Andy always rode?" one of the cowboys said. "Andy asked him not to do it, but Mr. Poindexter said he'd been offered a good deal by Mr. Norton, so he was going to do it. He asked Andy to take the horse over to Mr. Norton's ranch and Andy did, but what he done was—"

"What he done was, he fed the horse soap so's it would commence foamin' at the mouth," one of the other riders said, interrupting the first storyteller.

"And Mr. Norton said he didn't want no horse with the hoof and mouth," the third one said.

By now, all were laughing.

"And ole Andy, he had the horse all cleaned out when he come back. He told Mr. Poindexter that Mr. Norton accused him of tryin' to sell off a sick horse," the fourth said, concluding the story.

"Mr. Poindexter, he got all upset and wanted to go over and have a few words with Mr. Norton, tell him he didn't take to being accused of trying to sell a sick horse."

"But Andy stopped him, and said it was probably just Mr. Norton's way of backin' out of the deal." Again, all laughed.

"Andy rode that horse the rest of his life," one of the others said quietly, and the laughter stopped. "Mr. Poindexter, he sent me in today to tell Gene Crenshaw that he would take care of all the expenses of buryin' Andy, and he told me to bring back the horse."

"It is a good horse."

"Yeah. And Andy was a good man."

"Let's have a drink to Andy."

"Not just us, ever'body," one of the others said, and he turned and called out loud. "Ladies and gents! Ladies and gents!" After the second shout, all conversation in the saloon stopped.

"What is it?" someone asked.

The Poindexter rider held up his mug of beer. "I'd like for ever'one to have a drink to Andy Emerson," he said.

"I ain't goin' to drink to the son of a bitch," someone said. "Hell, we just had a fight last week."

"It was a fair fight, warn't it?" one of the other patrons asked.

The protestor thought for a moment, then nodded. "Yeah," he agreed. "Yeah, it was a fair fight. All right, I'll drink to him."

All in the saloon held their drinks high.

"To Andy," the Poindexter rider said.

"To Andy," the others repeated, and all drank the toast.

At that exact moment behind the jail, Smoke was looking at his watch when he saw the minute hand click onto the number one. He held the candle flame to the intertwined fuses of the two sticks of dynamite. As the fuses started sputtering, he ran back to Bloomberg's Mercantile, then stepped around the corner. He just made it around the corner when the dynamite exploded, the flash of the detonation momentarily lighting up the entire alley.

The alley was instantly filled with flying shards of brick and billowing smoke, even as the sound of the initial explosion echoed back and re-echoed, from both the Shoshone and Toiyabe mountain ranges.

The patrons of the Gold Strike Saloon had just finished drinking their toast to Andy when they heard the explosion. It was so loud that it caused all the bottles behind the bar to clink together.

"What the hell was that?"

"Someone blasting in the mines?"

"No, it's too late for that and that was too close."

The loud, stomach-shaking boom not only alerted those in the saloon, but awakened the entire town. Even before Smoke reached the three-foot-wide hole that was blasted in the rear of the jailhouse, he could hear people beginning to call out in surprise and alarm.

"What happened?"

"Hello?"

"What's going on?"

Smoke reached the hole quickly, then stuck his head in. A dim light still emanated from the hall lantern, though the smoke was so thick that it was difficult to see. He could hear coughing.

"Bobby Lee, are you all right?"

"Yes," Bobby Lee replied, and Smoke was pleased to hear that the young man's voice was just beside him. Bobby Lee emerged from the haze, and sticking out his hand, grabbed Smoke's hand. "Help pull me through," he said.

"Hey! What's going on back here!" Deputy Jackson shouted, coming from the front.

The deputy saw Bobby Lee escaping through the hole and he pulled his gun and fired, but by that time Smoke had already jerked Bobby Lee through, and out into the alley, so the bullets slammed harmlessly into the part of the wall not destroyed by the dynamite blast.

"Hurry," Smoke said. "Our horses are down here."

"Our horses? You mean mine too?"

"Yours too."

"Wow, my horse too. When you do things, you don't go halfway, do you?"

"You remember Preacher, don't you, Bobby Lee?"

"Yes, of course I remember Preacher."

"Preacher told me a long time ago, if you are going to do something, do it right the first time, because you may never get a second time."

By now, the town was alive with sound, from barking dogs, to screeching cats, to men and women shouting and calling out to each other.

"Was that a bomb?"

"It sounded like a bomb."

"What would a bomb be doing in Cloverdale?"

"The roundhouse? A boiler explosion maybe?"

Smoke and Bobby Lee climbed quickly into their saddles.

"This way," Smoke said. He had already spotted the quickest and easiest way out of town. The best way was not back down the alley, which was the way he had come in, but by riding between two houses that backed onto the alley and fronted on Vaughan Lane. By going this way, they would quickly find themselves in the long, snaking ravine that he had seen earlier. The ravine would give them cover and concealment for at least a mile.

A man, wearing a sleeping gown, was standing on the front porch of one of the two houses as Smoke and Bobby Lee rode by.

"Here!" the man called out. "What has happened?"

"I'm not sure," Smoke called back. "I think there may have been a boiler explosion down at the roundhouse."

"A boiler explosion? That don't make sense. What would they have steam up at this time of night for?" the man called back, though by the time the man finished his comment, his voice was behind them, because both Smoke and Bobby Lee had reached the ravine and were now bent low over their horses, riding hard.

Janet, who had been flirting with three men who were sharing a table, had joined the others in a toast to Andy. Minnie and Nabors had done the same thing, as had Doc Baker, who had playing chess. The piano player was turned around on the bench, with his back to the keyboard, when the explosion rolled through the saloon.

"Oh!" Janet shouted, startled so that she dropped her glass and put her hands over her ears.

"You think maybe it was the roundhouse?" someone asked.

Minnie and Nabors exchanged broad smiles, but said nothing. Looking toward Doc Baker, Minnie saw him glance back at her with the silent question in his eyes. She nodded, and he allowed only the barest suggestion of a smile to cross his lips, before returning to the game.

"Your move," he said.

"Damn, Doc, didn't you hear that?" Bryan Hughes asked. "Aren't you a little concerned as to what that was?"

"I'm more concerned about the fate of my bishop," Doc said. "I'm sure someone will tell us soon enough. Like I said, it's your move."

The pharmacist smiled, and captured Doc's bishop. "You had a right to be concerned," he said.

"Damn, I should of kept my mouth shut. You didn't even see that move until I called it to your attention."

"Doesn't matter," Bryan said, chuckling, as he held up the small chess piece. "I have your bishop now."

Sheriff Wallace was a single man, and he kept a room at Mrs. Kramer's Boarding House. He had just fallen asleep when the sound of the explosion awakened him. He lay in his bed for a few minutes, listening to the startled reaction of the town and trying to figure out what it might have been, when there was a loud knock at his door.

"Who is it?" he called, reaching over to pull his pistol from the holster.

"It's me, Sheriff. Deputy Jackson," a voice called from the other side of the door.

"Jackson, what are you doing here?" Wallace scolded. "You know better than to leave your post. I told you, anyone who has the night duty is not to leave the jail as long as we have a prisoner."

"Yes, sir, well that's just it, Sheriff," Jackson called back.

"What's just it?"

"We don't have us no prisoner," Jackson said. "Bobby Lee Cabot got away."

Getting out of bed, Wallace padded quickly barefooted over to the door to jerk it open.

"How did he get away?" Wallace asked angrily.

"Maybe you heard that loud boom a while ago," Jackson suggested.

"I heard it. What about it?"

"It seems like somebody blow'd a hole in the back wall of the jail."

"It *seems* like somebody blew a hole in the back wall? Or somebody *did* blow a hole in the back wall. Try and make sense when you talk to me."

"Yes, sir, well, I say it seems like somebody did 'cause somebody actual did blow a hole in the back wall," Jackson said, his convoluted explanation not much clearer than his original comment.

"Go get Harley," Wallace ordered. "Then get our horses saddled. We're goin' after him."

"Tonight? In the dark?" Jackson replied, surprised by the pronouncement.

"Yes, tonight in the dark. He escaped in the dark, didn't he?"

"Yes, sir. But which way will we go? How are going to catch him in the dark?"

"Will you get Harley and get our horses saddled

like I told you to?" Wallace said in exasperation as he began to pull on his pants.

"Yes, sir, I'll get Harley."

"Did you hear? The prisoner escaped! Bobby Lee Cabot got away!" someone yelled as they ran into the saloon, hitting the batwing doors so hard that they slapped back against the walls of the saloon.

"How did he get away?" one of saloon customers asked.

"Somebody set dynamite to the back wall and blew it plumb out!"

"Who done it?"

"Damn if I know," the bearer of the news replied. Turning, he left the saloon and started running down the boardwalk, the sounds of his footfalls receding in the distance.

"Jailbreak!" he was shouting into the night. "Bobby Lee Cabot broke out of jail!"

Nabors looked across the table to Minnie.

"Did you know that he was going to blow up the jail?"

"I was confident that he was going to get Bobby Lee out of jail. I didn't know exactly how he would do it."

Nabors chuckled. "You have to say this about him. When he sets out to help someone, he doesn't mess around, does he?"

"Who are you talking about?" Paul, the bartender, asked, coming over to join them then, not having heard the initial exchange between the two of them.

"The sheriff is goin' to come around asking a

lot questions," Nabors said. "You are probably better off if you don't have any answers."

"Do you have answers?" Paul asked.

"I don't have any answers," Nabors said. "I have lots of ideas, but I don't have any answers."

Doc Baker came over to join them then.

"I thought you were playing chess," Nabors said.

"I was, but Bryan cheats." Doc Baker didn't mean the charge seriously, and nobody took it so.

"I don't need to cheat to beat you," Bryan called back in good-natured banter.

"Did I hear that fella say a moment ago that the back wall of the jail had been blown out?"

"That's right," Nabors said.

"Do you think it might have been—"

"That's right," Nabors said again, interrupting him with a broad smiled. "There's no doubt in my mind who it was."

"Well, what do you know?"

Chapter Nineteen

Riding hard through the night, Smoke and Bobby Lee reached Lost Creek in the Sinkarata Valley at about four o'clock in the morning. They slept lightly through the rest of the night, then awakened just before dawn. Now, in the east, Smoke could see the long slab of the Shoshone Mountains outlined against the red-gold sky of sunrise. The De Satoya mountain range lay to the west.

They had made their camp under on a bench of rock overhanging the narrow stream, under a stand of great pines. Grasshoppers flitted about, and several yellow butterflies hovered over the water. A pair of eagles circled high overhead, while, somewhat lower, a much more active peregrine falcon snatched a fleeing grouse.

Smoke walked over to the edge of the creek, then lay on his stomach on a flat rock. Reaching down into the clear water and using his cupped hands, he scooped the water up, then splashed it on his face, finding the cold water invigorating.

"I want to thank you for answering my telegram," Bobby Lee said.

"You asked for help, Bobby Lee. Did you think I was going to ignore you?"

"Well, with Nicole being dead and all, I wasn't sure."

"Whether Nicole is dead or alive, you're still family."

Bobby Lee smiled. "I'm glad to hear that."

"What are you going to do now?" Smoke asked.

"I'm going to do what I started out to do," Bobby Lee said. "I'm going to hunt down and bring in Frank Dodd. I figure that's the only way I can clear my name."

"Sounds reasonable," Smoke said. "Do you have any idea where we start?"

"Where *we* start? Smoke, I appreciate you coming to get me out of jail, but I can't ask you to get involved."

"I broke you out of jail, Bobby Lee. Don't you think that makes me involved?"

Bobby Lee smiled again, and nodded. "I guess you are right," he said. "If you are sure you want to do this, I'll be more than glad to have you along."

"Tell me about Frank Dodd."

"He is as mean as they come," Bobby Lee said. "He led a group of raiders during the war, and he learned a lot about military operations. Now he runs his gang exactly like a military operation."

"Which side was he on during the war?"

"Ha!" Bobby Lee said. "He was on his own side. If it helped him to ride under the Confederate flag, he did. If it helped him to ride under the Federal flag, he did that as well. Mostly, what he was after was the plunder, and he didn't care which side he robbed from."

"Sounds like a real trustworthy man," Smoke said in a sardonic tone of voice.

"Yeah, he is."

"What about Sheriff Wallace?"

Bobby Lee ran his hand through his long, unruly, dark hair. "I should never have trusted the son of a bitch," he said. "I don't know why he didn't show up, or why he lied about our arrangement. Unless . . ."

"Unless he was in cahoots with Dodd," Smoke said, completing the sentence for him.

"Yeah," Bobby Lee said. "At my trial, they suggested that I was supplying Dodd with the information as to what train would be carrying money shipments. And of course, that has always been the big question. How did Dodd know? The suggestion was that I was providing him with information that I got from my association with the Western Capital Security Agency."

"Does the WCSA have that kind of information?"

"Yes, we are generally informed. Sometimes, we even provide additional guards, though most of the time the shippers just rely on one messenger."

"Would that information be available to anyone else?" Smoke asked.

Bobby Lee shook his head. "Not really," he said. "They are pretty close with it, only the people who need to know, like the WCSA and—" Bobby Lee paused in mid-sentence.

"And the sheriff?"

"Yeah," Bobby Lee said. "And the sheriff. I'll be

damned. That's why he wasn't in the express car with them. He was in cahoots with them."

"When I was coming down here, Dodd tried to hold up the train I was on," Smoke said.

"Really? Where?"

Smoke told him about the attempted holdup, including in his narrative the fact that Phillips and Garrison had been identified, while a third robber who had also been killed had not been identified.

"Hmm, Phillips and Garrison must have been new," he said. "I don't believe I ever met them. What did the other man look like?"

"He wasn't a very big man, had a pockmarked face, thin, sort of light brown hair."

"Had to be Wayland Morris," Bobby Lee said. "If you killed him, it was good riddance. He once killed a farmer, then raped his wife and daughter before killing both of them."

"Too bad I killed him," Smoke said.

"What?" Bobby Lee asked, surprised by the reply. "Why would you say that?"

"Shooting is too good for someone like that. That's the kind of person that the public needs to see hang."

Bobby Lee ran his finger around the collar of his shirt. "After seeing my gallows built, hanging isn't something I care to think about right now," he said.

Smoke laughed. "I don't blame you, but look at it this way. We did manage to spoil your hanging party, didn't we?"

"Yeah," Bobby Lee said. "Thanks to you, we did."

* * *

Eddie Murtaugh had been with the Western Capital Security Agency for three years. During that time he had often been partnered with Bobby Lee Cabot, in fact had learned everything he knew about the business from Bobby Lee. He considered Bobby Lee his best friend.

"He didn't do it," Murtaugh told Captain Bivens.

"I know how you feel, Eddie," Captain Bivens said. "I feel the same way. I've known Bobby Lee longer than you have. But the evidence is just too convincing. Frank Dodd has been terrorizing trains and stagecoaches all through Nevada. He always knows when they are carrying money. Last month, Frank Dodd held up a Nevada Central train and got five thousand dollars. Everyone had been wondering how Dodd was getting his information on which trains were carrying the money, and now it seems pretty obvious that he was getting it from Bobby Lee. And don't forget, Bobby Lee was with Dodd when he hit that train."

"Yes, but I believe Bobby Lee had worked his way into the gang in order to catch them," Murtaugh insisted.

Captain Bivens shook his head. "Eddie, you've been with us long enough to know that we don't operate that way."

"Maybe he didn't see any other way of stopping them," Murtaugh suggested.

"Why didn't he let us know ahead of time what he was doing?" Captain Bivens asked.

"You wouldn't have approved," Murtaugh said.

"No, I wouldn't have," Bivens agreed. "Our rules are very specific, Eddie, you know that. There is never any reason for joining with the criminal element. When you do so, you risk not only your own life, but you could wind up risking the lives of others as well, to say nothing of bending the very laws we are trying to protect. It could also jeopardize an ongoing investigation."

"There you go then. That's the reason Bobby Lee didn't tell you about it."

"There's one more reason we don't want our agents associating with the criminal elements," Bivens said. "Sometimes the pressures, and the temptations, can be overwhelming—so much so that a man might forget what side he is on."

"That did not happen to Bobby Lee. I know you have known him longer, Captain, but he and I have put our lives on the line together many times. I don't think anyone knows him better than I do, and I am telling you, he was not involved with Frank Dodd. He may have violated a WCSA rule, but if he did, I'm sure he thought that it was the only way he could bring Dodd in. I'll never believe he has gone bad."

"Your loyalty is commendable," Captain Bivens said. "But I have the integrity of the WCSA to think of. That's why I have offered a reward of five thousand dollars for him."

"Dead or alive," Murtaugh said.

"You understand the way it is out here," Captain Bivens said. "If we are to have any chance of bringing him to justice, we have to make the offer dead or alive."

"You are condemning him to death," Murtaugh said bitterly. "That takes on the role of judge and jury."

"He has already been condemned. He was found guilty of murdering the express agent and sentenced to be executed. He escaped, which makes him fair game for such a reward. I have assumed no role that is inconsistent with existing circumstances."

Murtaugh lowered his head and pinched the bridge of his nose.

"I know you are upset and concerned about your friend," Captain Bivens added. "But he made his own bed and now he must sleep in it. In the meantime, we go on. Are you willing to take on a new assignment?"

Murtaugh nodded.

"Good. I am putting you in charge. I want you to take two men with you. You will board the Virginia and Truckee Railroad at Carson City, and ride with it all the way to Columbus."

"You are sending three of us?"

"Yes."

"There must be quite a bit of money involved if you are going to use three of us."

"One hundred thousand dollars," Captain Bivens said.

Murtaugh whistled. "One hundred thousand dollars? That is a lot of money. Wouldn't it be safer to just keep the shipment secret?"

"Hard to keep it secret when you have something like this going out all over the state," Captain Bivens said, he voice registering his disgust. He picked up a newspaper from his desk.

"What is that?" Murtaugh asked.

"Read it," Bivens said, unable to hide the disgust he felt over the article.

Record Money Shipment

On Tuesday, the 4th of September, the Bank of Carson City is transferring one hundred thousand dollars to the bank in Columbus, by way of the Virginia and Truckee Railroad, such funds representing a record for the most money ever transported by that railroad. Mr. Matthews, owner of the Bank of Carson City, explained that the bank in Columbus, being newly charted, required the funds to ensure its solvency.

The train to be utilized, the Mountain View Special, will depart Carson City at 8 p.m. on Monday, September 3rd, and arrive at Columbus at 6 a.m. before the opening of business hours on Tuesday. Depositors in the Carson City Bank need not worry for the safety of their money for, as Mr. Matthews explained, this is but a loan from which interest will accrue.

Mr. Dempster, proprietor of the Bank of Columbus, has expressed his deepest gratitude for the loan, explaining that it will help bring business and prosperity to the community.

Murtaugh looked up from the newspaper article. "That's only four days from now," he said.

"Yes. Can you have your men selected and be ready by then?" Captain Bivens asked.

Murtaugh nodded. "I can."

"Then the assignment is yours."

"Thanks," Murtaugh said, turning away from the desk and starting toward the door.

"Mr. Murtaugh?" Captain Bivens called toward him.

Murtaugh turned back in response to the call. "Yes, sir?"

"I am sorry about your friend. But please don't

let friendship get in the way of your performance of duty."

"I don't understand, sir," Murtaugh replied. "How could my friendship with Bobby Lee affect this assignment?"

"If you are right about him, it won't affect it in any way," Captain Bivens said. "But, if I am right about him . . ." He let the sentence trail off.

"You think he might try and hold up the train?"

"There is that possibility, yes."

"If he does, he will no longer be my friend," Murtaugh said. "He will just be another train robber, and that is exactly the way I will treat him."

"You are a good man, Eddie Murtaugh," Captain Bivens said.

"Thank you, sir. But so is Bobby Lee Cabot. I'm not worried about my obligation, because he won't be the one robbing the train."

Chapter Twenty

At the Gold Strike Saloon, sun bars slanted in through the door and windows, highlighting the thousands of dust motes that hung in each beam of light. It was too early in the morning for customers, but that didn't mean that the saloon was empty. Paul, the bartender, was washing and polishing glasses. The handyman, Jesus Rodriguez, was working with a mop and bucket, making passes across the floor. Despite his best effort, the mop did little to clean the floor of expectorated tobacco juice and quid residue. Nate Nabors, who employed a piano player to keep the atmosphere lighthearted when he had customers, was actually quite an accomplished pianist himself, and often played for his own enjoyment. This was just such an occasion, and he was sitting at the piano playing the Reverie by Schumann. It was a quiet and relaxing piece, geared to the moment.

Of all the women who worked at the saloon, Minnie was the only one up at this hour, and she was sitting at a table near the piano, having her breakfast of biscuit and coffee while enjoying the music. It wasn't required that she be here yet, none of the women were required to be at work before noon, but Minnie thought she would rather be here than alone in her room, worrying about Bobby Lee and Smoke Jensen, wondering where they were at this exact moment.

Doc Baker came into the saloon then, smiling, and waving a copy of the *Cloverdale News Leaf.*

"Wait till you read this!" he announced loudly, though to no one in particular.

Nabors, having just finished his piece, got up from the piano and stepped over to the table where Minnie was sitting.

"What is it?" Nabors asked.

"Huh-uh," Doc Baker said, shaking his head. "Read it, then we'll talk about it."

"Do you mind if I read it over your shoulder, Nate?" Minnie asked.

"Don't mind at all."

Doc Baker laughed. "Knowing how much Marvin Cutler wanted to see Bobby Lee hang, it must have killed his soul to have to write this."

"What makes you think Marvin wanted to see Bobby Lee hang?" Nabors asked.

"Ha! Why do you even have to ask? You read that article he wrote about Bobby Lee. What was it he said in that last paragraph? Oh, yes, I remember." Doc Baker cleared his throat, then quoted the article in a stentorian voice, as if reading aloud. "A great crowd present to witness Cabot being delivered into the hands of Satan will send a signal to all who would contemplate duplicating Cabot's foul deed."

"Marvin Cutler is the consummate newspaperman," Nabors said. "He is sometimes prone to be a bit overblown with his stories."

"A bit overblown? He is a pompous blowhard," Doc Baker said.

Daring Jail Break

On the 28th, Instant, desperado Bobby Lee Cabot effected a daring escape from the jail at Cloverdale. The jailbreak came just three days before Cabot was scheduled to be hanged by the neck, the gallows having already been built and prominently displayed on Fremont Street in front of the jail.

The jailbreak occurred at five minutes after eleven p.m. of the clock. There can be no doubt of the time, as it is firmly fixed in the minds of the citizens of Cloverdale who heard the sound of the detonating dynamite, which explosion rent an opening in the back wall.

Deputy Jackson, who was the only eyewitness, states that he saw naught but the backside of Cabot as he made his egress through the aforementioned hole. Jackson discharged his pistol at the escaping prisoner, but the errant ball struck the wall with no effect. It is not known who helped the outlaw escape, but it is known that a telegram was dispatched on Cabot's behalf to Buck West. Though no one seems to have noticed when or if the man Buck West ever actually arrived in town, Sheriff Wallace harbors the suspicion that West is the one who enabled Cabot to thwart justice.

Bobby Lee Cabot was, at the time of the

commission of the crime, a railroad
detective for the Western Capital Security
Agency. It was the contention of the
prosecutor, and the conclusion of the jury,
that Cabot took advantage of his position
to gather information as to times and
routes of trains and stagecoaches, upon
which large amounts of money would be
transferred.

Because the Western Capital Security
Agency is well aware of its obligations to
protect its clients, the WCSA has put up
a reward of five thousand dollars for the
capture of their erstwhile agent.

"You know what I think?" Doc Baker asked.

"What do you think?"

"I think Wallace might have been involved with
the train robbery that they got Bobby Lee on,"
Doc Baker said.

"I'd be quiet about making that accusation,
Doc," Nabors said. "Wallace doesn't strike me as
the kind of man who would take too kindly to it."

"But don't you think he might be?"

"I have certainly thought about it," Nabors admitted. "But let's say you are right. What can we
do about it? Where will we go with our suspicion?
To the sheriff?"

"Ha, right," Doc Baker said sarcastically.

As the two men were discussing the subject,
Nabors started to fold the paper closed to return
it to Doc Baker. But just as he did, Minnie saw
an article that caught her attention.

"No, wait," she said, reaching for the paper.

"You can have the paper if you want it, but

that is the only article about the jailbreak," Doc Baker said.

"I saw something else I wanted to read," Minnie said without being specific. One article, in particular, had caught her attention.

Two New Riverboats Purchased

News from St. Louis is that on Friday last, the purchase of two new steamboats was announced by Thaddeus Culpepper. The boats, modern in every detail, will be floating hotels on the Mississippi River and none who ply that waterway for trade or pleasure will enjoy more commodious or luxurious staterooms. They will enter service from St. Louis to New Orleans with immediate effect. The boats will be named Kristina Dawn and Minnie Kay.

"You planning on taking a boat down the Mississippi River are you?" Nabors asked, chuckling, when he saw what she was reading.

"Why not?" Doc Baker asked. "I read that article. Those boats sound like they would be something just real grand. But I know what caught her attention. One of the boats is named after her." He laughed.

"What? Let me see," Nabors said. "Oh, the Minnie Kay. That's not named after her. Minnie's middle name is Lou, isn't it?"

"Yes," Minnie replied. "Minnie Lou Smith." She folded the paper closed and returned it to Doc Baker. "But it would be nice if I could make that claim. I'm sure those boats are just really grand."

* * *

The little sign had been professionally lettered, and it stood proudly just outside town.

Midas

POPULATION: 213

No-one is a Stranger.

It was Thursday, August 30th, when Smoke and Bobby Lee arrived in Midas, a community where false-fronted shanties and canvas tents competed with each other for space along the length of the single street.

"You ever been here before?" Smoke asked Bobby Lee as the two men rode into town. "The reason I asked is, is there anyone here who might recognize you?"

"I was here once, but that was a couple of years ago and I didn't stick around long. I doubt anyone would recognize me."

Despite the remoteness of the town, it seemed to be quite busy, as vehicles of commerce rolled up and down the street. In addition there were two new buildings under construction.

"I'll give the town this," Bobby Lee said. "It sure is a busy little place."

"Yeah, it is at that," Smoke said. He pointed to one of the more substantial buildings, which had its name, The Silver King, painted in red on the top of the false front. "What do you say we stop there?"

"Now that's the best idea you've had since the one you had about putting dynamite behind the jail," Bobby Lee said. He put his hand to his ear. "But my ears are still ringing."

"I could have left you there," Smoke said.

"No, no," Bobby Lee said, holding out his hand. "Don't get me wrong, believe me, I am not complaining."

The two tied off their horses, then stepped inside. If, as the sign outside town stated, there were 213 residents, Smoke figured that at least ten percent of them were in the saloon, even though it was just mid-afternoon.

The saloon was noisy with the sounds of idle men and painted women having fun. There was no piano, but a couple of men and a couple of bar girls were singing out of tune a song with ribald lyrics.

"Yes, sir, what can I serve you?" the bartender asked, sliding down toward them. He was carrying a stained and foul-smelling towel that he used to alternately wipe off the bar, then wipe out the glasses.

"How's your beer?" Smoke asked.

"Wet," the bartender answered.

"Sounds good enough," Smoke said slapping the necessary silver on the counter.

The singers let go with a particularly bawdy line, and everyone in the saloon laughed.

"That's some song they're singin', ain't it?" the bartender replied as he set two beer mugs in front of Smoke and Bobby Lee.

"The words are all right, but they need to work some on carrying a tune," Bobby Lee said.

The bartender chuckled. "You got that right," he said. "You boys just passin' through?" he asked.

"Could be," Smoke said. "Or it could be that we might stay for a while. This looks like a pretty lively town."

"It is. There was silver discovered three years ago, and that's what caused the town to come here in the first place. But that played out and looked like the town might die, but then some fellas come across a new lode no more'n a month ago and we've had some new folks come in." The bartender squinted at the two. "But I have to tell you, you boys don't look like no miners."

"We're just a couple of cowboys, looking for someplace that might need some riders," Smoke said.

"Not much in the way of ranching around here," the bartender said. "Not enough water, no grass."

"Yeah, that's about what we figured," Smoke said. "So I reckon we'll be riding on."

"Hey, you," someone at the far end of the bar called. "I know you. What's your name?"

Smoke laughed. "Well now, mister, if you know me, then you know my name."

"I know you all right. It just ain't comin' to me right now."

"Well, if you can't remember my name, it's not all that important, is it?"

"Don't get smart with me, mister," the man said. "I don't like people who get smart around me."

"Then you must not have many friends," Smoke said. "I can't imagine anyone around you who isn't smarter than you."

The others in the saloon laughed.

"What? What did you say?"

"Boomer, why don't you leave the stranger alone now?" the bartender said. "He ain't botherin' nobody. He and his friend just came in for a beer is all."

"You stay out of this, Abe, it ain't none of your

concern," Boomer said. "This here is between me and Mr. Smart Mouth there. Ain't it, Mr. Smart Mouth?"

"Boomer, is it?" Smoke said. "Boomer, why don't you have a drink on me. Abe, set him up with whatever he wants," Smoke said.

Boomer stared at Smoke for a long moment. Then his eyes flashed with recognition. He pointed his finger at Smoke.

"Wait a minute, wait just a damn minute here! I know who you are now. You're the fella they call Smoke Jensen."

"That's right."

"My name is Watkins. Boomer Watkins. That mean anything to you?"

"Can't say that it does."

"You killed my brother, Jerry."

"Jerry Watkins was your brother?"

"Yeah. Do you remember him now?"

"I remember him," Smoke said. "One of the ugliest men I've ever met. Of course, I suppose that is because his face was scarred with birdshot from a woman he tried to rape."[4]

"I'm glad you remember, 'cause I want you to know why I'm killin' you," Boomer said as his hand snaked toward his gun.

Boomer was fast, and he prided himself on his speed, but to his astonishment, Smoke had his gun out with the barrel inches from Boomer's face before he even cleared leather.

Boomer dropped his pistol back into his holster and threw his hands up.

"No! No!" he shouted.

---

[4]*Pursuit of the Mountain Man*

"Shuck out of that gun belt and walk out of here," Smoke said.

"Sure thing, mister, sure thing," Boomer said.

"I didn't mean nothin', I was just tryin' to scare you is all."

Boomer released the buckle, then let the belt fall. "Abe, I reckon I'll take that drink now," he said.

"I reckon you won't," Smoke said. "I told you to walk out of here and that's what you are going to do."

Boomer glared at Smoke for a long moment. "You ain't got no right to run me outta here."

Smoke pulled the hammer back and it made a deadly, double click as it rotated the cylinder.

"Then I'll shoot you and drag you out of here," Smoke said.

"No! I'm goin'! I'm goin'!" Boomer said as the laughter of the others in the saloon chased him out.

"Smoke Jensen, by God!" someone said. "That there is Smoke Jensen! I've he'erd tell of him. Ain't never seen him before."

"Well, we've seen him now," another said.

Bobby Lee chuckled, then spoke under his breath. "And you were worried about me being recognized."

"Are you really Smoke Jensen?" the bartender asked.

"Yes. And I'm sorry about running off one of your customers," Smoke replied.

"Don't worry none about that, Mr. Jensen," Abe replied. "If there was ever any sumbitch that needed runnin' off, it is Boomer Watkins. Hell, he runs off half my customers anyway, always bullyin' them. Yes, sir, it was worth it seeing him get his comeuppance. Besides which, you comin' here will be good for my business. I'll just put up a sign that said the great Smoke Jensen had a beer here."

"Or two," Smoke said. He put another dime down. "How about another for my friend and me?"

Abe pushed the dime back. "No, sir, Mr. Jensen, your money ain't no good in here."

"I appreciate that, Abe, but you aren't in business to give away your product. I'm more than glad to pay for it."

"Thanks," Abe said, taking the dime back. "What are you doing in Midas, Mr. Jensen? I mean really? 'Cause I know for sure you ain't a cowboy lookin' for work."

"Not looking for work, but I am looking for someone," Smoke said.

"Who would that be?"

"Frank Dodd."

The bartender nodded. "I reckoned that might be who it was, him being an outlaw and wanted and all."

"Have you ever seen him?" Smoke asked.

"He's been through here a time or two," Abe said. "He don't never stay long though. You after the reward, are you?"

"Yeah," Smoke replied without being more specific.

"Funny. I know'd you was on the right side of the law, but I never know'd you to be a bounty hunter, though."

"We do what we have to do," Smoke said. "Do you think the sheriff might have any information on Dodd?"

"He might," Abe replied.

"Where will I find him?"

"His office and the jail are at the far end of the street on the other side. You can't miss it—there are about six tents, then one brick building and that's the jail."

"Thanks, I believe I'll step down and pay him a visit."

"Bartender!" someone called. "A little service if you don't mind."

"Hold your horses," Abe said. "I'll be right there."

Smoke waited until the bartender moved down to answer the call. Then he spoke to Bobby Lee, speaking so quietly that only Bobby Lee could hear him.

"I'm going over to the sheriff's office to see if he has anything about your escape yet. That'll let us know how careful we have to be while we are in town. You stay here."

"Smoke, uh, I was in jail," Bobby Lee said. "So I don't have any, uh . . ."

Smoke chuckled. "I got it," he said. He took a twenty-dollar gold double eagle from his pocket and gave it to Bobby Lee. "Don't spend it all in one place," he teased.

"Thanks," Bobby Lee said.

Chapter Twenty-one

As soon as Boomer Watkins left the saloon, he looked up his brother Clint, who was at the moment in Tsun Woo's opium den, waiting for his time on the couch.

"Clint, guess who's in town!" Boomer said.

"I don't care who is in town. Can't you see I'm waitin' my turn here?"

"You'll care when I tell you," Boomer said.

"All right, who is in town?"

"Smoke Jensen, that's who."

The name got Clint's attention. "Smoke Jensen? Are you sure?"

"Hell, yeah, I'm sure. I recognized him. Besides which, he admitted it to me."

"Maybe it was just someone showin' off, someone who wanted you to think he was Smoke Jensen."

"No, it was him all right. He know'd exactly what Jerry looked like. I mean, he described him just right. Besides which he—I, uh . . ."

"What?"

"Well, I tried to draw on him, and he beat me. I ain't never seen no one as fast."

"If he beat you, how come you ain't dead?"

"I don't know. 'Cause he made a mistake, I guess. But I plan on it bein' the last mistake he ever makes. That is, if I can get you away from the Chinaman here. 'Cause if you don't, I'll just do it myself."

"Do what?"

"Wait for the son of a bitch to come out of the saloon, then kill him," Boomer said.

"Nah, you don't have to do it by yourself. Hell, it's liable to be another hour before I get my time on the couch. I reckon that's enough time to kill Jensen."

As Smoke stepped off of the boardwalk in front of the saloon, a bullet suddenly fried the air just beside his ear, then hit the dirt beside him before it skipped off with a high-pitched whine down the street. The sound of the rifle shot reached him at about the same time, and Smoke dived behind the water trough, his gun already in his hand. Crawling on his belly to the edge of the trough, he saw Boomer Watkins standing up on the roof of the Midas Mercantile just behind the false front and the sign that read GOODS FOR ALL MANKIND.

Boomer was holding a Henry rifle, and he operated the lever to jack in another shot. Before he could get off a second shot, Smoke fired, and he saw a little spray of blood from the hole that suddenly appeared in Boomer's forehead. The rifle fell from Boomer's hand as he pitched forward, turning a half-flip in the air to land flat on his back in a pile of horse manure.

Thinking that was his only threat, Smoke stood up, and had started across the street toward Boomer when another gunman suddenly appeared in the street, firing at Smoke. The would-be assailant's shot missed, and with lightning-quick reflexes, Smoke dropped to the ground, then rolled quickly to his left, just as the second shot hit the ground so close beside him that it kicked dirt into his face.

From his prone position on the ground, Smoke fired at the new gunman and hit him in the kneecap. The gunman let out a howl and went down, but he still had his gun and he was still shooting.

Smoke threw another shot toward the gunman, but as his attacker was lying in the street now, he made a more difficult target.

"Boomer! Boomer! Are you still alive?" the gunman lying in the street shouted.

There was no answer.

Not knowing if there was anyone else after him, Smoke got up and ran three buildings down the street, bending low and firing as he went. He dived behind the porch of the barbershop, then rose to look back toward his attacker.

His attacker had also managed to get out of the street, and now he fired at Smoke. The bullet sent splinters of wood into Smoke's face, and Smoke put his hand up, then pulled it away, peppered with his own blood.

"Listen to me!" the gunman shouted. "This here fella is a murderin' bastard! He kilt mine and Boomer's brother for no reason at all! I'll give a hunnert dollars to anyone who helps me kill the son of a bitch!"

"That's your battle, Clint, not our'n," someone shouted back. "Do your own killin'!"

Smoke stared across the street, trying to find an opening for a shot, but Clint had managed to crawl behind the porch of Miller's Feed and Seed Store. Smoke saw him get behind the porch, but there was no good shot for him. But that was a double-edged sword. He had no shot at Clint, which mean Clint had no shot at him, unless he showed himself. Smoke calculated the place along the length of the porch where he knew Clint would have to show himself. He took slow and deliberate aim, cocked his pistol, and waited.

Just as he expected, Clint's head appeared above the edge of the porch. As soon as it did, Smoke squeezed the trigger. His pistol roared and a cloud of black powder smoke billowed up, then floated away. When the cloud cleared, Smoke saw Clint lying on his back, dead in the dirt.

Smoke heard someone running toward him then, and he swung around ready, if need be, to take on someone else. When he saw that it was Bobby Lee, he smiled in relief, then stood up. Bobby Lee joined him and the two men, with pistols drawn, moved to the middle of the street, looking around for any others who might be gunning for them. They saw several people looking at them from the positions of safety they had taken, but not one soul presented an additional threat.

"Damn, brother-in-law, I can see right now that traveling with you is going to be just real excitin'," Bobby Lee said.

* * *

It was early afternoon and quiet in the Gold Strike Saloon. Nate Nabors was sitting at the piano playing the Moonlight Sonata by Beethoven, Paul was behind the bar polishing glasses, Doc Baker and Byron Hughes were engaged in their eternal game of chess, sitting near the piano enjoying the music, and Minnie was reading the newspaper.

"Where is she?" a loud voice called, disturbing the quiet afternoon and bringing Minnie out of her reverie.

Looking up from the paper toward the batwing doors, Minnie saw Sheriff Wallace standing there.

"Ah, there you are," Wallace said, looking directly at Minnie.

"Shh, Sheriff," Doc Baker said. "Enjoy the music."

"I don't want to enjoy the music," Wallace said gruffly.

"Well, maybe some of the rest of us do," Byron Hughes said.

"What are you doing here?" Doc Baker asked. "Why aren't you out looking for your escaped prisoner?"

"I am looking for him." Sheriff Wallace pointed to Minnie. "And you are going to help me find him."

"Me? How am I going to help?" Minnie asked.

"I want to talk to you."

"All right, Sheriff, have a seat," Minnie invited. "You won't even have to buy me a drink," she added with a smile.

"No, not here. Down at the jail."

"What?" Minnie gasped.

The music fell off with a couple of resonant chords and Nabors turned on the bench to look at Wallace. "What's going on here, Sheriff?" he asked. "Are you arresting Minnie?"

"Not now," Sheriff Wallace said. "But if she won't come down willingly, I'll arrest her."

"On what charge?" Nabors asked.

"For interfering with an investigation," Wallace replied. "And if any of you give me any more of your lip, I'll arrest you too."

"Now, by damn, you just hold on there, Sheriff," Doc Baker said. "You can't just—"

"Never mind, I'll come," Minnie said.

"I thought you might." Wallace made a motion toward the front door. "Let's go."

With a wan look toward her friends, Minnie followed the sheriff out of the saloon.

When they reached the jailhouse, Minnie noticed that the door was open between the front of the building and the cell area. Glancing through the door, she saw a bricklayer hard at work, repairing the hole.

"Have a seat, Miss—Smith, is it?" Sheriff Wallace began.

"Yes."

"Is that your real name? I know that most of the time whores take on phony names because they don't want their families findin' out anything about them."

"You know all about whores, do you?" Minnie asked.

"I know considerable about whores," Sheriff

Wallace said. "I'm a lawman. I have dealt with them quite a bit. Of course, I don't blame whores for changin' their name," he continued. "I don't reckon anyone who would whore has any pride left. But don't you think you could've come up with a better name than Smith?" Wallace laughed. "That's not what you would call just real original now, is it?"

"Why do you need to know my real name?" Minnie asked.

"Because I'm goin' to ask you some questions," Sheriff Wallace said. "And I'm going to have to know whether or not I can believe your answers. If I can't believe your real name, how am I going to believe you?"

Minnie didn't answer.

"Well, what is it?" Wallace asked, growing impatient at Minnie's long delay in answering.

"Minnie Smith is my real name," she said.

"All right, Miss—Smith," Wallace said, setting the name apart from the rest of the sentence and coming down on it with an emphasis that told her he didn't believe her. "I have a few questions for you."

Minnie said nothing.

"Why didn't you tell me that Buck West answered your telegram?"

"He didn't answer my telegram."

"Don't be coy with me, Miss Smith. I don't mean that he answered your telegram with one of his own. I mean that he came to Cloverdale."

"He didn't come to Cloverdale."

"Don't lie to me!" Sheriff Wallace shouted loudly, accenting his shout with the slap of his hand on his desk. "He damn sure did come here, and you know it!"

Wallace pointed through the open door to the hole in the back wall. "Who do you think did that, if not Buck West?"

Minnie shook her head. "I don't know."

"Somebody did it, because the blast came from outside the jail. That means somebody helped Cabot escape."

Minnie said nothing.

"You and Cabot were friends, weren't you?"

"I'm friends with a lot of men," Minnie said. "You said it yourself, Sheriff. I am a whore. I am paid to be friends."

"But you were sort of a special friend to Cabot, weren't you?"

"Sheriff?" the call came from the back of the building, from the man who was laying bricks in repair of the wall. "Could you come back here a moment?"

"I'll be right there," Wallace shouted in reply. He turned back toward Minnie. "You stay right here," he ordered.

"I'm not going anywhere," she answered.

"What do you want?" he called to the bricklayer.

"I didn't know the jail cell door was locked. I've about sealed myself in," the bricklayer said.

Wallace chuckled. "You'd be in a hell of a fix if I wasn't here, wouldn't you?" The sheriff opened the middle drawer to get the key.

"I'm not through with you yet," he said, shaking his finger at Minnie.

Minnie nodded, then, glancing at the open drawer, saw something that made her gasp. There, in the sheriff's drawer, was a letter from Bobby Lee, the mailing and return address on the envelope clearly legible.

She heard the talk from the back of the jail.

"Come back here," the bricklayer said. "I want to show you how I've had to dovetail these here new bricks in with the old ones. I need your approval."

"If the wall is strong enough to hold a prisoner, it's good enough for me."

"I want you to look at it anyway."

As the sheriff and the bricklayer carried on their conversation in the back, Minnie thought of the letter that was in his desk drawer. Dare she to open it?

Getting up from her chair, Minnie moved to the back door to listen to the conversation between the sheriff and the bricklayer. The sheriff was asking about something and the bricklayer was trying to explain it. It sound involved enough to give her the opportunity she needed, so she returned to the desk, where the drawer was still open, then, with another look back, she reached in and removed the envelope. Opening it, she pulled out the letter and began to read:

Dear Sheriff Wallace,
  I take pen in hand to inform you of a planned holdup of the Nevada Central train to be perpetrated by Frank Dodd and his gang. As we discussed, I have joined with Frank Dodd and his brigands in order to get the information we need to effect his arrest. The planned robbery will take place on Tuesday next, August 21st, at the evening hour of ten-thirty at the watering tower ten miles south of Lone City. I will be riding a gray, the only rider so mounted.

*Please have deputies on hand in the express car so
that we may apprehend Dodd and his men.*
                        Sincerely,
                        Bobby Lee Cabot

So the sheriff had lied during Bobby Lee's trial.
He had received the letter. She knew it! Oh, why
hadn't the judge let her testify?

"Whatever you are going to do, do it," Sheriff
Wallace called back to the bricklayer. "And don't
take all day to do it."

Minnie's heart leaped to her throat and with
nervous hands she replaced the letter in the envelope, then put it back in the drawer. But her
hand was still in the drawer when Sheriff Wallace
came back into the room.

"What are you doing in my desk drawer?" he
asked.

Seeing a pencil and a blank piece of paper,
Minnie pulled both from the drawer.

"I was going to leave you a note telling you that
I was going back to the Gold Strike," she said.

"You ain't goin' anywhere until I tell you that
you can," Wallace said. "Just put the pencil and
paper back in the drawer."

"All right," Minnie said, relieved that he had
not actually seen her with the letter. "It doesn't
matter now anyway, you are back."

"Now, I'm going to ask you one more time,"
Wallace said. "And if I find out you are lyin', I'll
send you to prison for helpin' Cabot escape. He
smiled. "Women don't do well in prison."

"I haven't lied to you, Sheriff."

"Did you send a telegram to Buck West?"

"Yes."

"Did he reply to the telegram?"

"No, and if you knew I sent it, then you also know that he didn't reply. I'm sure you checked with the telegrapher."

"Did you meet Buck West?"

"No."

It was easy for Minnie to say that she hadn't met with Buck West because, although she thought she had, she quickly learned that his real name was Smoke Jensen.

"Look here, Miss Smith, are you telling me that Buck West did not come to Cloverdale in answer to your telegram?"

"I'm telling you there was no Buck West," Minnie said.

"Do you know the penalty for lying during an official investigation?"

"Yes, I do. Do you?" Minnie asked pointedly.

"What is that supposed to mean?"

"You said you didn't get a letter from Bobby Lee. I know that you did."

"How do you know?" Sheriff Wallace challenged.

Minnie caught herself. She had almost given away the fact that she had seen the letter in his desk. If he knew that, all he would have to do is destroy it.

"I know it because Bobby Lee told me he mailed it to you."

"No, all you know is that he told you that," Sheriff Wallace said. "That didn't work for Cabot during the trial, and it isn't going to work now." Wallace pushed himself back away from the desk, ran his hand through his hair, and sighed. "Get out of here, Miss Smith. I don't have any more questions for you."

"That works out fine then, doesn't it, Sheriff?" Minnie said. "Because I don't have any more answers for you."

"If you hear from him, Miss Smith, I'll know about it," Wallace said. "Whether it's a letter or a telegraph message, I will know about it. So I'm tellin' you right now, if you do hear from him, you had better let me know right away."

With an angry glare at the sheriff, Minnie left the sheriff's office.

The gallows was still in place in front of the sheriff's office, but the sign had been taken away. Now it was little more than an ugly piece of construction.

Chapter Twenty-two

Doc Baker was gone by the time Minnie returned to the Gold Strike Saloon.

"Minnie! Thank God you are all right!" Nabors said. "Doc and I were worried about you."

"Where is Doc?"

"One of the workers down at the mine was hurt, Doc went to tend to him," Nabors said.

"Nate, I saw the letter," Minnie said.

"The letter?"

"The letter Bobby Lee had me send," Minnie explained. "I saw it. It is in the middle drawer of the sheriff's desk. I read it too, and it is exactly the way Bobby Lee told us. The letter tells what day, what time, and where the train was to be robbed. And in the letter, he asks the sheriff to be waiting in the express car with his deputies."

"Lord, Minnie, you weren't prowling around in Wallace's desk, were you? What if he had caught you?"

"I wasn't exactly prowling," Minnie said. "The sheriff got called away for a moment and he left the middle drawer of his desk open. I saw the letter in the drawer so, while he was gone, I read it."

Nabors hit his fist in his hand. "I knew he was lying," he said. "He stood right up there in court, under oath, and swore that he had never received that letter. I knew then, he was lying."

"What do we do with it now?" Minnie asked.

"Do with it? Minnie, you didn't take it from his desk, did you?"

"No," Minnie said. "I thought about it, but what good would that have done? That wouldn't prove that he had ever gotten it."

"You're right," Nabors said. He sighed. "This is frustrating. We now know for sure that he got the letter, but how are we going to prove it?"

"We've got to arrange for someone else to see the letter, someone the judge will trust. But I don't have any idea who that might be."

"I have an idea who it could be," Nabors said.

"Who?"

"Marvin Cutler."

"The newspaper editor?" Minnie replied. "Are you serious? You read his articles. He has it in for Bobby Lee."

"No he doesn't," Nabors said. "Not really. Like I said before, he is just a newspaperman. Why, he would jump at the chance to do a story like this, and the very fact that his previous stories seemed to be against Bobby Lee would just make him that much more credible. Yes, sir, if we can arrange for Marvin to see that letter, there is no doubt in my mind but that the judge will listen to him, and believe him."

* * *

"If there really is a letter, then yes, I would do the story," the newspaperman said. "As a member of the noble profession of the press, it is my duty to see to it that truth is told and justice prevails."

Doc Baker laughed. "You aren't running for office, Marvin," he said. "All we want to know is, will you do the story?"

"Yes. It would be a great story," Cutler replied. "And it might give me the opportunity to undo what damage I may have done by being so quick to judge."

"Good. Then all we have to do is give you the letter," Nabors said.

Cutler shook his head. "No," he said. "I can't take the letter from you."

"Why not? How else are you going to write about it, if you don't see the letter?"

"I have to see the letter in the sheriff's possession," Cutler said. "Otherwise, there would be no proof that it wasn't a plant."

"Are you accusing us of trying to plant evidence?" Doc Baker asked sternly.

Cutler held up his hand, palm out. "Heavens, no, my dear fellow," he said. "I am merely saying that, for the integrity of the story, I must personally see that the letter is in the sheriff's hands."

"How are you going to do that?" Minnie asked.

"Did you say you saw it in the middle drawer of his desk?"

"Yes."

"Then, somehow, I am going to have to get it from his desk."

"Do you have any idea how you are going to do that?" Nabors asked.

"Nothing comes to mind."

"Perhaps we can arrange a diversion," Doc Baker said. "Something that will pull the sheriff and his deputies away from the jail."

"Yes," Cutler said. "Yes, that would be a very good idea."

"You go on back to your office," Doc Baker said. "Let the three of us put our heads together. I'm sure we will come up with something."

"Very well. Get word to me when you have an idea," Cutler said. Standing, he started toward the door, but Minnie called out to him.

"Mr. Cutler?"

"Yes?"

"Where did you get that story about the two new riverboats in St. Louis?"

"What story is that, my dear?"

The newspaper was still lying on the table, and Minnie showed him the story.

"Oh," Cutler said. He smiled proudly. "My dear, disabuse yourself of any idea that because we are in a remote part of the United States that we are unable to report on the latest news from anywhere in the world. I'll have you know that this newspaper is a member in good standing of the Associated Press and because of that, we receive news articles such as the one you mentioned on a daily basis."

"I see."

"Why the particular interest in that article?"

"One of the boats is named after her," Nabors said.

"Indeed?"

"Not exactly," Minnie said. "But close enough that it got my attention."

"Well, I'm glad you enjoyed the story. I pay a fortune for the service, and one never knows if the stories I print from the Associated Press are even noticed by readers. I am pleased to see that they are." With a final wave, Cutler left the saloon.

"Now, all we have to do is come up with a diversion of some sort," Nabors said after Cutler left.

Nabors and Doc Baker began discussing ideas as to how to get the sheriff and all his deputies away from the jail, but Minnie wasn't listening. Minnie had drifted off to another time, and another place. She was remembering St. Louis two years ago.

Minnie's mother had died when she was eighteen. Three months later, her father shocked all of St. Louis society when he married a young girl who was not only the same age as Minnie, but who had been one of Minnie's high school classmates. She had graduated with Minnie, the graduation taking place just one month before she married Minnie's father.

The person everyone in Cloverdale knew as Minnie Lou Smith was not, as so many of the soiled doves, a young woman driven to the profession by a state of destitution. On the contrary, the young woman everyone knew as Minnie Lou Smith had come from one of the most affluent backgrounds in America. Her real name was Minnie Kay Culpepper, and her father, Thaddeus Culpepper, was owner of the Culpepper River Boat Company. Thaddeus Culpepper was a millionaire many times over.

"Minnie, I would like for you to meet your new mother," Thaddeus said, introducing his daughter to his new wife.

Standing beside him was Kristina Dawn Turner. Kristina Dawn and Minnie Kay had known each other for many years, and had long been adversaries, sometimes rivals for the attention of a young man, other times competitors in academic or athletic projects. Until the moment of her father's announcement, she had no idea that there was any kind of a relationship between Kristina and her father.

Her mother had only been dead for three months. How long had this relationship been going on? How could her father marry this person?

"Kristina is not my mother."

"I am now," Kristina said with a triumphant smile.

Minnie was shocked that her father had so dishonored her mother, and she wondered how he could have so betrayed her.

There was no doubt in Minnie's mind but that Kristina had married her father for his money. In fact, Kristina did not deny it when Minnie made that accusation.

"Tell your father that and see which one of us he believes," Kristina said with a malevolent smile.

"Be gone with you, girl!" Thaddeus Culpepper had said when Minnie indeed made the accusation against Kristina. "She is my wife, and more than that, she is your stepmother. You will honor her as you honored your own mother, and I will not listen to any more such scurrilous accusations."

"But Father, you must listen to me. This marriage isn't right," Minnie insisted.

"Minnie, if you cannot find it in your heart to accept this young woman who I love as a part of this family, then I will have no choice but to expel you from the family," Thaddeus said harshly.

Minnie gasped. She had no idea her father would ever consider such a thing.

Then, the longer Minnie thought about it, the more determined she was to deny him the opportunity to ever expel her from the family. She decided to expel herself. A week after that conversation, Minnie left home, taking a night train out of St. Louis. She had no particular destination in mind, but after a series of train rides, she stopped when the last train she boarded reached the end of track in Cloverdale, Nevada.

She had met Janet Farrell on that trip down from Battle Mountain, and Janet introduced her to Nate Nabors and "the life," as Janet called it. She lost her virginity the first night she went to work, but given everything else that had happened to her, that was almost insignificant. She had not been in touch with her father in the two years since she left St. Louis. She had no wish to be in touch with him now, because she did not want to give Kristina the satisfaction of knowing that she had become a whore.

"I've got it!" Nate Nabors said, pounding his fist in his hand. His loud outburst summoned Minnie back from her memories.

"You've got what?" she asked.

"Haven't you been paying attention, Minnie? I've got the solution to our problem. I know what kind of diversion to create in order to get the sheriff and his deputies away from the jail."

Although Minnie wouldn't admit it, she had been so lost in her memories that she had not been paying attention. She had to regather her thoughts to know what he was even talking about.

"What is the idea?" she asked.

"There needs to be a fight," Nabors said. "And it can't be just any fight. It has to be a fight that will get the whole town to come watch."

"Who are you going to get to fight that would draw the entire town to watch?" Doc said. "Hell, Nate, you know as well as I do that drunks get into fights every day without anyone paying the least bit of attention."

"Yes, but this won't just be a couple of drunks," Nabors said. "And I guarantee you that folks will come to watch these two fight."

"All right, now you have me interested. Who is going to fight?"

"Minnie and Janet," Nabors said.

"What? Are you crazy?" Minnie asked. "Janet is my best friend. I'm not going to fight her."

"I agree with Minnie," Doc said. "You can't ask her to pick a fight with Janet."

"It wouldn't be a real fight," Nabors said. "All it has to do is look like a real fight. And it has to take place outside so the whole town can come see it."

"I don't know," Doc said. "What do you think, Minnie? Would you go along with something like that? And do you think Janet would?"

"Janet would if I asked her to," Minnie said. "Especially now, after Sheriff Wallace killed Andy."

"Do you think you two could make it look real?" Doc asked. "I mean, real enough that the men who gather to watch it will be convinced that you two are actually fighting?"

Minnie smiled, and nodded her head. "Yes," she said. "Yes, women have been putting on shows for men since the dawn of time. I don't think we'll have any problems in convincing them that it is real."

"Will you arrange it with Janet?" Nabors asked.

"I'd be glad to," Minnie agreed.

Half an hour later, Minnie and Janet walked across the street to the Cloverdale Emporium. They found a hat that was the only one of its kind in the store, and both of them reached for it.

"I saw it first," Minnie said.

"No, I saw it first."

"I did."

"I did," Janet said, and she grabbed it.

Minnie pushed Janet down and picked the hat up from the floor. Screaming angrily at her, Janet jumped up, then pushed Minnie outside, where the fight continued until they were standing in the street, shouting at each other, pushing each other, and pulling each other's hair.

Though it looked as if they were very angry and doing their best to hurt each other, the pulling of the hair was very controlled. As Nabors predicted, though, the fight began to draw a crowd until soon, well over one hundred people, almost everyone of them men, were gathered in the middle of the street, shouting encouragement and laughing at the antics of the two women.

The young newspaper boy who worked for Cutler ran down to the sheriff's office.

"Sheriff, you better come quick!" he said. "They's two ladies fightin' out in the middle of the street and it looks like they are tryin' to kill each other!"

"A couple of women fightin'?" Deputy Beard said. "I want to see this!"

Sheriff Wallace came out of the jail and looked toward the crowd that had gathered at the far end of the street. The shouting and screaming, along with the shouts and laughter of the crowd, could be heard easily, even from this distance.

"What the hell?" Wallace asked as he started toward the disturbance.

Marvin Cutler was standing just behind the corner of the leather goods store, watching. As soon as Wallace started down the street toward the fight, he moved quickly to the front of the jail. Just before he stepped inside, he looked over at the newspaper boy.

"Tommy, you stay out here. If you see the sheriff comin' back, you let me know," Cutler said to his employee.

"Yes, sir," Tommy replied.

Cutler went into the sheriff's office, pulled open the middle drawer of the sheriff's desk, then saw the envelope.

"I'll be damned," he said quietly. He picked up the envelope, then removed the letter and began to read.

* * *

That evening, Marvin Cutler worked late in his newspaper office, writing the story even as he was setting the type. So familiar was he with setting type that he was able to read and proof the story, even though every letter and every word was backward. When he finished setting the type, he perused it once more, then, with a smile of satisfaction, put the platen in place, and printed the first issue. It was the first "extra" issue he had ever put out.

EXTRA – EXTRA – EXTRA – EXTRA

A Reconsideration of the Trial of Bobby Lee Cabot

Along with every other good citizen of the fair city of Cloverdale, this reporter sat in the court trial of Bobby Lee Cabot and not only watched, but celebrated the fact that Mr. Cabot was found guilty of the murder of August Fletcher. August Fletcher was, at the time of his tragic demise, a messenger for Western Capital Security Agency. This fine gentleman, a husband and father, was performing his duty aboard the Nevada Central train when, on the night of 21 August, the train was robbed and he was killed.

The Cloverdale News Leaf printed an article condemning Bobby Lee Cabot while praising the justice done in finding him guilty, and sentencing him to death by hanging. But recent evidence has come to light which convinces me that justice was not done. On the contrary, an innocent man has been found guilty, and he has been found guilty not because of a failure in the judicial system, but because of the perjury of one man, a man who, while purporting to be a servant of the people, has in fact been engaging in perfidious conduct that knows no bounds. That man is Sheriff Herman Wallace.

Those who followed the trial may remember that Mr. Cabot tried, on repeated occasions, to introduce into evidence the fact that he had sent a letter to Sheriff Wallace previous to the robbery, in which he disclosed all the information necessary to bring about the arrest of Frank Dodd and his gang. Sheriff Wallace claimed that there was no such letter, and indeed, without that letter in evidence, Cabot's defense was ineffective.

The Cloverdale News Leaf can now report that such a letter does, and in fact did exist. It was, even at the time of the trial, in the sheriff's desk, and had Mr. Cabot been fortunate enough to have been assigned a competent attorney, a simple warrant and search would have disclosed that fact.

This newspaper found the letter, in the sheriff's desk, not by writ of warrant as would be required of an officer of the court, but in the exercise of the freedom of the press. That letter, now in possession of the Cloverdale News Leaf, is included herein for the perusal of all justice minded citizens.

"Dear Sheriff Wallace,

"I take pen in hand to inform you of a planned holdup of the Nevada Central train to be perpetrated by Frank Dodd and his gang. As we discussed, I have joined with Frank Dodd and his brigands in order to get the information we need to effect his arrest. The planned robbery will take place on Tuesday next, August 21st, at the evening hour of ten-thirty at the watering tower ten miles south of Lone City. I will be riding a gray, the only rider so mounted. Please have deputies on hand in the express car so that we may apprehend Dodd and his men.

"Sincerely,
"Bobby Lee Cabot"

It is the sincere hope of this newspaper that Judge Briggs will declare the first trial to be a mistrial, and will by judicial fiat overturn the verdict of the jury. It is the further hope of this newspaper that Sheriff Wallace be arrested, removed from his high office, tried, convicted, and punished, not only for the perjury which condemned an innocent man, but for what may well have been his own complicity with Frank Dodd.

Cutler blew the ink dry on the single-sided, single-sheet extra edition newspaper, then smiled. He had been in the newspaper business for over twenty years, and this would be the biggest story of his life.

Chapter Twenty-three

"Sheriff, have you seen this?" Deputy Beard asked, stepping into the sheriff's office, carrying an edition of the extra Cutler had put out.

"No, what is it?"

Though the expression on Beard's face was one of great concern, he said nothing as he handed the paper over.

"I never read the newspaper," Wallace said, waving it away. "It's just a waste of time. If anything happens, people start talking about it anyway."

"You better read this one," Beard said. "And this ain't somethin' we want anyone talkin' about."

"All right, hand it here," Wallace said with an impatient sigh. He began to read, at first with bored indifference, though that quickly changed to anger and concern.

"What?" he called out in clear agitation over what he was reading. Putting the paper down, he jerked open the middle drawer of his desk. "Where's that letter?" he asked loudly.

"According the article, Cutler took it," Beard said.

"Why, that son of a bitch!"

"I told you, you should of got rid of that letter," Beard said.

Wallace pulled his pistol and spun the cylinder, checking the loads. "I think I need to pay Mr. Cutler a visit," he said.

"Huh-uh, I don't think you want to do that," Beard said.

"What do you mean?"

"Take a look down the street toward the newspaper office. There must be twenty or thirty men gathered there. They are talking about forming a citizens' committee to put you under arrest."

"Me? Don't you mean us?"

"Yeah," Beard agreed. "I mean us."

"Damn," Wallace said.

"What are we going to do, Sheriff?"

"I don't know what you are going to do, but I am going to find Dodd, get my share of the money, then get out of here," Wallace said. "I'll go to Arizona, or California, or some such place."

"I'm comin' with you," Beard said.

"Better get Jackson, he's as deep in this as we are. And until we get out of here, the more of us there are, the better it will be."

Smoke Jensen and Bobby Lee Cabot, unaware of the newspaper article that could clear Bobby Lee, had been on the trail now for just over a week. Needing to replenish their supplies, they stopped in the town of Lunning in front of Groves General Store, then tied their horses off at the hitching rail, then stepped up onto the porch. That was when Bobby Lee saw the poster.

"Smoke, take a look at this," he said, pointing to the wanted dodger that was nailed to a post.

WANTED DEAD OR ALIVE

Bobby Lee Cabot

Buck West

5000 *Dollar Reward*

"It has been a long time since there was last a reward out for Buck West," Smoke said.

"At least they don't have pictures or descriptions, and they don't have you connected to it," Bobby Lee said.

"Not yet anyway," Smoke replied.

When they stepped into the store, it was redolent with the familiar smells of cured ham and bacon, dried jerky, flour, spices, apples, onions, and tobacco. Smoke bought jerky, bacon, dried beans, flour, and tobacco.

"Hope nobody finds you," the small, middle-aged, balding man said as he piled all the purchases up on the counter.

"Beg your pardon?" Bobby Lee said.

The grocer chuckled. "Boys, you don't have to be coy with me. I been in this business a long time. I can tell by what you're buying, what you're up to. You've found a promising strike somewhere and you want to work it alone until it's developed. Like I say, I hope nobody finds you."

"Oh, uh, you're right. You startled me, I didn't think it was that obvious," Bobby Lee said.

"You can't fool an old man like me," the

grocer said. "I hope you have an authentic strike, but I have to warn you, I spent twenty years poking around up there in the Toquima Range, where I found a lot of places that looked promising, but I never found anything that paid out. That's why I give it up and come down here to run this store. Started out by just working here, but saved my money and bought it from the man that owned it first."

"Sounds like a smart thing to do," Smoke said as he paid for the purchases and began putting them into a cloth bag. "You would be Mr. Groves, would you?"

"No, sir, my name is Wagner. I kept the name Groves 'cause that's the name of the fella who owned the store first, and that's how folks remember it." Wagner smiled. "Plus which, I wound up marryin' Mr. Groves' daughter and keeping the same name of the store helps keep peace in the family."

"I notice you have three saloons in town," Smoke said. "Which one is the most popular?"

"The New York Saloon is the best," the grocer replied. "And it's always filled with people."

"What about the other two? The Lucky Chance and the Lost Mine?" Smoke asked.

"The Lucky Chance isn't bad," he said. "But the Lost Mine?" He shook his head. "I ain't never been in it, but from what I hear, there don't nobody but the dregs of the county ever go in there. They say it ain't nowhere near as nice as the New York."

"Thanks for the tip," Smoke said, gathering up his sack of groceries. Once outside, he tied the sack to the saddle horn, then untied the horse and swung into the saddle.

"What do you say we get us a beer?"

"Sounds good to me. The New York?" Bobby Lee replied.

"Not yet."

"Not yet?"

"You check out the Last Chance, have a beer, keep your ears open and see what you hear. I'll do the same thing at the Lost Mine. We'll meet in the New York in about an hour and compare notes."

"All right," Bobby Lee agreed.

The Lost Mine was at the far end of the street from Groves General Store. It was right across the street from the New York Saloon, and whereas the New York Saloon had a fresh coat of paint and a bright new sign, the Lost Mine was weathered and the sign was so dim, it could scarcely be read.

There was no piano in the Lost Mine, and there were only two working women. Dissipation pulled at both of them, and one had a purple flash of scar that started above her left eye, slashed down across her cheek, then hooked back toward her mouth. Upon seeing Smoke step into the saloon, the two women smiled and looked toward him. Smoke acknowledged their smile with a polite nod of his head, but as he approached the bar, he turned his body so that he presented his back to them, by way of letting them know that he had no interest in female companionship.

"What will it be?" the bartender asked. The bartender was wearing an apron that looked, and smelled, as if it hadn't been washed in months.

"Beer," Smoke said.

The bartender grabbed a mug from the bar. There was still an inch of beer at the bottom of the mug, and without pouring it out, he held the mug under the spigot of the beer barrel and started to pull the handle.

"A clean glass," Smoke said.

The bartender shrugged his shoulders and set the mug aside, then took an empty one from under the bar.

"A bit choosy, ain't you?" the bartender asked as he drew the beer.

"Let's just say that I want to drink my own beer," Smoke said, putting a nickel down as the beer was delivered.

"Prospectin', are you?" the bartender asked.

"I might be."

"All right, I understand," the bartender said, taking a step back from the bar, then lifting his hands, palm out. "Folks come here, absolutely certain they're goin' to get rich, they find 'em a spot they think nobody else has ever seen, then they want to keep it secret."

"You mean my spot isn't secret?" Smoke asked.

The bartender grunted what might have been a laugh. "Ha. More than likely there's been a dozen prospectors done busted their backs tryin' to prove out the very spot you're on now."

"Yes, well, I'll just keep it secret if you don't mind," Smoke said, responding to the bartender's reasoning.

The bartender drifted away and Smoke nursed

his beer, listening in to a dozen different conversations to see if he could pick up a clue as to
where to find Frank Dodd.

Fifteen miles southwest of Lunning, in the small
town of Marrietta, Emmett Clark was having his
lunch in the Silver Palace Café. Dodd and Conklin were over at the Hog's Head Saloon. Since
joining Dodd, Clark had been involved in four
more robberies—two additional stagecoaches,
one freight office, and a grocery store. The shotgun guard riding on the second stage had tried to
defend the coach against the robbers and Clark
had shot and killed him.

In Clark's mind, his descent into hell was complete. No longer did he try to maintain the fiction
of being "drawn onto the outlaw trail by events
beyond his control." He now considered himself
to be a man without conscience or honor, and
he was not in the least disturbed by that.

Clark had just finished his supper when a newspaper boy came in peddling his papers. Sum-
moning the boy over, Clark bought a paper.

"Gee, thanks, mister," the boy said when Clark
gave him a dime and told him to keep the
change.

Drinking a second cup of coffee, Clark began
perusing the newspaper.

> Queen Victoria, now sixty years old, has
> worn the crown of England for forty-two
> years, a longer period than that known to
> any other living European monarch.

Clark wondered what it would be like to be a monarch for forty-two years. Maybe not as good as it sounded.

The next article also caught his attention.

Mr. Thomas Edison, the inventor, has been exhibiting in New York his improvement of Mr. Alexander Graham Bell's telephone. Mr. Edison's instrument is said to be of such power that the receiver need not be placed at the ear in order to catch the sounds. He also says that he has nearly perfected his new electric light. He claims that he has supplied six lights from one horse power, and that the cost of the light is not more than one-third that of gas. Mr. Edison has stated that it will soon be time to let the public realize the benefit of these marvelous inventions.

Clark had never seen a telephone, but he had heard of it. He knew that a telephone was something like a telegraph, only you could actually speak through the wires, though he had no idea how that would work.

He was about to lay the paper aside when he saw an article that began with the headline "Record Money Shipment." He read the article with a great deal of interest.

Folding the paper over, Clark left his meal half-eaten and hurried over to the saloon. Conklin was sitting alone at a table in the back, eating cracklings and drinking beer.

"Where's Dodd?" Clark asked.

"He took a whore upstairs," Conklin said, though as his mouth was full, he mumbled his words.

"What room?"

"How the hell do I know what room? It could be any of 'em. Far as I know, ever' room up there is a whore's room."

"He needs to see this," Clark said, holding up the paper.

"What is it?"

"Like I said, it's something Dodd needs to see." Clark started toward the stairs.

"I wouldn't go up there if I was you," Conklin called out to him. "I've known Dodd a long time. He don't like bein' bothered none when he is with the whores."

"He'll like this," Clark called back.

Clark went up the stairs, taking two steps at a time. Not knowing which room Dodd was in, he began knocking on all of them. "Dodd," he called, banging on one door after another. "Dodd, get out here!"

"Go away, I'm busy," a muffled voice called from inside one of the rooms.

"Dodd, open the door," Clark called again, moving to the room where he heard the voice. "You aren't going to want to miss this."

A few seconds later, Dodd, wearing only his trousers, and with a disgruntled expression on his face, jerked open the door. Behind him, sitting up in bed but with the sheet down so that one of her breasts was fully exposed, a saloon doxy waited for him.

"You better have a good reason for this," Dodd said.

"How about one hundred thousand reasons?" Clark replied, showing him the newspaper.

* * *

Less than one hour after Clark showed the newspaper article to Frank Dodd, Herman Wallace, Harley Beard, and Loomis Jackson rode into Marrietta.

"What makes you think Dodd will be here?" Beard asked.

"He told me he would be," Wallace said. "He always kept me posted as to where he would be. How else do you think I got the information to him?"

"What's he goin' to think now that you don't have no information to give him?"

"I don't care what he thinks," Wallace said. "The son of a bitch owes me money, and we're going to need money to get out of here."

"Where do we look first?" Jackson asked.

"Where do you think?" Wallace replied as he turned his horse toward the Hog's Head Saloon.

Chapter Twenty-four

Having heard nothing of particular interest while spending time in the Lost Mine Saloon, Smoke moved from the Lost Mine to the New York Saloon. The New York Saloon was considerably larger than the Lost Mine, and much more crowded. It took Smoke a few seconds to locate Bobby Lee, who was sitting alone at a table in the middle of the crowded room.

Smoke nodded at him, then walked over to the bar. The bartender was wearing a clean white apron and a clean shirt, the sleeves of which were held up by garters. He had slicked-back coal-black hair, and a waxed handlebar mustache.

"Beer," Smoke ordered, and he smiled as he saw the bartender, very meticulously, select a new, clean mug, then hold it under the spigot. The bartender was careful to build a head, but not spill any of the beer. The difference between the New York and the Lost Mine could not be more strikingly manifested than in observing the procedures of the two bartenders.

With his beer in hand, Smoke crossed over to join Bobby Lee at his table.

"Anything?" Smoke asked.

"Nothing. How about you?"

"I didn't hear anything usable either," Smoke said, just before he took a swallow of his beer.

There were three men at the nearest table, and something one of them said caught Smoke's attention.

"I can't believe they would put in the paper about carryin' all that money on the train. Don't they know that's just askin' to have someone rob it?"

The speaker holding forth was a big, bearded man. The two men with whom he was sharing the table were also bearded and nearly indistinguishable from each other except for a large mole on the face of one, and a three-corner scar on the face of the other. The speaker's face, though rough hewn, was unmarked.

"I know people who have been workin' the mines for near fifteen years, good productive mines they were too, and they haven't taken out as much money as is goin' to be on that train. All a fella would have to do is rob that train and he'd have enough money to spend for the rest of his life."

"You want to rob a train, Cooley?" one of the others asked, and all three laughed.

"Hell, no, I ain't no train robber," Cooley said. "I'm just sayin', it don't make no sense to me for the newspaper to put in a story about shippin' one hundred thousand dollars. Just 'cause I ain't no train robber don't mean there ain't folks who won't do it."

"That's true. But I'm sure they'll have it guarded. I figure anyone who plans on robbin' that train is goin' to have to be awful smart, or awful dumb."

"Yeah? Well, I know a feller that sure fits that description," Cooley said. "If he finds out about this train carryin' all that money, why, he'll rob it in a heartbeat."

"You're talkin' about Frank Dodd, aren't you?"

"Maybe I am, and maybe I ain't," Cooley said. "To my way of thinkin', it ain't none too smart to be throwin' that fella's name around."

"No, I ain't goin' to be throwin' it around neither."

"Tell me, Owen, what would you do if you had that much money?" Cooley asked.

"I don't know. Maybe buy some new equipment for my diggings," Owen said.

Cooley laughed.

"What's so funny?"

"Hell, if you had that much money, why would you spend any more time trying to scratch a living out of a mine that ain't hardly payin' nothin' at all?"

"Yeah," Owen said. "Yeah, you're right. I'd probably go back East somewhere, maybe get me a haircut and a beard trim, some new clothes, and then eat me a lobster."

"A lobster?"

"Yeah, I've always wanted to eat me a lobster."

The other two men at the table laughed.

* * *

"Did you hear that?" Smoke asked Bobby Lee. Smoke's question was asked quietly, so that only Bobby Lee heard.

"Yes, I heard it. Something about a train carrying one hundred thousand dollars."

"We need to have a look at that newspaper," Smoke suggested.

"I saw someone bring a pile of them in a while ago. He left them on the end of the bar. I'll go get us one," Bobby Lee said.

Bobby Lee walked up to the bar, picked up a paper, and dropped two pennies into a jar that was sitting beside the papers. Taking the paper back to the table, he and Smoke began looking through it.

"Here it is," Smoke said. "It's reprinted from the *Carson City Gazette*. The money is being shipped from Carson City to Columbus. How far is that?"

"It's just under a hundred and fifty miles," Bobby Lee said.

"Do you know the route?"

"Not really, but back in our Reno office, we have a map of every railroad in Nevada. I just remember seeing it."

Bobby Lee looked back at the paper, then noticed another article of interest.

"Smoke, look at this!" he said excitedly. "Here is a reprint of an article from the *Cloverdale News Leaf*! I think I've been cleared!"

Smoke read Cutler's article, then nodded.

"I think you have too," he said. "So, what do you want to do now? Do you want to go back to Cloverdale?"

Bobby Lee drummed his fingers on the table for a moment, then shook his head.

"No, not yet," he said. "This may be the best opportunity we will ever have to get Dodd. I started out to get him and I intend to do just that."

"What was that date again?" Smoke asked, checking the article.

"The third of September," Bobby Lee replied. "Wait a minute. That's—tonight," he said, just realizing it.

"Yes," Smoke said. "What do you say we walk over to the depot and get a map and a schedule?"

"Good idea," Bobby Lee said.

Five minutes later, the two men were at the Lunning depot, perusing the train schedule and studying the railroad map.

"You know how Dodd works," Smoke said. "Do you have any ideas how he'll plan to do it?"

"From the look of this map, I would say he will try it at Hawthorne," Bobby said.

"Hawthorne?"

"Yes, look here," Bobby Lee said, pointing to the map. "It is forty-five miles from Cleaver to Hawthorne, with no water tanks in between. Forty-five miles is just about the limit an engine can go without refilling its tank, so the train is going to be awfully thirsty when it gets there. And because it will come through at eleven p.m., most of the town will be asleep. Dodd will wait until the train stops, then he'll hit it."

Smoke nodded. "That sounds reasonable," he said. "How far is Hawthorne from here?"

"Twenty-five miles according to the map."

"If we want to be there by eleven, we had best be going."

* * *

The Mountain View Special consisted of the Baldwin engine, a four-four-two named the *Eric McKenzie*, a wood tender, an express car, a baggage car, two sleeper cars, and two day cars. With a full head of steam, it hurtled south through the night on the Virginia and Truckee Railroad as sparks flew from the smokestack and glowing cinders fell between the tracks. By sight and sound, the behemoth made its presence known to man and animals alike.

"You've got a good fire stoked there, R.A.," the engineer said to his fireman, having to shout to be heard over the hiss of active steam, the clatter of steel pistons, wheels, and couplings, and the gush of wind. "We're making near thirty miles to the hour!"

"I'll keep the pressure up as high as you want it, Clyde," R.A. said as he threw in more chunks of wood. "There's not an engine on the line that can top the *McKenzie*."

In the express car behind the tender, Eddie Murtaugh and two other agents of the Western Exchange Security Agency sat on the floor against the wall of the car. The door was open slightly. Murtaugh stood up, then stepped over to the open door to look outside.

"Whooowee, those boys up front have us going lickety-split," he said.

"I wonder how fast we are going," one of the other agents said.

"I don't know, but it's fast."

"Mr. Murtaugh?" the railroad express man said.

Murtaugh turned toward the express man.

"You wanted to know when we came to Hawthorne? According to my watch, we will be there in about five minutes."

"Thanks," Murtaugh said. "All right, boys, get ready."

"I hear the train," Smoke said. "Get ready."

Smoke and Bobby Lee were behind the feed and seed store that was directly across the tracks from the water tower. They were on the same side of the track as the door to the express car. That way, they would be able to observe any approach to the car.

"I haven't seen anything, have you?" Bobby Lee asked.

"No, I haven't."

"I know they are here, though," Bobby Lee said. "They have to be here. There is no other place where they will have the train stopped like this."

The train approached the water tower, its speed already greatly reduced, the wheels and couplings squealing in protest as the brakes were applied.

"We had better get mounted," Smoke said. "We may have to move fast."

Smoke and Bobby Lee swung into their saddles as the train rumbled by, then came to a complete halt. It sat there for a moment with the engine issuing loud, rushing sighs as the relief valves opened and closed, emitting large clouds of steam. The steam clouds were so white that, in the dark, they looked almost iridescent.

The fireman came out of the engine cab,

climbed up on top of the tender, brought the great water spout down to the tank opening, then pulled on the rope to lift the gate and start the flow of water. Even from here, and even above the puffing sounds of the engine at rest, Smoke and Bobby Lee could hear the splashing of water into a tender that was nearly empty. As Bobby Lee had pointed out, the demand for water at this stop was at its maximum.

"See anything?" Bobby Lee asked.

"Not a thing," Murtaugh answered the same question that had been put to him by one of his men.

"Maybe Dodd isn't going to rob the train," one of the others suggested.

"He's not going to rob it," Murtaugh replied.

"What do you mean he isn't going to rob the train? Isn't that why we are here?"

"He is going to try to rob the train," Murtaugh said. "But he is not going to, because we aren't going to allow it."

"Well, if he isn't going to try it here, where is he going to try?"

"I don't know," Murtaugh admitted.

"How far to the next water tank?" Smoke asked.

"It's all the way back in Lunning," Bobby Lee said. "Damn, if they are waiting there while we came up here, I'm going to feel pretty foolish. I'm sorry, Smoke, looks like I led you on a wild-goose chase."

"Don't worry about it, Bobby Lee. We'll just do what has to be done," Smoke said.

"What would that be? If Dodd is waiting in Lunning, there's no way we can get there in time to stop him. The train will run twenty-five to thirty miles per hour, we would kill the horses trying to keep up that pace."

"We aren't going to try and keep up with the train," Smoke said.

"We've lost the opportunity, haven't we?"

"No," Smoke said. "The train hasn't been robbed yet, has it?"

"No," Bobby Lee said. "If it had been, the express man would have made a report as soon as the train arrived. But nobody came out of the express car."

"Then it isn't too late to prevent the robbery."

"How?"

"Simple," Smoke said. "We'll just ride on the train. I'll get us a couple of tickets."

"What about our horses? There's no stock car on this train."

"We'll board them here, then take the next train back."

Chapter Twenty-five

Bobby Lee took care of boarding the horses while Smoke bought tickets. The train was already rolling out of the station when the two men ran down the platform, then leaped up onto the rear mounting step of the last car. There was a porter standing out on the rear platform, and he reached down to help each of them board.

"Thanks," Smoke said.

"Yes, sir, glad to help," the porter said. "You gents just barely made it."

The passage of the train and a twist of wind caused a plume of smoke from the engine to whirl around onto the platform, burning Smoke's nose and eyes. He coughed and waved his hand. "Let's get inside," he said.

"Where should we go?" Bobby Lee asked.

"If we can find a seat in this car, this is where we should be. That way, if Dodd does try anything, he will be in front of us."

"Good idea," Bobby Lee said. He saw a couple

of seats halfway up the car on the left-hand side. "How about if we sit there?"

"Good choice," Smoke replied.

"Wait a minute, do you really intend to wreck the train?" Emmett Clark asked after Dodd explained his plan to the others.

"Yes."

"Why? All you have to do is wait by a water tower. You know the train is going to stop there."

"This train is carrying one hundred thousand dollars," Dodd said. "That means it is going to be full of guards, all of them riding in the express car. And every one of them will be expecting us to hit the train at one of the watering stops. They won't be expecting us to wreck the train. And chances are that after we wreck it, they won't be in any condition to stop us."

"You mean they might be killed in the train wreck," Clark said. It wasn't a question; it was an accusatory declaration.

"Yeah," Dodd said. "I wrecked my share of trains and killed my share of people during the war. What's different about this one?"

"There are innocent people on this train," Clark said.

"There were innocent people on the other trains I wrecked too," Dodd said. "Do you have a problem with that?"

"I don't have any problem with it," Wallace said. Wallace, Beard and Jackson had joined up with Dodd on the same day Clark took him the newspaper article about the money shipment. "I need money if I am going to get a new start somewhere, and I don't care what I have to do to get it."

"Look, Clark, if you don't want to be a part of this, you can ride out now," Dodd said.

"What is the breakdown again?" Clark asked.

"There are six of us," Dodd said. You will each get fifteen thousand dollars, and I will get twenty-five."

"I don't like that," Clark said.

"Then ride out now," Wallace said. "That will just be more money for the rest of us."

"I didn't say I wasn't going to do it. I just said I didn't like it."

"All right, then stop worryin' about who might get hurt. Ain't nobody ever goin' to get out of life alive anyhow."

"Dodd, I hear the train a' comin'," Conklin said.

"All right, the palaverin' is over now. Get back, all of you," Dodd said.

As the others got back out of sight, Dodd bent down over the detonator generator. A wire from the generator ran to sticks of dynamite that had been carefully placed on a wooden trestle that spanned a gulley forty feet deep and 150 feet long.

Clark watched as the train approached the trestle. He had an inclination to suggest that Dodd blow the bridge now, for doing so would prevent the train from going any farther and might spare the lives of the passengers. But he said nothing because he knew that Dodd was right. With a shipment of money as large as this train was carrying, it would be heavily guarded, and simply stopping the train wouldn't be enough. They would still have to deal with the guards. Clark drew a deep breath, then let it out slowly. His share would be fifteen thousand dollars. He concentrated on the amount he would get from this job. Fifteen thousand dollars.

As the train approached the trestle, Clark thought he had never seen anything so beautiful in his life. It was like a painting, the engine headlamp stabbing forward, the boiler shimmering in the moonlight. Some of the car windows were glowing, but most were dark.

By the orange light of the cab, Clark could see the engineer leaning out the window of the cab, looking forward down the track with the stump of a pipe clamped securely in his teeth. It was, Clark knew, the last few seconds of this man's life, and he felt an intense pain, not only over what was about to happen, but that he was a part of it.

The train moved onto the trestle, and Clark saw Dodd push down on the generator handle. Instantly thereafter, the dynamite exploded in a great, bright flash. A moment later, the sound of the explosion reached Clark's ears, but even as he was listening to the blast, the trestle began to give way, first the supports that were directly involved with the blast, then the others, upon which the total weight of the train had been transferred. Unable to accommodate the increased weight, the remaining timbers also buckled and the engine, with the wheels still turning, left the bridge.

Back in the rearmost car, Smoke and Bobby Lee were engaged in conversation, and Smoke was telling his brother-in-law about Sally, Pearlie, Cal, and his ranch.

"I'm glad you've got a new family, Smoke," Bobby Lee said. "And Sugarloaf sounds like a great place to live."

"It is a great place to live," Smoke said. "You'll have to come visit me there, maybe stay for a while."

"Ha. If I found a place like that, I would be likely to stay for years, not just a while," Bobby Lee said.

"You are family, Bobby Lee. You are welcome as long as you—"

Smoke's reply was interrupted by a loud crashing sound. The car came to an abrupt halt, and he and Bobby Lee, along with several other passengers in the car, were thrown from their seats.

His attention fixated on the events unfolding before him, Clark watched as the engine plummeted downward, moving slowly as if time had been suspended, until it hit the ground below. The boiler exploded, and bits and pieces of the engine and the first two cars were blown high into the air, chunks of wreckage seeming to hang in place for a long moment before tumbling back down, many of them falling dangerously close to Clark and the others.

The other cars were dragged down into the gully, the first two telescoping, with one car sliding into the other, the remaining cars buckling and breaking before coming to a smashing rest. As the sound of the gushing steam and explosion drifted away, nothing was left but the wails and cries of the injured.

Smoke banged his shoulder on the seat in front of him, then barked his shin painfully as he was thrown to the floor. Even before the sounds of splintering wood, breaking glass, and twisting metal subsided, there were the screams and shouts of surprise, fear, and then pain from the other passengers in the car.

"Bobby Lee!" Smoke shouted. "Are you all right?"

Bobby Lee was lying facedown in the aisle. Getting up slowly, he turned toward Smoke, and Smoke saw blood coming from a wound over his eye. Closer examination of the wound, however, showed that it appeared to be superficial.

"What happened?" Bobby Lee asked.

"We've had a train wreck," Smoke said. "I think Frank Dodd has just hit the train."

"Let's go," Dodd called to the others. "Let's get the money and get out of here."

The others started toward the wreckage, but Clark hung back.

"Come on, Clark!" Dodd called. "That is, if you want your share of the money."

"My God," Clark said under his breath. "What have we done?"

Clark had come too far and sunk too low to back out now. Taking a deep breath to steel himself, he joined the others as they hurried toward the wreckage.

* * *

"Help me! Help me, mister, help me!" a man said, lying under a twisted mass of wreckage. His right leg was grotesquely twisted almost all the way back.

Clark stumbled over something and looking down, saw that it was a severed head. When he saw the pipe, still clenched in the teeth, he realized it was the engineer's head.

"Oh, my God!" Clark said.

"Hurry up!" Dodd called. "Let's get the money and get out of here!"

When they reached the express car, Clark saw that the messenger and all three of the guards from the Western Capital Security Agency were dead, but the safe was under the bulk of the overturned car. It was going to take all of them several minutes to pull the wreckage aside so they could reach the safe.

"We're never going to get this out of here!" Conklin complained.

"Get to work! Stop complaining and start moving the wreckage aside!" Dodd ordered. "We don't have all day!"

Smoke and Bobby Lee managed to work their way out of the last car by pushing through a large rent in the side. At first, the scene that greeted them was unbelievable, wreckage strewn about everywhere, men, women, and children lying dead, dying, or badly injured. The moans and cries created a terrible din in the night air.

Bobby Lee pointed to some men who were standing in a pile of wreckage that was once the express car. They were working intensely, throwing aside pieces of timber in a desperate attempt to get to something underneath. Smoke thought they must be trying to rescue someone and he started toward them, but Bobby Lee grabbed his arm.

"Smoke!" Bobby Lee said. "That's Dodd and his gang!"

"Dodd!" Smoke shouted.

Upon hearing his name called, Dodd, without hesitation, pulled his gun and fired.

That was the opening shot of a deadly battle, with Smoke and Bobby Lee on one side, and Dodd, Clark, and the others on the opposite side. The surviving train passengers, dying, wounded, and unwounded, had orchestra seats while the muzzle flashes of rapidly firing pistols illuminated the faces of eight desperate men. For fully thirty seconds, the roar of pistol fire overcame even the wails and cries of the wounded.

Smoke and Bobby Lee stood side by side, exchanging fire with Dodd and the members of his gang. Gradually, the flashes grew fewer, and the exchange of gunfire slackened as, one by one, the would-be train robbers fell in their tracks from well-placed .44-caliber balls.

Errant pistol shots whizzed by Smoke's ears, or hit the ground, sending up tiny fireballs before careening away with a high, keening sound, missiles of death in the darkness. Smoke felt, rather than saw or heard, Bobby Lee go down beside him, and he responded by shooting and killing yet another of Dodd's gang.

Finally, the last of Dodd's gang went down, and the shooting stopped. Smoke stood in place for a long moment afterward, holding a smoking pistol as the final echoes of gunfire rolled back from the nearby Excelsior Mountains. Now, even the cries of the injured had quieted, and as Smoke stood there, the only one doing so, it was as if someone had arranged a giant and very macabre tableau.

Suddenly, and totally unexpectedly, Dodd sat up and pointed his pistol at Smoke. Smoke reacted quickly by pulling the trigger on his own pistol, but the hammer fell on an empty chamber.

"Well, now," Dodd said. "Look at this. Ain't I the lucky one, though?"

The outlaw pulled the hammer back, but before he could fire, another shot rang out and a black hole appeared in his forehead as he fell back.

Thinking it might have been Bobby Lee, Smoke looked down at his brother-in-law, but saw only open and opaque eyes, looking up in their death stare. Bobby Lee was dead.

"I owed you that, Mr. Jensen." The voice came from one of the outlaws with whom Smoke had just done battle. Looking toward the sound, he saw that one of the other outlaws had managed to raise himself up onto his elbows. It wasn't until then that Smoke recognized him.

"Clark?" Smoke called out. "Emmett Clark?"

Clark coughed before he answered, and as he did, his cough spewed out blood.

"Yeah, it's me," he said.

"You were riding with Dodd?"

"Yes."

"I don't understand. If you were riding with him, why did you shoot him?"

"Like I said, I owed it to you. Call it a matter of honor," Clark said, and with another spasm of coughing, he fell back with one final, gasping breath.

When Smoke returned to Sugarloaf, he learned that both Pearlie and Cal had won everything in their events at the rodeo. In addition, Pearlie had won "Most Outstanding Cowboy," which came with a prize of a silver-studded saddle. Pearlie let it be known that he planned to give the saddle to Smoke. Smoke told Sally that he didn't feel right taking the gift, but Sally convinced him that it was very important to Pearlie, so Smoke agreed. With great pomp and ceremony, Pearlie presented the saddle, and Smoke saw that Sally was right. There was genuine joy in Pearlie's face when Smoke accepted it.

For the first several days after returning, Smoke was a bit pensive, thinking not only about the events of the previous few weeks, but also about the fact that Bobby Lee's death had severed the last living connection to Nicole. At first, he found the thought rather melancholy, but the more he contemplated it, the more he was able to find peace with the idea.

The door to that part of his past was forever closed.

Smoke had been back at Sugarloaf for three weeks when he received a letter that had no return address, but was postmarked from St. Louis, Missouri. Not until he opened it did he see that the letter was from the young woman he had met in Cloverdale.

> *Dear Mr. Jensen:*
>
> *I want to thank you, very much, for everything you did. You answered my telegram on behalf of Bobby Lee, and, like a true friend, or as I later learned, a true brother, you came to help him. And while Bobby Lee was killed, he was at least spared the humiliation of being hanged for a crime he did not commit.*
>
> *I also want to thank you for giving me the reward money, though there aren't words enough to express the depth of my gratitude for that gesture. The money has enabled me to leave the life I had begun and start anew. To that end, I have returned to St. Louis where I intend to, when the time is right, reestablish contact with my father, Thaddeus Culpepper.*
>
> *You may be surprised to learn, Mr. Jensen, that my father is a very wealthy man, so I feel guilty about having taken the reward money from you. I assure you, though, that the money was put to immediate and good purpose. And I promise, that once I am reestablished, I will give every cent of the money you gave me to a worthy charity.*
>
> > *Your Friend,*
> > *Minnie Kay Culpepper*

"Smoke, is everything all right?" Sally asked when Smoke finished the letter.

"Yes," Smoke replied. "Everything is fine. It's from Minnie Smith, the girl I told you about."

"The girl who worked at the Gold Strike Saloon? The girl you said was a very pretty girl?"

"Yes, that girl," Smoke said.

"And she is now writing you letters?"

"Just one letter—so far," Smoke said, holding the letter up teasingly.

"Oh, my. Should I be jealous?" Sally asked, but the smile on her face told Smoke that she understood he was teasing, and was merely joining in the banter.

Smoke got up from his chair, walked over to her, put his arms around her, and pulled her to him for a very deep kiss.

"What do you think?" he asked.

THE MOUNTAIN MAN SERIES BY
WILLIAM W. JOHNSTONE